D0953327

the 9:09 project

ALSO BY MARK H. PARSONS

Road Rash

Parsons, Mark H.,
The 9:09 project /
[2022]
33305254237542
mi   02/13/23

the 9:09 project

MARK H. PARSONS

DELACORTE PRESS

This is a work of fiction. Names, characters, places, and incidents either are the product of the author's imagination or are used fictitiously. Any resemblance to actual persons, living or dead, events, or locales is entirely coincidental.

Text copyright © 2022 by Mark H. Parsons
Jacket art copyright © 2022 by Ray Shappell

All rights reserved. Published in the United States by Delacorte Press, an imprint of Random House Children's Books, a division of Penguin Random House LLC, New York.

Delacorte Press is a registered trademark and the colophon is a trademark of Penguin Random House LLC.

Visit us on the Web! GetUnderlined.com

Educators and librarians, for a variety of teaching tools, visit us at RHTeachersLibrarians.com

Library of Congress Cataloging-in-Publication Data is available upon request.
ISBN 978-0-593-30975-9 (hardcover) — ISBN 978-0-593-30976-6 (ebook)

The text of this book is set in 11-point Maxime Pro.
Interior design by Cathy Bobak
Jacket art reference photo © 2022 by Jochen Conrad/EyeEm/Getty Images

Printed in the United States of America
10 9 8 7 6 5 4 3 2 1
First Edition

Random House Children's Books supports the First Amendment and celebrates the right to read.

Penguin Random House LLC supports copyright. Copyright fuels creativity, encourages diverse voices, promotes free speech, and creates a vibrant culture. Thank you for buying an authorized edition of this book and for complying with copyright laws by not reproducing, scanning, or distributing any part in any form without permission. You are supporting writers and allowing Penguin Random House to publish books for every reader.

For Mom

CHAPTER 1

It is not enough to photograph the obviously picturesque.
—Dorothea Lange

"CAN STUPIDITY MAKE YOUR HEAD HURT?" SETH ASKED ME.

"Only other people's heads," I said. "Never the stupid guy's."

He looked toward the other end of our table. "Well, *that* explains a lot."

We were in the cafeteria, eating lunch while trying to ignore Beal Wilson and his buds and their rating game. Those geniuses had started a ten-point system at the beginning of the school year. Who knows why . . . maybe they saw it in a movie and missed the entire point? Now, a week in, they'd finalized it. According to them, any girl under a five was so far below grade she wasn't even worthy of notice or discussion. (As a corollary to this, by doctrine they'd hook up with anyone five or above. So really, it was a binary go/no-go system, not a ten-pointer. But it was useless trying to tell them this. Trust me—besides being sexist asshats they aren't exactly La Montaña High's best and brightest.)

They continued with their hot-or-not bullshit while I looked for the chance to practice my street photography skills. Given the choice I'd rather use my Nikon but there's no way I'm dragging it around all day in my backpack, so I'm not above using my phone.

I'd just snapped someone walking toward the exit with a tray in her hand. I hadn't seen her before, but something about her walk caught my eye. Like she meant business. Okay, and maybe something else. Just before I hit the button I reframed it so she was leaving the frame instead of entering it, and panned with her so she was sharp and the background was blurry. Like she was almost too fast to catch. After I snapped it, I took a quick peek at it. *Yeah, that works.* Underneath it all I could still hear Beal yakking away . . .

". . . so, I'd say that's a seven-five. Well, at least a solid seven."

"Solid," his buddy Tristan said with a snort, like the word was somehow funny.

I looked up. They were talking about the girl I'd just photographed. I never joined their rating games, but I couldn't imagine thinking of her as "nice and ordinary," or whatever they thought a seven was supposed to be.

"You'd better not let *her* hear that," Riley said. "They call her AK-47 for a reason." Riley is Beal's other sidekick.

"So?" Beal said. "There's nothing wrong with that. I'm just saying she's fine. She'd rate even higher if she wasn't so damn scary." He looked down toward our end of the table. "Right, Seth?"

"You're clearly the expert, dude," Seth said.

Beal nodded, missing the irony. "J? What do you think?"

"Hmm. *I think* . . ." I paused, considering my impression of the girl. Leave it to my weird brain to come up with a cartoon image of a tour guide leading people through dangerous territory. "I think if I suddenly had to survive in an undisclosed jungle location in Argentina and could take just one student from this cafeteria, I'd choose her." They stared at me. "She has a little Che Guevara in her," I added for clarification.

Beal shook his head. "Man, you're *weird*."

With a few minutes left before the bell Riley suddenly came to life, all excited. "Dude, look at that! Is she new? Man, I'd be *all over* that. She's an eight. At least. Maybe an eight and a half."

"Eight and a half?" Seth replied, without looking up from his phone. "So, she's not quite uber-hot, but still clearly hotter than just hot? Like, semi-uber-hot?" He paused his sarcasm long enough to glance up at the girl in question. He isn't the type to make rude comments, but I could tell she had his attention.

Beal weighed in. "Eight-five, easy." He paused for dramatic effect. "I'd let her give me a sleeper."

". . . says the guy who couldn't get a labradoodle to lick his noodle even if he put peanut butter on his balls," Seth muttered to me.

I turned my head for a look. It was Ollie. Of course. And she was coming this way. She'd started high school with a fashion-forward vengeance last week and apparently aimed to keep it that way. Today she was messy-blond-hair/surprised-eyes/preppy, like Taylor Swift's little sister who'd been out too late the night before.

"She's a freshman," I said.

"That don't plug no holes" was Beal's brilliant retort.

"Wow—you make that up just now?" Seth asked.

They suddenly ran out of things to say as she approached our table and walked up to me. "So," she said quietly. "Do you suppose I could get a ride from you after school?" You'd have to know her to realize the microscopic crinkles in the corners of her eyes meant she was smiling underneath the puppy-dog face. She knew what she was doing, and I knew it. And she knew I knew.

I paused, like I had to think about it. "Okay," I finally said. "I'll wait for you in the parking lot."

She nodded. "Thanks." She turned and walked away without ever making eye contact with any of the other guys.

Once she left, they all turned toward me with that *What the hell?* look. And never one for subtlety, Beal said, "What the hell, J? You're all like Mister Quiet Loner all the time and it turns out you got a little hottie in your back pocket or what?"

I just shook my head, like *You dumb bastards,* then grabbed my backpack and stood up. "Like I said, she's a freshman." I headed out to my fifth-period class.

It's not that I was trying to mislead them. I just wasn't in the mood to deal with a pack of loser horndogs trying to get me to hook them up with my little sister.

* * *

History class. There are a few secrets to it, at least at La Montaña
High School:

1. Know the important names and dates of the
   major events. (Subtle hint: these are the ones
   they tell you.)

2. Maybe also remember the barest facts about
   them if you're really shooting for an A+.

3. Let the teacher know you know. Don't hide in
   the back of the class. Don't sit front and center—
   unless you're an unrepentant kiss-ass—but
   second or third row, maybe one seat off center,
   will work fine. And engage, or what's the point?

4. But don't piss the teacher off. Okay, I'm not
   great with this one. Or even moderately good.
   Like the fact that Mr. LaRue was born without a
   sense of humor is somehow my fault?

That's it. Not much heavy lifting involved, just regurgi-
tation.

Like today. I was gazing out the window at some hills in
the distance, still thinking about those idiots in the cafeteria,
when LaRue said, "Who can give me a military leader after the

Civil War who rose to political prominence?" He looked at his seating chart—for the biggest offender, apparently—and said, "Jamison Deever?"

I swung my head around. "Huh?"

"Civil War. Military leader. Rose to prominence after." He literally snapped his fingers, like I was a trained seal or something. "Weren't you paying attention?"

The moment he said *Civil War* a timeline popped up in front of my eyes—the latter half of the nineteenth century. The timeline scanned to the Civil War era—early 1860s. It was blue. Which makes no sense, as you'd think a war should be red due to blood and violence, but it had more to do with the fact that the letter *C* is definitely light blue. A famous name from the war still stuck out *after* the war was over. *Ulysses S. Grant.*

The phrase *8+8* hovered in front of my eyes. In light gray, of course, as eights are. I knew the Civil War started in 1861 (see Secret #1, as previously stated), and the phrase reminded me that Grant became president eight years afterward, for eight years. "Grant. He became president of the US in 1869 and served two terms, until 1877."

LaRue studied me for a moment. "That's correct. But I suggest you keep your attention within the room from now on." He turned away. "Now, who can tell me about the reconstruction effort during . . ."

Okay, there's another secret. Maybe.

> 5. Have the neurological condition known as synesthesia.

It's not contagious. Or fatal. Or even harmful. In fact, if there were a cure, I wouldn't take it—life would seem too bland. And my grades would probably take a dive.

For as long as I can remember, certain things—like letters, numbers, days of the week, months of the year—have had definite colors. And those colors don't change. Like, *A* is sort of a pastel orange, like orange sherbet mixed with vanilla ice cream. Always. Just like *7* is always a thin sort of purple, and *Wednesday* is a broad, boring, light brown/tan. Just like the day itself feels. And when someone says "Wednesday," I instantly see it in a little box, with Monday and Tuesday in their own boxes to the left of it (in gray and yellow, respectively), and Thursday and Friday to the right (blue and brown . . . duh). It might sound goofy, but I have no control over it.

There are other manifestations. Like when someone talks (especially droning on in a boring way, like a certain US history teacher I know), I see the words spooling by as they speak, spelled out in bold, black letters like the captions at the bottom of a newsfeed. And sometimes I see ideas played out as strange little cartoons, like my brain was an anime studio on drugs or something.

My mom said most of this was the same for her. I can remember sitting with her at the kitchen table when I was a little kid, comparing notes. Like, "What color is Tuesday to you?" And she'd say *Green*, and I'd say "No way! It's totally yellow. What about November . . . ?"

I never gave it much thought—I guess I'd assumed it was pretty universal. When I learned otherwise, I've got to tell you, I was kind of stunned. I was helping my dad in the garage where he had an NPR science program on the radio and they were talking about how some people had this condition where they associated colors with letters or numbers, or sometimes with sounds or other cross-sensory stuff. I remember thinking *This is news?* but then they said it was a neurological condition called synesthesia, and apparently it only affects a small percentage of the population. I'll admit for a second there I was a little worried because it sounded like some sort of disease—somewhere between amnesia and diarrhea. But then they said there were no known negative side effects, blah blah blah . . . possible correlations with creativity or memory . . .

But all I could think was, you mean *everyone* doesn't do this? Seriously, it'd be like seeing the headline, *Scientists report some people can breathe through their nose!*

"I'd kind of figured most people saw things that way," I said to my mom, "but I guess not. Apparently, it's pretty rare."

She looked at me with the same little crinkle in her eyes that Ollie'd had today and nodded. "I knew that. I never made a big deal out of it because I didn't want you to feel 'different.' But you have to admit it's pretty cool, don't you think?"

Yes, I did. But now that feeling was gone—along with my mom—and no one else seemed to have her ability to understand me or help me feel less alone in the universe.

As for my sister, sure enough she was waiting in the parking lot, leaning against Mom's old Subaru Outback. Yeah, it still kind of weirded me out, driving it. But it beats walking. I guess.

As I unlocked the car, one of the seniors rolled by in a new

Camaro. What my dad called a Faux-maro. Bright yellow. We both watched it, appraising the potential perfection of this particular hue.

"Perfect?" Ollie asked.

I shook my head. "It's a couple shades too dark."

Ollie shot me a look. "It's always something with you, isn't it?"

CHAPTER 2

Photographers stop photographing a subject too soon,
before they have exhausted the possibilities.
—Dorothea Lange

AS SOON AS I ROLLED OUT OF THE PARKING LOT OLLIE
had her face in her phone. I figured she was texting, like always.
But when we stopped at a red light, she held it up and showed me
a pic of a model. She was Latina, professional-grade hot. Wild
dark hair, with some sort of smoky thing going on around her
eyes. Just this side of a raccoon. But a really attractive raccoon.

"Judge," she said. Probably because I tell her *Don't be so judgy*
at least three times a week. "Which do you like better? This one,
or"—she scrolled to another pic—"this one?" If the first one was
"sultry," the second was at the other end of the continuum, over
toward "fresh-faced" or whatever. A white girl—beachy-blond,
blue eyes, big smile. Also, professionally hot.

"So, am I judging the pro hair and makeup, the studio light-ing, the fan-in-the-face, or the Photoshop skills?"

She took her phone away and pulled a face. "Can't you be serious for once?"

"I am. No one looks like that in real life."

"Well, duh. But if they did, which one would look better?"

I was about to render a preference, then stopped. Did I really want to come off like Beal? "They both look great." And regard-less, they were both way out of my league.

"J!"

"Okay. Maybe the first one? Something about the look in her eyes . . . she seems smart."

She leaned back in her seat and folded her arms, looking away. "You're useless."

I glanced over at her. "This is for you, right?" She was still looking forward, but her head bobbed almost imperceptibly. "Look. You're my sister, so to me you're not even like a real girl." She started to say something, but I kept going. "However, some of the guys at school seem to like the way you look—God knows why—so maybe you should consider just sticking with whatever you're doing now. If it even matters to you, I mean."

I was expecting her usual pushback, like *Fashion is an art form* and *It's not about hotness,* but instead she said, "They do?"

I had her full attention now, so I told her all about their messed-up rating system.

"What did I get?" she asked.

"Seriously? You care what Beal Wilson—who's grown into an

all-around snarky dickwad—gave you on his patented hotness scale?"

"No. I was just curious. But if you don't want to—"

"Eight."

Her eyes narrowed. "So that's it? I'm eighty percent? Like a B or something?" This from a girl who cares about her grades almost as much as her fashion. Not quite, but it's close.

I shrugged. "Like I said, I'm genetically blind to it. Besides, I think it might have been an eight and a half, so—"

I realized the mistake the second it was out of my mouth. We have a saying about things that are okay but sort of second-rate. Like a decent movie that drags in the middle with some cheese on the ending. We call it *pretty B-plus*. It's right up there with *just fine* and *not bad*.

"So they're saying . . ." Long pause while she breathed in slowly through her nose. "I'm a *B-fucking-plus* . . . ?" Wow. Ollie was officially pissed off—she never drops f-bombs.

I shrugged. "Hey, most girls don't even rate a seven with them."

That apparently wasn't helping. "Who do they think—" She spun in her seat and faced me, speaking quietly. "You can tell your friends that on a scale of one to ten, they're probably a three. Maybe a four on a good day. If they've had a shower. And Beal drops to a two, because there's absolutely nothing hot about being a total dick."

"I'll be overjoyed to pass that along, but they're no friends of mine."

"You're the one hanging with them, not me."

"I'm not *hanging* with them." I shrugged. "I gotta eat some-where and there's usually room at the end of their table. They don't even know you're my sister, so how much of a friend could they be?" Which was a good question, come to think of it.

"Whatever. Just tell them."

I glanced over at her. "So, are you pissed because those de-meaning randos are sitting around rating girls . . . or because of the rating you got?"

She snorted. "What do *you* think?"

"I think you didn't answer."

We were approaching Happy Jack's Burger Bistro. I pulled into the right lane and slowed way down, pointing at the drive-thru. "Don't make me buy you a burger. Because I will."

It's doctrine at La Montaña High that anytime someone takes you through the drive-thru at Happy Jack's and buys you some-thing, you're thrown into an instant round of Truth or Dare from the time you order until you receive your food and drive off. And since most of the Happy Jack's crew are stoners—because Jack himself is a big-time stoner from way back—the service isn't ex-actly as fast as your average McDonald's or Taco Bell. At school they call it the *no-lie drive-by.* Stupid, I know, but add girls and alcohol on a Friday night and it can be randomly amusing. Or so I've heard.

She looked at me, then at Happy Jack's, then back to me. "Okay, if you really need to know," she finally said, "mostly be-cause it's such a dick move." She paused. "And maybe a little about the B-plus."

I wasn't expecting that much honesty. Once in a while I felt close to Ollie. Like right after Mom died. Not as much lately—not sure if that was me or her—but right now, hearing her admit that, I did. And I felt sad, too. "Look, I get why it pisses you off, seeing those jerks sitting around reducing girls to a number and analyzing their flaws . . ."

"Like they're all perfect themselves," she threw in.

"Exactly. Which is why I kind of hate that you care what they think."

She was silent for a minute. "To the extent that I do . . . so do I."

I changed the subject. "So, there's a new girl at school—"

"There are hundreds of them," she interrupted. "Including me. They're called freshmen."

"Shut up. You know what I mean. She's about my age, and I've never seen her before."

"Well, *that* really narrows it down."

I let it go. "She has a weird nickname. AK-47, I think."

She nodded. "I heard some of the girls talking about her. I guess she's pretty quiet." She got a funny look on her face. "Why?"

I shrugged. "I don't know. Just curious."

"Uh-huh . . ."

When we got home, I dropped my backpack and flopped on my bed, staring at the ceiling. Ollie had a point about the whole "friends" thing. She didn't exactly say it, but it was hovering there, like a fart in an elevator—why was I hanging anywhere near these guys, if we weren't friends?

If I'm being honest, the answer's simple.

It's because I don't *have* any real friends.

Because maybe I'm too disconnected to even try.

And because I don't feel like I fit in at *any* of the tables.

I mean, it was bad enough before. But these days . . . man, I don't even fit in at the lame-o loser table. What's up with *that*? Not that I was totally textbook normal before, but after something like this happens to you, can you ever get back to normal . . . or are you somehow changed forever?

That table of losers are what my dad would call low-hanging fruit. Okay, not Seth. He has his own issues, but he can be funny as hell—in his semi-cynical way—and he's a computer wizard. He's actually a pretty good dude . . . he was in my math class last year and we bonded over corny jokes about stuff like pi and irrational numbers, and we've been eating together on a casual basis since then. So he's probably the closest thing I've had to an actual friend in quite a while. Ever since . . .

It suddenly occurred to me that maybe Ollie felt sad for me the same way I felt sad for her.

This line of thought was interrupted by the entrance of Her Royal Brattiness. "Hey, J—I need a new selfie."

"So? You've got a phone."

"Not a selfie-selfie. A quality selfie."

"Didn't we just do that? Like last week when school started?"

"I'm going for a new look now."

"Oh. Now that your old look has been rated as—"

"Don't say it."

"—B-plus?" I cracked up.

"Shut up. That's not it and you know it."

"You shut up."

"Can you do it or not?" she asked.

"When?"

"Half an hour?"

"Don't you have anything better to do?"

"Sure. But you don't." Followed by a snicker, which made it even worse.

I lay back down and closed my eyes. "Whatever."

"Thanks!"

She left and I resumed staring at the ceiling. Sad to say, but she was right—my life had devolved to that wonderful point where I had nothing going on. Unless you counted AP language homework as "something." Which I didn't.

The first time Ollie asked me to take a pic of her, maybe six months ago, she ended up telling me what to do every step of the way. I put up with it for a while—my mom's hoarse whisper saying *Go easy on your sister* had been playing in my head for at least a year by then—but finally I just set the camera on a tripod, handed her the remote, and left her on her own. She was happy to be in charge, snapping away for fifteen minutes before telling me she was through.

I picked up the camera and scrolled through the shots. They looked like a bunch of B-plus selfies only with better resolution.

You know . . . camera too close, nose/lips/chin exaggerated, staring at the camera with a semi–duck face, cluttered background, flat lighting, etc.

"Cool," I said. "Mind if I take a few?"

"Go ahead."

I went with a longer focal length, pulled the tripod back several feet, sat her in a different chair, and spun her so the window lighting was at an angle to add depth. I set the camera to manual and opened the aperture to the max, then focused on her eyes so her face was sharp but the background was blown to a blur. She was looking at something across the room and I took a few quick pics before she realized what I was doing.

"I wasn't ready!"

"I know. That's the point. Okay, you can look over here." She did, automatically going into her Donald Duck impersonation. "Now smile, as big as you can." She grimaced like a fool. "Stop smiling and look *into* the lens." She dropped the stupid grin, cocking her head as she looked, and I caught it. I took a dozen more, but I was pretty sure that was it.

"Let me see!"

I held the camera up out of reach, like playing keep-away with a terrier. "As soon as they're done. Give me half as long as it took you to get ready, okay?"

She snorted and ran off while I got to work. The first thing I did once I'd loaded them into my computer was zip through all the ones I'd taken. The warm-up shot I'd caught of her was okay, and one or two of the later ones were pretty good. But the first one of her actually looking at the lens had something cool going on, so I worked on it.

I forgot it was Ollie and approached it like something I'd taken on the street. I decided on full monochrome but made it warm-toned, like an old-school black-and-white fashion print. Then I bumped up the contrast but made sure the skin tones stayed smooth. Some mild cropping had the head fill most of the frame, and edge burning highlighted the face as it emerged from the dark blur of the out-of-focus background. Not over-the-top Hollywood, but pretty dramatic in an organic way. I pushed my chair back and looked at the image on my monitor. Not bad.

I put her selfies into a folder along with the one I'd worked on before I called her over.

She pulled up a chair next to mine and I started clicking through her selfies as she judged and commented. "Okay . . . next . . . not bad . . . wait, back up a sec . . . let's see the next one . . ."

Then I opened the one I'd worked on.

"Huh" was all she said. She stared at it for a while. Then she reached over and scrolled backward, glancing at the last three or four she'd taken, then back to the one we'd been looking at. She examined it for several seconds, then tapped the screen.

"Send me this one."

"You're welcome," I said to her back as she walked out of my room.

She ignored me, but that was the last time she tried to over-direct my photography.

* * *

She walked into the kitchen where I was setting up my gear. "I'm ready."

"Okay, let's bang this out," I said, like I had important stuff to go do. Yeah, *right*.

I looked up from messing with my camera—she was a beach bunny with raccoon eyes. Or a raccoon with beach bunny hair. Like she was trying to look like one of the models in her magazines. "Don't you think maybe you're overdoing the whole burglar-mask thing?" I felt silly saying that but . . . well, Mom had asked me to look out for her. What does that even *mean*, "looking out" for someone?

"Shut up and shoot." I guess Ollie didn't know either.

I shrugged. "Famous last words."

Since that first session we've developed a process. The monitor on my camera is too small to see from several feet away, so I put a vanity mirror on a stand next to the camera. That way she can get in position, check her look, then shift her eyes back to the lens. That wouldn't work with most people, but she has definite opinions on what she's going for—and she has good instincts, to be honest—so I put up with it.

We've done this a bunch of times (whenever she feels the need for a new profile pic, which seems like a couple times a month) so it goes pretty fast. We were about done when she said, "Can you make my eyes bigger? Like with Photoshop or whatever?"

A hundred replies flew through my brain, but I just shook my head. "Nope—not going there."

"Why not?"

"Maybe because it'll actually make your eyes look *smaller*?" She did that *Huh?* squint. "You know, that moment when people see you in person and you're, like, fundamentally different than your photo?"

"Ninety percent of the people who'll see the pic will never see me in real life."

"In that case, how about we just do a search and find a girl who looks a lot like you . . . only better. Then we post her pic and say it's you. Done."

She just glared at me.

I thought for a second. "Okay . . . wait here."

I came back in a minute with a hand towel, a spray bottle full of water, and a hairbrush.

"What are you doing?" she asked.

I threw her the towel. "Just an idea. Cover your face, then wet your hair and brush it back."

She looked at me like I'd suggested dunking her head into a bucket of cold chicken soup. "Do you know how *long* it took me to get it this way?" she said, whirling her hand around her hair.

"Yup, and we just took a ton of pics with it like that. Time to try something new."

She finally did, wetting and combing her hair until it was slicked back off her face. Then I got behind the camera. "Okay, keep your head tilted down like that, now look into the lens. No duck face, no smile."

I didn't have to tell her twice. *Click.*

Later, when we were reviewing the processed photos, she looked at the wet-head one and said, "*Wow,* J—that's great. How did you know that would work?"

I shrugged. "Just a lucky hunch . . . I figured smaller hair might equal bigger eyes."

She looked back at the pic. "Hmm . . . so what if you Photoshopped *this*?"

"Forget it," I said as I finished putting away my stuff. "I'm okay with taking your picture. I'm not okay with making you into something you're not."

CHAPTER 3

Pick a theme and work it to exhaustion... the subject must
be something you truly love or truly hate.
—Dorothea Lange

"HEY, JAMISON, HOW'D SCHOOL GO TODAY?"

I was in the garage with my dad. I'd heard him come home while I was stashing my gear so I went out there and sure enough, he was doing something with a drill press in the corner.

"Fine," I said. The *truth* is, I was feeling crappy. Which is why I was out there in the first place.

He raised an eyebrow. "So give me an update—what did you do today?"

I shrugged. "Nothing much. Aced my history quiz. Mostly just hung out with friends."

That last part was because I knew he wanted to hear it. Okay, the *truth* is, once upon a time I could have said that without lying. Because once upon a time I had a few friends. Sort of. But during the whole time Mom was sick—and especially after—they basically quit hanging out with me. It was like they forgot how to talk to me. Or maybe I couldn't talk to them.

He lifted the cover of the drill press. "Good. Having friends might be even more important than a history test."

In which case I was totally screwed.

Because my dad is probably my best friend. At least now that Mom's gone. Not that he knows it. And what's really weird about it—besides the obvious—is that we don't sit around having deep, self-revealing conversations about the meaning of life while we drink beer or smoke weed or go on epic road trips. Or whatever best friends do.

The *truth* is, we mostly just hang out in the garage and talk about movies or photography or music or—in my dad's case— antique British motorcycles. Which—in *truth*—is pretty redundant, because they quit making motorcycles in England over fifty years ago, so they're *all* antiques.

Not to him. He's into what he calls the postwar classics, from the fifties and sixties. Not that he has one. He just has books. And magazines. And videos. And posters. *Lots* of posters, all over the garage. Once a year he takes the six-hour round trip to San Jose, where they have this big vintage Brit Bike show. And even though I don't give a shit about antique motorcycles I usually go with him. Because that's what friends do. But don't go thinking it's an epic road trip where we talk about the meaning of life or anything. Because it's not, and we don't.

My dad loosened the drill press belts and moved them to different-sized pulleys, which changed the speed of the drill press. There was a big chart on the inside of the cover showing which combination of belts and pulleys equaled which speed, but he never looked at it. He just moved the belts from one pulley to another, stared at them for a second, then tightened them up and closed the cover. He's like that with machines. They speak the same language.

He nodded up at a new poster on the wall as he wiped his hands on a rag. "Did you see that?" It was a picture of a girl on a motorcycle. A bright yellow motorcycle.

There's one other thing we talk about—the color yellow.

You know how some old ladies are obsessed with purple? Well, my dad has this thing about yellow, and apparently he's had it since he was a little kid. I don't know . . . maybe he had a toy truck that was yellow and he imprinted on it like a baby duck or something? All I know is, he loves yellow, but it has to be the pure, primary color. *Straight, no chaser,* he says. Which is really hard to find, so it's been a game since we were little. Ollie or I would see a yellow car going by and we'd holler, "Hey, Dad—look!" and he'd say, "That's pretty cool, but it has a little too much white in it." And sure enough, if you looked close you could tell it was a tiny bit creamy . . . just enough to dilute the magic of the perfect yellow. Ollie and I got really good at being able to tell if a yellow was really "yellow," and in which direction it was off. (Like *that's* a useful job skill.)

"That's a beauty, don't you think?" he asked.

I examined the poster. The model on the bike had on knee-high brown boots and a tiny matching miniskirt, with a super-wide belt and some sort of weird flowery top. And mountains of poofy blond hair. Like something out of an over-the-top movie about the swinging sixties, *baby*. Underneath it all she was probably hot, but the effect was ruined by all the corny stuff she had on. And the knowledge that she was at least seventy by now.

"She looks nice, Dad. But not my type—a little too Austin Powers for me, ya know?"

He thought that was funny. "I meant the bike." Which I totally knew. I mean, my dad is like the opposite of Beal and his buddies—the last thing he'd ever do is talk about women, at least not in that *Look how hot she is* way. I'd never really thought about it before, but I guess maybe that was out of respect for my mom.

The one thing we *don't* talk about very often is Mom. She was like the perfect yellow. And while there's a ton you can debate about something that's flawed, there's not much you can say about perfection.

And *that's* the truth.

I checked the time on my phone as I approached the corner of Fig and Gardena—it was a couple of minutes past nine—then put it back in my pocket and pulled my Nikon out of my backpack.

Finch Coffee Company had a pretty good crowd inside, sucking down lattes and munching on the best paninis in town. I didn't want to stand around in front of their big window like some sort of creeper so I moved down to the corner and leaned against the brick wall of a clothing store that was closed for the evening.

This corner was turning out to be a good choice for a night-time photo project. At 9:09—when my phone alarm started vibrating in my pocket—there was a college-age couple crossing the street, walking toward me.

I took a few snaps as they approached, then when they got near me I said, "Hi. Would you mind if I took a quick photo of you two?" They gave me a look, like *Who are you and why do you want to take our picture?* and I quickly added, "It's for a school project." They looked at each other and kind of shrugged, like *Sure . . . why not?*

"Cool, thanks." As I pulled back to the edge of the sidewalk and brought my camera up, my brain presented an image of two little number creatures. They were both the number *1*. Not that they had T-shirts with digits printed on them, but I knew. Plus they were both white, instead of green or purple. Anyway, when they merged they were *still* white and not yellow, which a *2* would be. Maybe imagine the equation *1+1=1*, only animated? It's hard to explain, but it made me think this couple was legit.

"Stand however you want," I said, "and look however you want. Just be yourselves." Which is hard to do when a stranger is pointing a camera at you from eight feet away, but my hunch was right and they were better than most. The guy leaned back against the wall, looking up at the top of the building across the street, and the girl faced him—her back completely to the camera—and wrapped her arms around him, resting her head against his chest.

I fired off a couple of frames, then moved a little to the left and took a few more. For the last one the guy looked directly at the camera. Not exactly smiling. But content.

I brought the camera down. "Thanks. That was awesome."

The girl nodded. "No problem." They walked on, hand in hand.

It's been almost two years since Mom died. People tell me I'll get over it, but I don't even know what that means. Or if I want to. I mean, imagine you're dying and the people you love most in the world are gathered around you, and everyone's sad. Then someone says, "Don't worry—we'll be over it in a couple of years."

You don't think a term you've never heard before can change everything, but if I never hear *metastatic invasive lobular carcinoma* again for as long as I live, it'll be way too fucking soon.

It was near the beginning of my freshman year when we got the news. At first they told Ollie and me that Mom was going to be sick for a while. But pretty soon they couldn't hide it anymore. We'd overhear them talking about stuff like *stage four* or *palliative treatment* or *hospice*. Plus you'd have to be a zombie not to notice *them* walking around like zombies. Within a few weeks it was out in the open—Mom was going to die, and there wasn't shit anyone could do about it.

That last part was the hardest. You see all these shows where people have diseases way more exotic or rare than breast cancer, and all the smart scientist/doctor types bust their ass and figure out some way to fix it. Or you'll read about all these amazing medical breakthroughs on the internet. But with Mom, it was like none of that applied, almost like they didn't even try. Oh, they gave her some options. Two of them.

They could do their best to make her comfortable, and she would die within a few months. Or they could give her treatments that would make her sicker than a dog, and chances were she would die within a few months.

Mom, being the smartest person I've ever known, chose Option A.

I, on the other hand, held out for Option C: *None of the above.* Something—*anything*—that didn't include *and she would die soon* as part of the prognosis. I remember talking to my dad, insisting there must be something they could do, and he told me as gently as he could that the cancer had spread throughout her body and there really wasn't anything that could be done.

"Well, I . . . I just refuse to accept that!" I said, tears running down my face.

He came over and surprised me by giving me a fierce bear hug, then he took a step back, his hands still on my shoulders. "And that's one of the many things I love about you, J."

She made it four months, passing away after winter break had ended. She'd been in the hospital for the last week and Dad practically lived there too. I was there the last day. I make it a point to *never* think about that day (let alone talk about it) but the one thing I remember after she'd died was the doctor looking at a clock and saying to the nurse, "Notate the official time of death as 9:09 p.m."

At the time I thought, *Why does it even matter? We all knew she was going to die—it's not like it's a murder mystery or something.* But it eventually did matter, at least to me. Because the hardest part—besides the unreal fact that she was gone from us forever—was that the rest of the universe kept on going. I mean, after the doctor had said that, I'd looked out the window—we were four stories up—and in the distance I could see people walking past the corner of Fig and Gardena like everything was fine. I couldn't get over the fact that the world hadn't stopped spinning on its axis at 9:09.

That thought ate away at me for over a year, and the feeling of missing my mom got worse—not better—as time went on. Like, she was my mom and I loved her, sure, just like Ollie and Dad loved her. But she was also my translator and my tour guide . . . the only person I knew who *got* me . . . who could explain the world to me and help me make sense out of it.

When school was starting and I was feeling totally shitty and alone—I decided to do a photo project, more out of desperation than anything else. I knew I wanted to do a street thing, capturing images of ordinary people like Dorothea Lange had done, but other than that I had no idea. Then it hit me. My mom was the big supporter of my photography—she was the one who got me my Nikon three or four years ago, she was the one who bought me photo books, and she was the one who was always telling me I had talent and encouraging me to "do something with it."

So I settled on that one little corner of the world I saw from her hospital room. I go there at 9:09 p.m. and I capture whoever happens to be there. Which has turned out way more interesting than you might think. Because when *you* pick the subjects, you can end up sort of filtering them. Like maybe going more for interesting gnarled old faces or cute girls or just people who look similar to you . . . what my psych teacher calls selection bias. But with the selection being done by the randomness of time, I actually get a really cool, diverse cross-section of subjects.

The first time I did it I brought my tripod but it seemed to make people self-conscious, which is the kiss of death. So instead I shoot handheld with the effective speed cranked way up. Sure, the image can get a little noise in it, but I'm doing this whole thing in black-and-white—I'm looking more for "dramatic realism" than "studio smooth"—so it's no big deal. Plus I really like the freedom of holding the camera.

Maybe I lose a little resolution, but I gain a lot more connection with the subject. And I'm okay with that, because *that*—some sort of connection—is what I'm looking for.

Does it work? Honestly, I have no idea, because so far the only real viewer is me.

I settled on the "school project" line last week. I was trying to explain to some guy what I was doing, but it was a total fail—I began talking about my mom and suddenly found it hard to speak and I started to tear up. You better believe that dude got out of there, fast.

Luckily the next person was a woman with a little more patience. I tried again, but ten seconds in I could tell it was headed for the same location, so out of frustration I blurted out that it was for a school project and she just nodded and said, "Okay, sure." And that was that.

So yeah. This is something I do, but I don't ever talk about it. I don't even know what the project really is, or when it'll be finished. I only know that each and every day of my life will have a 9:09 p.m. And I know one more thing . . .

I know I don't ever want to be over my mom.

CHAPTER 4

The camera is an instrument that teaches people
how to see without a camera.
—Dorothea Lange

TURN AROUND, YOU DORK!

The text was from Ollie. I stopped in the middle of the cafeteria, set down my tray, and sat on the nearest table, waving my arm without turning around. Within fifteen seconds she plopped down next to me.

"You could do *so* much better," she said, looking at Beal and the guys across the room. Which was the general direction I'd been heading when she'd texted me.

I looked at her. "Remember this moment," I said solemnly. It's a phrase we use when one of us wants the other to take a mental snapshot to capture a specific moment, for better or worse.

She nodded just as seriously. "Done." Then she went back to her buoyant self. "You can come sit with us!"

"Naw . . ." Was eating near the usual losers any worse than sitting with a bunch of kids?

She must have read my look. "C'mon, it's not just freshmen." She glanced back at her table. "Really." Then her voice got sort of singsongy. "Kennedy Brooks is there."

Kennedy Brooks—a junior like me—is also the only certifiable nine-plus at La Montaña High, at least according to Beal and his cronies. And she's no dummy, either. We went to school together when we were kids, and I always wanted her in my group whenever we did team projects in class because she had great ideas and worked hard.

Okay, and maybe I'd had a serious crush on her through the last year or two of elementary school. Okay, and maybe beyond. But once she hit eighth grade she became popular and started running with a different group of kids, and she hasn't said much to me since. It's not like we were ever best friends or anything, but these days she acts like she doesn't even know who I am.

I shrugged. "So what?"

"I'm not going to beg." She stood up. "I just thought you could use a change."

I stood up too. "You know what? Maybe I could."

She smiled her crinkly half smile. "Cool." And if I'm being honest, it made me feel good that she wanted me to join her.

We grabbed seats near the end of the fashionista table and she was right—at least half the girls were my age. Leave it to

Ollie—and her superior social skills—to somehow end up sitting with the popular girls within a week of starting high school. Even if table talk seemed to be on a strict rotation between clothes and makeup and hair and who's-hooking-up-with-who.

The girl Riley had called AK-47 was at the far end. Okay, actually at the table next to it. And she seemed more interested in whatever she was reading than in the gossip-girling around her. Not that I looked at her. At least, not more than two or three times.

Somewhere in there Ollie pulled out her phone and passed it around, with her latest head shot called up. When Kennedy got it, she looked from the pic to Ollie and back to the phone. "Wow. Is that even you?"

Ollie squinted—subtle, but I could tell it was the opposite of her crinkle. She nodded. "Yeah. My brother Jamison's a photographer—he did it."

One of the other girls asked, "Would he do ours?"

Ollie stuck her thumb in my direction. "He's right here—why don't you ask him?"

And they did. All at once.

Something about it was hilarious. I mean, who knew that taking free photos of girls who think you can make them look better than they really do could turn you into a popular guy? By the time lunch was over I had three girls—including Kennedy Brooks—scheduled to shoot at three o'clock the next day, after sixth period let out.

And one full-blown strikeout with that AK girl.

I'm not even sure why I asked. Maybe I was feeling bad that she seemed excluded from the others . . . something I could totally relate to. Regardless, I don't usually go up to girls I don't know and start talking to them. Trust me on this.

Anyway, she was still sitting there reading after everyone else had left, and for some reason as I walked by her on my way out I stopped. She looked up from her book.

"I'm taking head shots of some of the girls here tomorrow right after school," I said, pointing back toward where they'd been sitting, "and, um, maybe you'd like to join in?" The minute the words came out of my mouth I realized how weird it sounded. I suddenly felt my face get hot and I wanted to run from the room.

She didn't exactly help the situation, either. She didn't consider it for a few seconds and then decline. She didn't ask anything about it, like why we were doing it or if it cost or anything. She didn't say yes, and she didn't even lie and say maybe, to make me feel good. She just said, "No thank you," and turned back to her book without another glance. Like I didn't exist.

I mentally shrugged and kept going, but inside I felt stupid. What was I thinking?

"Promise me—no black-and-white," Ollie said. "That's *my* thing."

"Hate to break it to you, but for like the first hundred years of photography, that was *everybody's* thing. Still is, for lots of people." I looked over my shoulder and pulled into traffic from the school parking lot.

Ollie didn't budge. "But none of them go to La Montaña High. Here, it's my thing."

"Did it ever occur to you that it's actually *my* thing? Like, it was my idea, and—"

"*I* bring you to their table, *I* show off my pic, *I* tell them you did it . . ." She paused, and I looked over at her. Mistake. "J . . . can't you let me have just this one thing?"

I slammed the steering wheel with both hands. "I cannot *believe* you just used the fucking puppy-dog look on me! I showed *you* that when you were six and you wanted a My Little Pony bike."

She laughed. "And it worked, too."

I sighed. "Okay—no black-and-white for these head shots. But you've got to meet me halfway—I can't stand that uber-fluorescent stuff. At a minimum I'm doing them in low saturation."

"What do you mean?"

"Pastel. You know—soft color? I don't know . . . sort of like Joyce Tenneson, but not."

She looked up something on her phone. "Oh. Yeah, that would be fine."

I glanced over. She had a Tenneson pic up, one of the angel-looking ones. "I'm glad you're good with it, but I wasn't asking permission."

She knows when she's won. "Sure, cool, whatever you want . . ."

* * *

"You don't have to smile," I said. "Unless you're actually happy about something, I mean." She stopped smiling and went into her version of the duck face. Which—if possible—was even worse than Ollie's version of it. "On second thought, you have a great smile . . ."

I was in the cafeteria after sixth, doing the head shots I'd promised the day before. And stressing out over it. Sure, the original premise sounded awesome: *Be a cool fashion photographer for the afternoon, taking photos of hot girls.* But I hadn't read the fine print: *These girls will not be models, they have no clue what they want, and if you don't magically make them look pro-grade hot, they're going to tell everyone what a phony you are.*

I mean, I know how to take pictures, but talking to girls—let alone telling them what to do—was *not* something that came naturally to me.

But I did my best—I focused on the technical stuff to try and lower the awkwardness of the whole thing. I set up my Nikon on a little tabletop tripod and had them sit near the big north-facing windows. Getting back a ways with a longer lens framed their face against the darkened empty stage at the far end of the room, and opening up the lens threw everything behind them out of focus.

It took a while but I finally got some decent results with the first two girls . . . once I'd talked them down from the whole "suck in the cheeks and make a kissy face" thing. But working with Kennedy turned out to be a breeze—she knew what she wanted, and she actually took direction well. It was almost like shooting Ollie. Except Kennedy was a smoking-hot girl my own age and *not* my sister, which made it way more, uh . . . interesting.

Adding to the interest level was that fact that, when I was done, she came around to sit next to me and review the session with me on my camera's monitor. I mean, like *right* next to me. Which I'll admit made me really nervous and really excited at the same time. I started showing her what we had, lowering expectations with "It'll look way better on a bigger screen, especially once I've had a chance to work on it a little."

She smiled at me. "No worries. I saw what you did with Olivia. That was pretty incredible." She picked up my phone and put a number into it. "Let me know when it's done—I'm really looking forward to seeing it."

"Well . . . thanks." I was already thinking about how I'd lower the color saturation in her head shot—*except* for her amazing blue eyes—when I realized she was still talking . . .

". . . you know," she continued, "I think you're really good at this. Do you ever do it professionally?"

I didn't know what to say. "I've never really thought about it."

She put her hand on my shoulder as she stood to leave. "Well, you should."

* * *

I was still thinking about what Kennedy said when I got downtown that evening. I had forty-five minutes to kill, so I went into Finch Coffee Company and got a chai, then took a stool at the window counter because it was crowded. (I guess there are some loyalty benefits to being an indie coffeehouse in a college town, because they came back strong after the whole lockdown thing and they've stayed that way.) I didn't mind the window stool because I could watch people go by and try to do the street photo thing in my head.

A few years ago my mom gave me a book about a photographer from the 1930s who talked about photography happening more in the mind than in the camera. The photographer was Dorothea Lange. Every time I crack that book I find something worth taking away. Lange was a street photographer before street photography was a thing. And an activist. That famous depression photo, *Migrant Mother,* that you see in every US history book ever? Look at it sometime. I mean *really* look at it. She took that. Like twenty minutes from here. She captured way more than a face with that—she captured the entire era. What a badass.

As I sat there, people-watching out the window and practicing taking pictures without a camera, trying to figure out what my project was about, it occurred to me that people spend a lot of time on their phones trying to make everything in their lives look better than it really is.

It also occurred to me that Dorothea Lange did the exact opposite—she tried to show things as they really were.

I made a decision—*that* was my mission statement for the

project: *Show life as it really is.* Don't polish it or varnish it or make it look better than it is. Not worse, either. Just tell the truth. Not the surface truth. The *deeper* truth . . . the stuff that makes you feel like you might have a chance of actually understanding the other person . . . of feeling what they feel.

I felt like my mom would've approved of this.

No. It felt like she *did* approve.

A chill ran down the back of my neck and I had to blink a few times to clear up my eyes.

A little while later I found myself wondering what Kennedy was doing. Right now. Then it hit me. I had her number—I could text her.

I agonized over it, trying to strike a balance between friendly and professional without coming off like a creeper. I finally decided on hey, was fun working with you today. hope we got some stuff you like! I sent it and just sat there, waiting for a reply. Nothing. Waited several more minutes. Checked my phone like five times. Still nothing.

I finished my chai when the clock above the barista station showed the little hand on the nine and the big one on the twelve. Time to go. I went down the street and parked myself on the corner, camera in hand, and waited.

The corner was empty at the moment, but a few seconds after my phone alarm vibrated someone came out of a side street up ahead and started walking toward me. They were dressed like me, only their hood was pulled up over their head—I couldn't even tell if it was a guy or a girl. I raised my camera and took a few shots as they approached.

As they got closer I could tell it was a girl underneath the hood—dark eyes, dark hair, strong features. I held out my camera and said, "I'm working on a school project—would you mind if I took your—?" And then I recognized her. AK.

She looked over and was about to reply when I could tell she suddenly recognized *me*. Probably as the guy who'd already asked if he could take her picture yesterday, since that was the only interaction I'd had with her. Like, ever.

"Hey," I said, "I didn't realize it was you. Sorry. I just thought . . ."

She just glared and shook her head once, then looked down and sort of snorted, like *I don't believe this.* She kept going, hands thrust in her pockets, without a word.

Talk about awkward. I wanted to disappear.

CHAPTER 5

The words that come direct from the people are the greatest. . . . If you substitute one of your own vocabulary, it disappears before your eyes.
—Dorothea Lange

I GOT UP EARLY THE NEXT MORNING AND CHECKED MY phone. Nothing. But so what . . . it was a Saturday and Kennedy probably slept in.

I opened my computer and found myself going over the head shots I'd taken at school.

Okay, I found myself going over the head shots I'd taken *of Kennedy* at school.

Either way, there was one I kept coming back to. I'd had her sit facing sideways and sort of look over her shoulder at the camera, but in one she'd also scrunched her sweater up under her chin. Almost like she was flirting. It gave me a little of that "can't look away" feeling, and I wanted to amplify that vibe. I cropped in close so her face filled the image as it was framed between the white fabric and her blond hair. Awesome.

I lowered the saturation but kept some color in it so I wouldn't be intruding on Ollie's precious "territory." I wanted the color soft but the image itself sharp, especially the eyes. Then I brought the irises back up to realistic color saturation (okay, maybe a touch more) so they really grabbed you.

Or at least, they really grabbed me.

Then I zoomed *way* in and smoothed out any imperfections on her face I could find. Not that she really had any—plus she'd touched up her makeup just before the session—but when I was done her skin tone was flawless, like the cover of a glossy magazine. With street photography I'd consider this cheating. I know I'm sort of a beginner at portraits, but for a fashion image like this, every other shot you're up against has been Photoshopped to death, so I figured a little touch-up was allowed.

When I was finished I leaned back and took in the image.

Yes. The "can't look away" feeling was definitely stronger. I found myself staring at her face on my monitor until I had to shake my head to break away.

My stomach growled and I glanced at the time on my phone. I'd been at this for a couple of hours already. I quickly saved what I had and headed for the kitchen, and when I returned with a stack of toaster waffles Ollie was in my room, looking at the image on my computer.

"Remind me to close my door next time," I said.

She ignored my comment as she grabbed a waffle off my plate and pointed at the screen. "That's amazing." She peered closer. "Wow, is that even her?"

"Don't be a smartass."

"I wasn't. Okay, I was, but she deserves it. Either way, that's an awesome photo."

"And it's *not* black-and-white."

"No, it's not. So where are the others?"

"Um, others?"

"You did three girls, right? So where are Chloe and Sofia?"

"Oh yeah. I haven't gotten to them yet."

She smiled as she left my room. "*Uh-huh.* Love to see them when you're done . . ."

It took me about twenty minutes to finish the other two. I told myself that was only because I'd already built up a template with all the work I'd put into the first one. Although without as much attention to the eyes. Or the skin tones. But still, I thought they looked pretty good. Although I was going to hold off on showing Ollie for an hour or so.

In the meantime, I sent the head shot to Kennedy. Okay, I spent half an hour drafting a message to go with it, *then* I sent it . . .

Dear Kennedy . . . *God no!*

Hi, Kennedy . . . *Still not right.*

Hey, Kennedy . . . *Better, but still no. I think she knows her name by now.*

Hey . . . *Yeah. Casual. Like you're friends.*

I just spent two hours working on your photo . . . *No way—do you want to come across as whipped or what?*

I finished working on your head shot. *Better . . . more direct. And if she wants to think I'm a photo genius who can just gin this stuff up on the spot, let her.*

I love it. *No! Soft/mushy. Non-pro.*

I'm really happy with it . . . *Good. Set expectations. If the photographer likes it, that sort of implies it's a quality image, right?*

and I hope you like it too. *Nope. Insecure. You want to look like a pro . . . be confident.*

and I'm confident you will be too. *But don't actually use the word* confident, *you dumbass. Sounds like a salesman.*

and I think you will be too. *Okay. Strikes a balance between wimp and jerk.*

I think it shows your inner . . . *Stop. Just . . . no!*

It demonstrates the aspect . . . *Too pretentious.*

I feel like it shows something unique . . . *Not quite. Maybe make it a team effort—give her some credit too.*

I feel like we captured something unique here. *Yeah, plus we* links *the two of you. Go with it.*

Best, *No! Too old-fashioned.*

Cheers, *Ugh. Are you suddenly British or something? Go for casual and just get it over with, you dumb shit.*

So:

Hey, I just finished working on your head shot. I'm really happy with it, and I think you will be too. I feel like we captured something unique here.

—J

Thirty minutes for thirty words. At this rate it'd take me a week to do the essay I had to turn in on Monday. Man, I needed to get my act together.

I sent it, then I sent the other two photos with quick *Here ya go, hope you like it* messages. And by lunchtime I'd heard back from both Chloe and Sofia. Turns out they were really happy with their head shots, and they each sent me a nice reply, basically gushing over the pics and thanking me for taking them. Which was cool. But still nothing from Kennedy.

I distracted myself with my usual go-to—vegging online—starting with one of my favorite photo sites, a forum called SSA, which stands for Street Shooters Anonymous. Except the *A* part isn't all that accurate—some pretty famous photographers hang out there, and it's cool to see them toss different workflow ideas back and forth. (I never post, I just lurk—those guys are way above my head.) For some reason I couldn't focus on the discussions so I bailed and spent the afternoon hanging with my dad in the garage. Then Ollie came home from who-knows-where and my dad said, "Thai, sushi, or Mexican?"

Ollie said "Mexican!" right when I shouted "Thai!" We both turned to Dad. He made the sign of the cross over me as he broke the tie.

"Sorry, my son. Mexican it is."

"Tacos de, at least . . . ?" Might as well try for a consolation prize—Tacos de Ensenada was a hole in the wall, but it had the best Mexican food in Vista Grande. Which was actually saying something. (There was another restaurant we all loved—Thai

Sister. But it had been my mom's favorite place, and by unspoken agreement we haven't eaten there since.)

He nodded. "Sure, why not?"

We went, and I just sat there—staring at the finest pollo colorado within a hundred miles—while Dad and Ollie joked around and talked about school and stuff. And all I could think about was my stupid phone and how it sat there, doing nothing at all.

Just like me.

Later that evening, at home, I finally heard back from Kennedy.

thx

"... so it would appear that most of you enjoyed the essay, based on your comments."

"*Enjoyed* is a strong word," a girl somewhere behind me said. Everyone laughed, including Ms. Montinello. I turned to see who'd said it and about fell out of my chair—it was the girl who blew me off at 9:09 last Friday. AK-47 or AJ-74 or whatever she called herself. And why did she suddenly appear in my AP language class after school had already been in session for two weeks?

Whatever. I faced forward before she saw me looking. The teacher was still talking.

"... which brings us to the formal form of the essay. Who can speak to the rhetorical triangle?"

A brown triangle took shape in front of me. Brown for the *R* in *rhetoric,* of course. My synesthesia kicked, practically forcing my hand up.

"Mr. Deever?"

Instead of words, there were little pictures, like panels from a comic book. On one point of the triangle was a person writing a book, on another was the book itself, and the third was someone reading the book. "There are three elements to classical rhetoric." An old Greek guy appeared with a robe and a long gray beard. "Aristotle first described them—and named them in Greek—but basically you have the speaker or writer; the text itself; and the listeners or readers."

"Exactly," Ms. Montinello said. "The communicator, the message, and the audience. It applies regardless of medium." She looked up, then nodded at someone behind me who'd evidently put their hand up.

"That's great, but does the so-called communicator have any responsibility to know who their 'audience' is," AK said, "or can he just keep throwing his ideas out there, regardless of whether or not anyone wants to hear them?"

Ms. Montinello looked amused, but it was subtle . . . more like Ollie's crinkle than Kennedy's smile. "Well, I suppose communication is more effective if there's a willing audience."

"Exactly," AK said. I didn't have to turn around to tell she had her arms folded and was glaring at me.

I stopped as I entered the cafeteria and glanced over at fashion central. I had an eye out for Kennedy. I was also looking for Ollie and that AK girl. None of them were there yet. I actually felt relieved as I grabbed some food and headed over to my usual table, where Beal, Riley, and Tristan were eating at one end and Seth was parked at the other.

Beal looked over as I sat by Seth. "Ooh, look who's here! I thought you were too good to sit near us."

"I am, which is why I'm over here," I said as I sat down.

Apparently he was absent the day they explained irony. He sneered. "So why aren't you over at the 7-Up table, then? Those hotties kick you out?"

I nodded. "Yup."

He looked confused. "Uh . . . they really, like, kicked you out of their table?"

"Well, I volunteered to move back." He still looked confused and I sighed, like I was explaining something to a small child. "You're not the only one who rates people, you know. They decided someone had to come over here and raise the table average back up to at least five, so I took one for the team." I indicated his little group. "Seems you guys lost points for dickishness."

He just stared at me for a minute. "You're *so* weird."

I looked over at Seth. "You know, some days this isn't even fun anymore."

He rolled his eyes. "Tell me about it."

I never thought I'd say it, but I was glad to see Ollie walk into the cafeteria. Even if I almost didn't recognize her. Her look this week was apparently Euro-waif: skinny black jeans, little pointy elf shoes, sleeveless vest, hair—platinum blond—slicked back off her face, and dark makeup, almost goth.

She saw me and I gave her a tiny *Come over here* head tilt. As she walked up I said, "So back me up . . . you can lose a couple of points for being a dick, right?"

She nodded, straight-faced. Micro-crinkle. "At least. Maybe more." She quickly scanned the rest of the group, then looked back at me. "If you're a *real* asshole, you can sink below zero." She kind of shuddered. "Then you'll die a virgin for sure." I nodded and she turned and left without another word.

I went back to my food like nothing had transpired, thinking *Wait for it . . . incoming in three . . . two . . .*

"So they can just decide who's a dick and who's not?" Beal said, right on cue.

"Yeah," Riley chimed in. "What gives them the right?"

"Wow," Seth said. "That totally sucks, doesn't it? I mean, they're sitting over there in Hot Land, getting all judgy on *us*?" He shook his head in disgust. I looked at him and waved my hand above my hair, like *That went completely over their heads, man.*

He just laughed.

Suddenly a pair of hands reached around from behind me and covered my eyes. Soft hands. "Guess who?" a girl's voice said.

The immediate vicinity went dead quiet, which in itself was a clue. "Help me out," I said. "Are you here in gratitude, maditude, or some other attitude?"

"Mostly the former. We'll see about the latter later."

"Aha! I believe we have a satisfied customer." So it was either Chloe or Sofia or . . .

She removed her hands and I looked up.

. . . Kennedy.

"A *very* satisfied customer," she said, grinning. I couldn't help it—I smiled back . . . even though I was a little confused. "You were awesome, J. Thanks again!"

"Uh . . . no problem."

"You have plans this evening?"

When a girl like her asks you a question like that, there's only one answer. Plus I never had plans. "Not really."

"Great. I want to talk to you about something. Okay if I call you later?"

I shrugged, trying to be cool. "Sure."

She smiled. "Thanks." Then she walked away and you could hear the sound of four necks turning at once to watch.

Okay, five.

Seth leaned over. "You know," he said quietly, "you can stop anytime . . . this isn't even fair."

"I know."

"And I have to warn you, I'm going to carry your books around from now on, hoping some of it rubs off on me."

"Cool. Every superhero needs a sidekick."

"So, what did you do to leave her a satisfied customer?"

"*Very* satisfied," I reminded him.

"Sure, whatever. But . . . ?"

"I took a head shot of her." I pointed to the 7-Up table. "Over there, last Friday after school. Then I did some work on it and sent it to her. Came out pretty good. No charge, either."

He nodded. "Good move, man." He paused. "So . . . who's the other girl?"

"Chloe or Sofia. Don't know their last names, but I photographed both of them, too."

"No, the one that was just here. The cute little blond . . . I think you gave her a ride home last week?"

I shook my head. "Off-limits."

"Hey dude, I'm not horning in on anyone. Just curious who she is—never seen her before."

"You have to promise to not hit on her."

He waved me away. "Don't worry about it."

"I'm serious."

"Okay." He held his hand up like he was taking a solemn oath. "I promise."

"Her name's Ollie. Short for Olivia."

"*Ollie* . . . I like that. So, does Ollie have a last name?"

"She does." Pause. "Deever." I watched his eyebrows go up. "She's my sister."

He just stared at me, then slowly shook his head. "Man, I hate you . . ."

CHAPTER 6

As photographers, we turn our attention to the familiarities of which we are a part.
—Dorothea Lange

I LOOKED AT THE GIRL ON THE MOTORCYCLE POSTER AND I had to admit, she was pretty hot. I tried to picture her as a girl today—instead of fifty years ago—and for some reason she kept morphing into Kennedy Brooks.

"Dad?"

He looked up from the workbench where he was fixing something. "Yeah?"

"How did you and Mom meet?"

He seemed surprised by the question. *I* was surprised by it. "We met at work—at the plant. I've told you that."

"That's *where* you met. I was wondering *how* you met."

"Hmm." He put down the screwdriver and turned on his

stool so he was facing me. "Are you talking the mechanics of it, or the social part?" Spoken like a true engineer.

I shrugged. "I don't know. Both, I guess."

He looked up at the ceiling for a second, then nodded. "Okay. I was a junior engineer, doing junior engineer stuff like delivering plans. I had to run them by the business office, which was in the next building over. Your mom was the engineering liaison, so I turned the plans in to her when I was done, and we'd talk. Just small talk at first. But I found myself looking forward to running plans, because it gave me an excuse to see her." He smiled. "After a while we started talking about not-so-small stuff."

"Like . . . ?"

"Whatever was important to us at the time. Books, music, films. Whatever."

"That's it? I mean, just talk?"

"No, we started having lunch together pretty regularly, and then we started going out . . . dinner, movies, going to clubs to see bands. You know—the usual stuff."

I *didn't* know—not firsthand—but I nodded anyway.

"But the important thing was the talking," he said. "Your mom was funny and creative and cheerful, and sometimes silly in a really adorable way. She was also one of the smartest people I've ever known." He paused for a second, as if deciding what to say. "Pretty people are everywhere." I must have looked confused, because he said, "What I mean is, your mom was beautiful, absolutely, but she also had so much more going on. And that's what made me want to get to know her better. Which is why the talking part is so important. She became my best friend, right around the time I fell in love with her . . ." He stopped and looked around the garage, like he suddenly remembered where he was. "So, does that answer your question?"

Wow. He'd never talked even half that much about my mom before. It was kind of embarrassing, to be honest. "Uh, yeah. Thanks."

"No problem." He gave me a funny look. "What brought it up?"

"I don't know . . . Just curious."

"Hey, Miss B-Plus! How's it going?"

Ollie glared at me as she walked by my room. "Better'n you, Mister C-Minus."

"Ha! I'm carrying a four-point-two . . . and climbing." Okay, mostly due to the fact that I was taking more AP classes now that I was a junior, but still . . . "Anyway, I think your stock is going up," I added.

That got her—she turned around and came into the room. "What are you talking about?"

"You might even be out of B-plus territory soon." I snorted. "Not that there's anything wrong with that."

"Shut up." But she sat. "What do you mean?"

"I feel like such an enabler even telling you this . . ."

"Telling me *what*?"

"I heard someone refer to you today as 'the cute little blond.'"

"Who?"

"Obviously someone with bad vision." She just glared at me and waited. "Seth," I finally said. I could tell she wasn't sure which one he was. "He's a junior. White guy, dark hair, talent for sarcasm. Not quite as tall as me. Actually really smart—a computer geek—nothing like Beal and those other asswipes."

"Oh yeah, I know who he is. Hmm . . ." I sensed she was waiting for me to make another joke about it, but I passed. For now, anyway.

"That's all. Sorry I can't report you've risen to the rarefied level of a nine . . ." Which reminded me of something I wanted to ask her about. But I couldn't just come right out and say it—I had to sneak up on it. "So, what's Chloe like? I mean, I just met her, but she sent me a nice message about her pic . . ."

"Oh, she's great." Ollie looked up like she was trying to remember something. "Good at math. Wants to go to UCLA and major in premed. Seems pretty cool." She gave me just a hint of a crinkle. "Why? Do you like her?"

"No, I don't really know her. Just asking. So, what about Sofia?"

"Sofia's a crack-up! Always joking around, but doesn't put other people down. I really like her."

"Cool. So, uh . . . what about Kennedy?"

"What about her?"

"What's she like?"

"You're the one who had a crush on her—you tell me."

I snorted. "Yeah, like in sixth grade."

She snorted right back, like we were a pair of dueling pigs. "*And* seventh. *And* eighth. *And* . . ."

I waved it away. "Doesn't matter. We haven't really talked since we were like twelve. I was just asking what she's like now, that's all."

"I don't know." She shrugged. "She's really popular. All the guys think she's totally hot."

Because she is. "Okay, but what's she like?"

She thought about it for a minute. "She's like someone who's really popular, who all the guys think is totally hot." She looked at me, but this time there was no trace of a crinkle. "Why? Do you like her?"

I shook my head. "Nope. Just asking." Then I said, "One more. That AK girl . . . I saw her at your table. She seems a little, uh . . . different."

Ollie nodded. "I suppose so."

"What do you mean?"

"She's just . . ." She paused. "She's just herself. Not part of any clique. Which isn't necessarily a bad thing." Then she asked the required question. "Why? Do you like her?"

I shook my head. "And it wouldn't matter if I did, because she sure doesn't like *me.*"

"How do you know?"

"Let's see . . . I've talked to her exactly twice in my life. The first time she ignored me. The second time she gave me the *Eat shit and die* look. And then ignored me. Subtle stuff like that."

Ollie nodded. "Sounds like her. She's a bit of a loner."

"If that's what she's like, then . . ." I stopped, because someone was texting me. Which—other than Ollie looking for a
ride, or occasionally my dad—was a rare thing. I looked at my
phone—Kennedy. hey j, do you have time to meet with me this
evening?

"I have to go," I said to Ollie. "We can talk about your loner
friend later . . ."

She left but I barely noticed because I was busy texting. sure.
Then I thought about how much fun we'd had, doing that head
shot session. should i bring my camera? ☺

no, just talk. meet me somewhere?

ok. finch coffee? on fig, near your place

half an hour?

I checked the time. 8:15. sure—see you there!

I brought my camera anyway since I thought I might do a
9:09 shoot, but I kept it in my backpack. I got there ten minutes
early and dropped my stuff at a table in the corner. i'm here, I
texted. ordering a drink. can i get u anything?

non-fat sugar-free mocha

ok!

I got her drink—and a chai for me—and sat at the table, wondering why she wanted to meet with me. Several scenarios ran
through my head . . .

    1. She'd suddenly realized she couldn't live without
       me, and was breathless to see if I felt the same
       way. *(Yeah . . . right.)*

Or . . .

> 2. She had an essay due tomorrow and wanted me to write it for her. *(Much more likely. And yeah, I probably would.)*

Or . . .

> 3. She needed to borrow money and thought I was a likely chump. *(Yeah, I probably was.)*

Or . . .

Someone plopped down across the table from me and I looked up. Right into the most amazing blue eyes. I just about handed her my wallet and said *Here—take whatever you need.*

She smiled at me. "Thanks for meeting me."

"No problem." I vaguely wondered why my cheeks hurt.

"I meant what I said at school. You do great work—I really loved the head shot."

I nodded, like it wasn't a big deal. "Awesome. Thanks."

"So I was thinking . . ." She looked down at the table, then back into my eyes. *Zap.* "Promise not to laugh?"

"Promise."

"Well, I was thinking it might be fun to try some modeling."

"Oh, you'd be great at it!"

She smiled shyly. "You really think so?"

"Definitely."

She let out a deep breath like she'd been holding it. "Oh, thank you! You never know if people are going to laugh at your ideas." She took a sip of her mocha. "I looked online, and everyone says the first step is to get a model portfolio." She wrinkled her nose. It was adorable. "Whatever that is."

I've never done one but I've read all about them on photography sites. "It's when you put together a book of photos showing you with different looks. Like, some are kind of casual, and some are more dressed up. And a head shot or two. Maybe a dozen shots, total."

"I'm so glad someone understands this." She paused. "So . . . do you think you could help me put one together?"

I didn't even think about it. "Sure!" Then I stopped. "Well, I don't have a studio or lights or anything, so we'll have to do it on location somewhere . . ."

And then we started talking about where to shoot it. In the middle of all this my alarm buzzed at 9:09 but I shut it off and kept on talking. We batted ideas around until our drinks were gone—including the refill she let me get her—and then it was time to go.

When we were leaving Kennedy gave me a hug outside and said, "I'm glad I have you in my life, J."

What do you say to that? "Uh, me too."

She smiled. "Thanks. Let's talk soon." Then she left.

I turned and headed back the way I'd come. I was on Fig—within fifty feet of Gardena—and I'd never even made it to the corner.

When I got home I found Ollie looking at her phone, as per always.

"Hey, Ollie, I have a favor to ask."

She didn't even turn around. "What?"

"I want to borrow some of your magazines."

"Huh?" Nose still in the phone.

"Fashion magazines."

She turned. "Why?"

"I want to get some photo ideas. Because I, uh . . ." Because what? *Because the hottest girl in school wants me to help her with a project and I find myself unable to say no?* Somehow I didn't think she'd understand. "Because I need to put together a model portfolio. That's all."

Now I had her attention. "For who?" I didn't say anything. Her eyes narrowed, then she nodded slowly. "For the hottest girl in school. Of course—who else?"

"Hey, don't give me that. I'd do it for you. Heck, I pretty much already have. And I'd do it for Sofia or Chloe too, if they asked."

"If they asked." She shook her head. "That's the point. They wouldn't ask. At least not without—" She stopped. "So how much is she paying you?"

I shrugged. "We didn't talk money."

She smirked. "I'll bet you didn't."

CHAPTER 7

*The good photograph is not the object. The consequence
of the photograph is the object.*
—Dorothea Lange

I DIDN'T GET THE CHANCE TO HAVE DINNER WITH DAD
and Ollie the next day. Or maybe I *arranged* to not have the
chance, because I needed some alone time. Either way, I found
myself downtown that evening thinking about what Ollie'd said.
I mean, she'd basically implied Kennedy was taking advantage of
me. But was she? Because she sure didn't have to twist my arm or
anything . . . I was apparently more than happy to help her put a
portfolio together—for free—because . . . why?

I mean, was I like *in love* with her or something? That was
stupid. I didn't really know anything about her . . . not her middle name . . . not what she wanted to do after high school . . . not
even if she was a dog person or a cat person. She'd hardly said a
word to me in years until a couple of weeks ago.

But I was sure feeling something. And it wasn't good. Okay, there were a few minutes where it was, but the rest of the time it just . . . hurt.

That was it. I was in *hurt* with her. And I hated it. Because she sure as hell didn't seem to be hurting for me. Man, this felt like eighth grade all over again . . .

The more I thought about it, the worse I felt. I didn't know if I was pissed at her or mad at myself or what, but I was definitely in a mood.

I was distracted from my cheerful thoughts when my alarm vibrated at 9:09 as I stood near the corner of Fig and Gardena. It was a slow weeknight but there was one guy approaching in the distance, so I waited for him.

I took a snap as he crossed the street toward me, then I lowered the camera as he approached. He was around my dad's age—maybe a little older—and by the looks of it he'd had a hard life. He was a big guy—a little heavy, and pretty rough around the edges. Maybe a construction worker, I don't know.

"Hey, do you mind if I take your picture?" I sort of wiggled the camera. "It's for a school project."

He gave me a hard look but finally held his hands up, like *Whatever.* "Don't matter to me."

"Thanks." I brought up the Nikon as he folded his arms and stared back at me, almost belligerently. I fired three frames, then lowered the camera. Suddenly I thought about why I was doing this. I mean, the *real* reason, not just that it got me out of the house and gave me something to do in an otherwise random, meaningless life.

"I'm doing this to honor my mom. Is your mom still around?"

He shook his head. "Nope. Died a few years ago. Stroke."

"I'm sorry. I really miss mine, and I'm sure you miss yours, too."

He suddenly softened and his eyes got big and round. "Yup." He glanced at the sky for a moment. "Every day." Then he nodded at me and I nodded back, and he moved on.

Someone else was coming up the sidewalk, but 9:09 was past so I didn't really look at them. Besides, I was still thinking about that big rough guy, missing his mom. When I finally glanced up I immediately wished I hadn't. It was AK/whatever-the-hell-her-name-was. The last thing I wanted was her thinking I was trying to take her picture *again,* so I looked back down at my camera, ignoring her entirely.

She went past—carrying a backpack—and turned into Finch Coffee.

I'd really been looking forward to that chai, too. I packed my stuff and got ready to walk home, then stopped. *Screw it—I've got as much right to be there as anyone else.*

Ten minutes later I was sitting in Finch, looking at what I'd just shot, when I noticed someone standing next to my booth. I glanced up. It was AK.

She didn't move to sit, and I sure wasn't going to invite her. She nodded at my Nikon. "Don't even ask."

I turned it off and set it down. "Wouldn't dream of it, especially after yesterday in class. You're clearly not part of my 'willing audience.' "

She gave me a funny look. "You were actually paying attention. That's a start."

I ignored that. "If you hate that class so much, why'd you even transfer in?"

She seemed surprised. "I don't hate that class at all—"

"Could have fooled me," I muttered.

"—and I want to be a writer. As soon as they told me AP lang is a prerequisite for AP lit, I put in for the switch."

"Well, *I* want to be a photographer." I held up my camera. "And taking pictures is a prerequisite for *that*."

Okay, that might have come off a little snarky and I thought she might leave, but she just nodded. "Fair enough. So . . ." She tilted her head toward the street outside. "I've seen you there twice. At the same time. Why are you out on the corner taking pictures at nine o'clock?"

I thought about being snarky again. I thought about blowing her off with some lie. I briefly considered telling her the whole thing, but NFW. A little cartoon dude popped up in my mind's eye, holding a big stack of papers labeled *Story,* then he faded away. But a different guy took his place holding a single page labeled *Synopsis*. He stuck around. Okay . . .

"It's actually at 9:09," I started. She just looked at me, waiting. "Because, uh . . . that's sort of an important time for me." Still waiting. "Something significant happened . . ." I suddenly had a hard time talking.

"To you?" she finally asked.

"No." I paused. "Well, yes. I guess. But to someone else." She just stood there patiently. I might have caught a little nod. "So, um . . . I try to take a . . . well, I try to honor . . ." God, this wasn't working at all—I could barely get the words out, and I ended up just sitting there, blinking at her.

"I think I understand," she said quietly. "Even if I don't understand." She just looked at me for a long time, and for a moment I believed she got it. Which was goofy . . . how could she? "Something doesn't have to be physical to be forever," she finally added, then nodded and walked away.

I got home and decided to check in with my dad before going inside. As usual he was at his garage workbench, doing who-knows-what with a pile of old metal parts. What *wasn't* usual was his attitude.

"Hey, Dad—how's it going?"

He looked up like he'd barely heard me. "Huh?"

Wow. Had he been crying? It was hard to say . . . and of course I'd never ask him. "Just saying hi. What are you working on?"

"Sorting some parts. Why don't you go inside. I'll be in after a while."

"Uh . . . okay. See ya." He didn't even reply.

I went inside and saw Ollie sitting in the kitchen, scrolling through her phone. For some reason there were flowers in a vase on the counter.

"What's up with Dad? He sure is quiet tonight. And what's with the flowers?"

She spun on me and it looked like she'd been crying, too. *"What's up with Dad?"* she said, mimicking me. "What do you *think's* up? It's Mom's birthday, you dumb shit! Which is why I bought flowers. Why don't you get your head out of Kennedy's perfect ass and pay attention to your own family?" She stormed off to her room, slamming the door behind her.

Shit. I didn't even bother going to my room—I just plopped down at the table with my head in my hands. I mean, how could I forget my own mother's birthday? Especially considering her final words to me? I suddenly had this panicky feeling in my chest, like she was slipping away from me . . . like I was going to forget her and it'd be like she was never my mom.

All these ideas went through my brain, like maybe I could make a post about how important she was to me or something. Which would be gone in a day . . . *great.* I needed something permanent, maybe not directly about her, but somehow related to her so every time I saw it I'd be reminded of her. So she couldn't slip away. Maybe like planting a tree in her honor? Man, I didn't know *what* I wanted . . . I just knew I needed to put all these feelings into something or I was gonna seriously fucking lose it . . .

I thought about it some more, then finally got up and went to my room, where I loaded tonight's pics into the folder on my computer labeled *Corner Pics.* Then I did something I hadn't done since I started doing the street shots—I opened up the folder and spent half an hour going through everything. They weren't all complete crap. Okay, some were. And a lot of them were just plain B-plus. But a few of them were pretty good.

I leaned back and thought about what I was really trying to

do on that corner at 9:09 every night. I dug into the folder again. The hardest part was deciding what to include. There were pics that worked in a technical sense, that were well composed or balanced or had good exposure. But what were their *consequences*—would they mean anything to anyone?

I thought about my mission and decided to simply go with the ones that made me feel something in common with the people in them . . . some connection. And once I started really looking, I realized I didn't care as much about technique as I'd thought.

I looked at the photo of the construction worker. It was a little dark, a little gritty, and there were some weird lights from a car off toward the edge of the frame. Some of that could probably be fixed or cropped, but what really mattered was how it made me *feel*. At first glance the guy seems angry, but then you get the sense that it's more like he's challenging you—or maybe the whole world—right through the camera lens. Like he's actually trying to prove he isn't afraid. Which hints that maybe he *is* afraid. All of which led me to see a man who'd worked hard his whole life but probably didn't have a lot to show for it. Except his pride.

What I liked about the image was it wasn't all obvious. It drew you in, trying to see the guy's entire story in 1/100th of a second. That's what Dorothea Lange did . . . not that I was anywhere close to her league.

But it gave me a starting place . . . a bar to shoot for. I made a subfolder and named it *keepers*. Whenever I saw an image that actually made me feel some sort of connection with the subject—*any* sort of connection—I put a copy into the sub-folder.

Believe me, I ended up cutting a lot of stuff.

I got to work on what was left, and I ended up doing everything in black-and-white. It's just more graphic. Maybe because it's more stripped down, it's closer to the truth?

By the time I was done I was left with about thirty photos that I still thought were keepers. And it was three o'clock in the morning. After I'd shut everything down and was lying in bed in the dark, certain images still kept popping up in front of me . . .

The couple I'd photographed against the building. Where she has her back to the camera and he looks like he has everything he's ever wanted or needed right there . . .

A woman walking home with a sleeping baby against her shoulder. She's really happy and peaceful. In the image she puts out this vibe like she's a saint or something . . .

A round-faced girl with freckles and curly hair and the most amazing smile. You look at her and you can't help but think *She's super nice—I just know I'd really like her if we met in person* . . .

A homeless guy with an old dog. He *wasn't* a saint and he *didn't* have everything he'd ever wanted and you might *not* like him in person, but there was a real bond between him and his dog. I was glad they'd found each other. I'd bought him a cup of coffee and a sandwich at Finch after I'd photographed them, and he immediately gave half his sandwich to the dog.

The girl in the black hoodie crossing Gardena toward me, somehow looking fierce and thoughtful at the same time . . .

Those images did something to me. They did something *for*

me. I fell asleep feeling like I'd finally found something worth-while . . . maybe even *done* something worthwhile. I wasn't sure yet exactly what it was or what I was going to do with it, but for the first time in a long time, I felt like I had *something*.

I wished I could show my mom this . . . but somehow it felt like maybe she knew.

I woke up totally out of it when my alarm went off a few hours later. Then it all came back to me and I suddenly had to open my computer and check. What if I'd been fooling myself in the middle of the night and it was nothing but junk? I could feel my heart speed up as I opened the folder, then I let out my breath. They were good.

I went to school with this weird feeling, like I was carrying around a secret. Like when you first learn that your mother's a superhero and you inherited some minor superpower. I spent most of the day thinking about what I wanted to do with the photos.

Well, except during AP language. Ms. Montinello was de-bating something with a student while I was in the middle of thinking about whether I wanted to work on more images or just do something with what I had, when she said, "So, Mr. Deever, what's your opinion on this?"

I almost said *Whaaa?* or *Huh?* or even the old *Could you re-peat the question?,* but the one percent of my brain that actually *was* in the present saved my ass at the last second. "It's a broad issue. Which part, specifically?"

She folded her arms. "*Specifically,* we were discussing the benefits of using the passive voice in a logically applied rhetorical essay. What say you?"

Pick a position and defend it. Passive . . . Active . . . I saw a sleeping little cartoon animal—like a goofy Dr. Seuss character—sprawled across a desk with a book lying next to him, and one who was awake, leaning forward and reading with interest. The sleeping guy was a pale yellow, almost transparent. For *P.* And the alert one was a creamy orange, like an ice cream push-up. For *A,* of course. "I say no. Active is better."

"That's it? Just 'better'? Even for logical rhetoric?"

Show confidence. "For anything. If you don't engage the reader, you're lost before you start. They probably already know the facts—the important part is making a compelling case. Don't be afraid to take a stand . . . passive voice is weasel-wording. 'Mistakes were made,' right?" I snorted. "Sounds like a politician." I smiled. "In my opinion."

She smiled back, so I figured I was okay. "Yes, but how do you really feel?" A few people snickered. "So, we have at least two students who feel rather, uh . . . *strongly* that passive voice should be avoided." She glanced at someone behind me.

I took a quick peek. Of course. Her.

"Does anyone else have a strong opinion on this?"

Apparently not . . .

I'd been thinking about what AK had said when I'd tried to tell her about my street photos—about something not needing to be physical to be permanent—and if nothing else, by the end of fourth period I'd come up with some vague ideas about the images. Maybe something sort of like SSA? But not? I don't know . . .

I went to the cafeteria, got some food, and sat at the far end of the usual losers' table, where Beal and Riley were already busy ranking and yanking at the other end. After a couple of minutes Seth sat next to me.

Did I really want to do this?

I glanced over at him. "So . . . you still interested in that sidekick gig?" Which I guess answered my question.

"No cape. And I'm still up in the air about the tights. But otherwise, maybe."

"Nothing too exciting. I'm not sure, but I think I want to build a website."

"Dude, that's my definition of exciting." He paused. "Not really. But it's better than carrying your books around. What do you need it to do?"

I shrugged. "Host some photos. Probably some text to go with them. Maybe a place for comments. Has to be easy for me to update pretty often, maybe once a week."

"Should be no problem. How about the layout—you okay with simple?"

"Sure. Probably a clean, graphic look. Don't want to detract from the pictures anyway."

"Yeah, and it'll load faster than a bunch of fancy crap. Where're we doing this?" He looked around. "Not here, right?"

I shook my head. "I'm thinking my place. How about today, after school?"

"I'm in," he said a little too quickly.

"Thanks." I fixed him with a look. "But I'm still holding you to your promise."

"Yeah, and I still hate you. But okay."

CHAPTER 8

To be good, photographs have to be full of the world.
—Dorothea Lange

SETH KEPT HIS PROMISE—WE WORKED IN MY ROOM AND he stayed focused on helping me figure things out. We started with a template that I wasn't crazy about at first, but it was like watching Ollie turn a bunch of random scraps into a cool outfit. Every time I'd complain, he'd say "Just give me a minute." And then he'd change the color scheme or tweak the layout a little and sure enough, it'd be better.

We were mostly done with the basics when my dad came home from work and stuck his head in my room. "Hey, J, how's it going?" If he was still upset about yesterday he was hiding it pretty well, and as usual we didn't discuss it.

"We're good. Working on a project."

His glance took in Seth, still hunched over my computer, tapping away. "Cool. Who's your friend?"

Seth turned and nodded to my dad. "Hi, I'm Seth." He indicated my computer. "J wanted help building a porn site," he explained with a straight face. *Great.*

My dad didn't even blink. "That's fine, as long as you can find a way to monetize it. College is expensive."

Seth laughed like that was actually funny.

"It's a school project," I said, glaring at both of them. "And we're almost done."

Dad ignored me and turned to Seth. "So, you like Thai, sushi, or Mexican?"

"We've got work to do," I said.

"You've still got to eat, and your sister and I are hungry." He looked at Seth. "So?"

I was mouthing *Thai* at him, but he said, "Mexican sounds good."

Dad grinned at me. "Sorry, mijo. It's three to one."

Damn.

"So, what do you want to do?" my dad asked Seth as we dug into our food at Tacos de.

Having someone else with us made it feel more like a family meal, not less. Like it was nice to have someone else there, even if it wasn't Mom.

Seth was good about not sniffing around Ollie. But it'd never occurred to me that there could be the opposite issue. Even I could tell that Ollie had gotten herself dressed up a little, even though Tacos de was just a mom-and-pop joint where you'd be fine wearing shorts and a T-shirt. And she paid attention to him when he spoke—at least, a lot more than she ever does to me. Like when Seth answered my dad's question about what he wanted to do.

"Not positive about the details yet, but something to do with computers for sure."

My dad nodded. "You mean like coding or computer engineering?"

I was waiting for Seth to agree, which would totally get him some dad points because Dad was for anything with the word *engineer* in it, but he shook his head. "I don't think so. Coding is awesome, but I'm more into the aesthetics of it. I want to do something with graphic design."

Ollie looked at him and nodded sagely. "Good design is *so* important . . ." She went off on a little lecture about design and its significance in modern society, while Seth mostly just listened and nodded occasionally.

In the middle of it all my dad caught my eye and winked. It was such a small thing but it kind of floored me, like he was saying *I know exactly what's going on here and Ollie is so serious and trying so hard to show she's an adult and it's really kind of cute, isn't it?* I mean, *I* knew what was happening, but I figured people my parents' age were oblivious to it, so having him just casually admit that he was aware of it all—and that he was aware that I was aware—was, I don't know . . . not necessarily bad, but weird. Like I'd suddenly been promoted to an adult or something.

I wasn't sure I was ready for it.

* * *

After dinner Seth and I were back in my room, finishing up the basic template of the site. We had the page layouts mostly done and we'd loaded the first gallery of pics when Seth turned to me. "So what tags do you want on it?"

"What do you mean?"

"Besides whatever text you're going to add—which I guess'll have words like *photograph* and *street photography*—are there any other terms you want connected to the site? Like for people searching for something that's not included in the text. You know, for SEO?" He caught my *Huh?* look. "What's this site *about*, besides being a collection of random shots taken at night?"

I just shrugged, not sure what to say. I'd never really told anyone what the project was actually about.

"Okay, let's back up," he said. "What are you calling the site?"

I hadn't really thought about that, either. I mean, I knew I didn't want to call it Corner Pics or something, because that was just boring. I'd begun to think of the photo project as the 9:09 thing, so . . . ? "How about the 9:09 Project?"

"The 9:09 Project," he repeated, trying it on. "I like that. But why 9:09? I mean, I get that you take the pictures at night, but why that particular time?"

I was going to blow him off with some bullshit about it just being a time I chose because I liked the sound of it. Like how I tell people it's a school project—it's easier than the truth. I started to feed him that line, then it hit me: I used to have friends. At least, a few guys I could sort of call friends, on a good day. Right up until that horrible night almost two years ago. At 9:09 p.m. When I boxed myself up.

He was looking at me, waiting, when I heard myself say, "Because that's what time my mom died."

"What?"

I told him. All of it. About my mom, about starting the photo project to honor her, about my private little meltdown when I'd forgotten her birthday . . . and about me deciding to put my project up on a site as a memorial to her.

When I finished he sat back and didn't say anything for a while. "Wow. I had no idea," he finally said. He leaned forward. "Why're you keeping it such a tight secret? Sometimes a little sympathy can be a good thing."

I shook my head. "Not looking for that."

He shrugged. "Okay, maybe *understanding* is a better word." He pointed to my computer, where the gallery of pics was still open. "And knowing the backstory gives this more . . . I don't know. Gravity."

"Don't need that, either—I feel heavy enough as it is." I was already regretting telling him. "Look, I only told you because you said you needed to know what it was about for the tags. Not for sympathy, and not for anyone else to know. Got it?"

He motioned like he was zipping his mouth shut. "Got it." He swiveled back toward the computer and put his hands on the keys and paused for a second, then kind of nodded to himself and started typing a list of phrases into the field on the website template. I looked over his shoulder.

Loss.

Grief.

Loss of loved one.

Missing loved one.

Honoring loved one.

Grieving for loved one.

Memorial for loved one.

Remembering loved one.

Coping with loss of loved one.

And so on . . .

"Not sure what that's going to do," I said.

"Maybe nothing—who knows? But it might help someone in a similar situation find your site, even if they're not actually looking for *street photography* or whatever."

"I still don't get how that helps."

He gave me a weird look. "You know, I didn't come over here just to try and get into your sister's pants—"

"Hey! You said 'just,' " I interrupted. "Which indicates—"

"Which indicates *nothing*." He waved it aside. "Look, J . . . You're a good guy, you're generally smart, and you're even slightly funny at times. But you also have a supreme talent for missing the whole point."

If I were a dog I would have tilted my head. "I'm sure missing this one."

He sighed. "People want to help other people. Like, I came

here to help you. And did you ever think that maybe—just maybe—this site might help someone else?"

I sat there for quite a while, thinking. Remembering how lost and alone I'd felt after my mom died. Then I nodded at him. "Thanks, man. For the help. And . . . for the help."

That didn't mean I was going public with everything. Well, I guess technically I was, but anonymously. After Seth left I got back to work, writing a little overview for the main page of the site. I didn't want anything fancy or long-winded, but Seth had a point.

Artist's Statement

This page is where I'll post some of my work from what I call the 9:09 Project. My mother passed away at 9:09 p.m. and I honor her by taking a photograph at that time as often as possible. I go to the same corner night after night and do my best to capture whatever's there at 9:09. Perhaps that sounds pointless, but it does two things for me . . .

It reminds me that life keeps on going, even after we're gone.

It also reminds me that, in some ways, it doesn't.

Anyway, here is my work, presented as honestly as possible.

Who am I? Just someone who's lost someone. Like many of you . . .

Right after I'd gotten it to load, Ollie walked into my room. She glanced at my computer. "What were you guys working on?"

"We were putting up a page for . . . for a school project." I didn't want to get into it right then.

"Were you guys studying together or what?"

I shook my head. "The project was for me. Seth was helping me with it, because he's a computer wizard."

She nodded. "Cool." Then she asked, "So what's he like?"

It was my turn to ask her favorite question. With a smartass grin on my face, of course. "Why—do you like him?"

I was expecting instant denial, so I was surprised when she shrugged and said, "I don't know." I looked close—there was a trace of a crinkle. Possibly. "So, what's he like?"

"According to Shakespeare, if I tell you he's a decent guy you'll run the other way. But if I say he's a bad-boy loser, you'll be attracted to him like a magnet."

"Screw Shakespeare. If you don't want to tell me, don't tell me." She turned to go.

I flashed on my promise to my mom, about looking out for Ollie. But then I thought about my promotion, at dinner. Maybe there was more to it than that.

"Hey."

She turned back. "Yeah?"

"I think he's a good guy."

"Okay then."

After Ollie left I had the urge to head down to Fig and Gardena. Like *right now*. I guess knowing these street pics were a part of something bigger made it feel more important. Like I had some sort of purpose. As I walked downtown it hit me that I felt better—about myself, about my life, about *anything*—than I had in quite a while.

When my alarm went off a group of kids was crossing the street toward me.

There were five of them—all dudes—around thirteen years old. "Hey guys, mind if I take your picture? It's for an art project." (Kids don't give a shit about school projects.)

"Sure," one of them said.

"As long as we get a copy," another one added. "We're a band."

"No problem," I said. "Why don't you stand over there."

There was a little jockeying for position as they lined up against the wall—the one who'd demanded a copy of the pic clearly wanted to be in the middle—and once they got that worked out they just stood there side by side, staring at the camera and looking serious. I guess that was the male eighth-grade version of the duck face. I took a couple of quick snaps, then said, "No posing. Just be yourselves."

They shuffled around a little but ended up with the same basic look. I sort of shrugged and figured that was as good as it was going to get, so I fiddled with the exposure and the aperture to try and at least get a halfway-decent picture. Then my brain gave me this weird image, sort of a split-screen thing with writing on both halves. One side was covered with typed exposure equations, all math-y and blue and precise, and the other side was a bunch of handwritten poetry, sort of warm-colored and ragged and torn. It hit me—technique is good, but only in support of the human element. By itself it's just an exercise, with nothing at the center.

I stopped what I was doing, brought the camera down, and looked right at the quiet kid on the end. "So, what's the dumbest thing *this* guy ever did?" I asked, indicating the one in the middle.

"Oh dude! There was this one time where we played at a pool party and he thought he could stand on a raft in the middle of the pool and sing . . ." And they forgot all about being photographed and started riffing on each other. Pretty soon they were cracking up and yelling and pointing like a pack of wild monkeys and I was shooting away, only stopping to ask *And then what happened . . . ?* to keep them going.

After a few minutes they wound down, but by then I'd fired off twenty or thirty frames. I got a number to send them a photo and they went on their way, still laughing and making fun of each other as they wandered down the street.

I was feeling pretty good as I went to Finch so I splurged on an extra-large chai and grabbed a booth, where I started reviewing the pics. The first ones were what you'd expect—they looked like every crappy amateur band photo ever. But some of the later ones had a different vibe . . . they'd forgotten to try and be cool or badass or whatever. They were just themselves—thirteen years old and full of life. You could see it in their faces—the energy and the humor and the excitement. You could also tell they really liked each other. There was one shot where the kid on the end was pointing at the one in the middle and saying something, and all the others were cracking up. Even the kid in the middle.

I was reviewing a few more, thinking *There's definitely something here,* when I realized someone was standing next to my booth. I looked up. Her.

"You know, you did it again today in language class. With the passive voice thing."

I shrugged. "Questions were asked. Opinions were rendered."

She actually smiled at that, which did something to me. Kind of like my dad's wink at dinner. But not.

I held up my camera. "We all know what *I'm* doing here." I nodded at the laptop under her arm. "So what about you? Homework?"

She shook her head and blinked at me, and for some reason I had the impression she felt like I'd felt the night before, trying to talk about why I was doing my photo project. "No," she finally said. "I'm trying to . . ." She paused. "I guess I'm doing the same thing you are."

What do you say to that? I shrugged. "Well . . . good luck." Then out of my mouth came, "You know, I'd love to see whatever you're working on sometime. Really." Wow. Where did *that* come from?

She just stared at me, and all of a sudden I could hear the clank of dishes back in the kitchen . . . the front door swinging shut . . . the barista calling out someone's order . . .

"Thanks," she finally said, and things went back to normal. For a second she looked like she was going to say something else, then she turned and walked down the aisle to an empty booth.

I went back to my camera and tried—without much success—to focus on my photos.

When I got home the light was still on in the garage so I wandered out there.

"Hey, Dad?" He was messing with an ancient wind-up phonograph scattered in pieces across his workbench. What did he see in that pile of junk that I didn't?

He turned to face me. "What's up, son?"

"I have a stupid question. What exactly is an AK-47? I mean, I know what it is, but . . ."

He seemed surprised. "It's a Kalashnikov. 7.62 by 39." He must have seen my confusion. "You know . . . from Russia, with love? Designed to be cheap and reliable more than anything else."

"Is it like popular or something?"

"Popular? Hmm . . . It's certainly the hardware of choice for much of the world." He suddenly looked concerned. "Why are you asking?"

What do you say to that? *Well, there's this girl at school and she's a bit of a loner . . . maybe sorta like your only son, now that I think of it . . . and for some reason that's her name and she's really severe and intense and she hates me and she never smiles—well, except for tonight—and sometimes I find myself agreeing with her in class but that only makes it worse . . . ?*

I sure didn't say *that*. "It's no big deal. It's the nickname of somebody at school and . . . I don't know. I was just wondering."

He wasn't willing to let it go yet. "So is this something I should be worried about? Do you think he might be violent, or—"

I laughed and waved it away. "No, nothing like that." *Anyway, it's a she, not a he. And she doesn't seem violent at all. Well, other than sometimes it seems like she might want to go a couple rounds with me . . .*

But I didn't say *that*, either. I just added, "I promise. It's nothing to worry about."

CHAPTER 9

I believe that what we call beautiful
is generally a by-product.
—Dorothea Lange

"COOL," I SAID. "I THINK WE GOT EVERYTHING WE NEED for that one. Ready to change into the fancy-pants stuff?"

Kennedy and I were at Mission Park after school. It was down by the creek and had lots of good scenery for backgrounds, plus it had a restroom she could use as a changing room. And it was way less crowded during a weekday afternoon than it would be on the weekend.

As she changed, I previewed what we'd just shot. We'd started with the sporty look—basically her in running shorts and shoes with a sports top—and I got her standing, stretching, drinking out of a water bottle, and posing with a tennis racquet. Then we went for the casual look, which was a slightly dressed-up version of what she normally wore to school. So far, so good. Next up was the more formal look.

She sauntered out of the restroom and I couldn't help it. *"Wow . . ."*

Her hair and makeup were similar to when we'd done her head shot, but she had on some sort of flowing thing that was more like a giant scarf than a dress. It had wild jungle colors, and you could see right through most of it. It went down to her calf in the back but was short in front, and it swept back and showed her legs all the way up when she walked. Her shoes were like clear sandals, only with four-inch heels.

"You look . . ." How did she look? "You look gorgeous," I finally said. And I meant it.

She gave me a shy smile and glanced away. Then we got to work.

I tried everything I'd learned from Ollie's fashion magazines and from studying things online. I shot her full-length, from the front, from the rear, from each side. Then the same thing in three-quarter-length. Then head shots, just because. Then walking, dead-on—like on the runway at a fashion show—and from the side. Then in some relaxed poses, leaning against a railing, with ducks on the grass in the background. Then I gave her a wineglass to hold and had her stand among the trees and look into the distance as I worked around her in a semicircle.

All in all we spent at least an hour on that one look alone, and by the time we were finishing, the sun was low in the sky and the lighting had that magical warmth to it.

And—any love/lust/longing aside—she really was great at it. Okay, I haven't photographed a ton of models—my experience has been limited to Ollie and Sofia and Chloe and a few dozen random people during my nighttime street shoots. But I could tell Kennedy was different. Like, I could say, "Why don't you start at that tree and walk toward me?" and instead of looking self-conscious or bored or having a big fake smile on her face, she'd stride across the grass like a queen reviewing her troops or something—head high and arms swinging—like she *owned* the place.

I don't know if she binge-watched runway reality shows all day or just had a natural talent or what, but she was seriously good at it.

After we were packed up, I looked over at her.

"You know, you're really good at this."

She looked down but I caught her smile. "Thanks. I don't . . . well . . ." She looked up at me. "Really?"

I nodded. "Absolutely. So, uh . . . when do you want to get together and go over these? To see which ones make it into the portfolio, I mean."

"You're the expert, not me. Why don't you pick the ones you think are best and go with those?" She gave me that shy look again. "Besides, I hate looking at pictures of myself."

"I'll do my best."

"I know you will." She paused. "So when do you think it might be ready?"

I hadn't even thought that far. I'd figured we'd get together somewhere—maybe the coffee shop, or even her place—and look at all of them. Then she'd take a file home and narrow it down a little. Then another meeting, for final decisions. Then talk about the layout and the order in the book.

"I . . . I'm not sure."

She smiled. "Maybe next week?"

"Uh . . . okay."

She placed her hand on my arm and looked at me. "That would be nice." Then she leaned in and gave me a kiss. On the lips. "I'm really excited to see it."

"Me too."

Have you ever edited down several hundred photos, trying to decide on the top ten? Nothing to it. All you have to do is . . .

1. Review all pics and throw away the obvious trash.
2. Sort all remaining photos into folders by style (Casual, Sporty, Formal).
3. Make another pass and toss the bottom 50 percent of each folder. (This was hard. I sort of fell in love with each shot of her, to tell the truth.)
4. Sort each folder into subfolders, by pose.
5. Decide on the best three poses for each style.
6. Review and decide on the best single photo of

each of the above poses. (This was even harder. I'd pick one I loved by itself, but then for some reason it wouldn't look right with the rest. So I'd change it. Or maybe change one of the other finalists. And look at the whole thing all over again.)

7. Add head shots. I used the one from the school session, and the best of the ones I'd shot when she had her formal look on.

8. Arrange the final pics in order. (According to the experts: Start strong. Finish strong. And no filler in between—if something doesn't live up to the best, toss it.)

9. Do processing on every photo in the portfolio to (a) make it look as good as possible, while (b) making it look like no work was done, and (c) making them all have the same feel, so they go well together.

When all this was done (a few hours a night for four nights), I ordered three sets of 8x10 pro-quality prints of each. One for the portfolio, one as a backup for Kennedy, and one for my resume. Then I went online and bought a couple of stylish-looking presentation books to hold the prints, and paid for rush shipping. By the time everything was done and ready to go, I'd spent a ton of time on this thing.

And a couple hundred bucks, easy.

* * *

I'd be lying if I said money wasn't an issue.

Something you don't immediately think about when faced with terms like *metastatic invasive lobular carcinoma* is that, along with the earthshaking loss-of-life issue, at some point you also have to face the trivial loss-of-income issue. Mom and Dad had both been working when they met, and that hadn't really changed after they'd married and had kids. So along with ripping out the heart of our family and stomping it to a bloody mess, as a little bonus cancer also cut our household income in half.

Kind of like he did right after Mom had been diagnosed, Dad had tried to shield us from the worst of it. But just like it was impossible to hide the fact that something had been seriously wrong with Mom, it was hard to hide the fact that Dad was working a lot more overtime . . . that going out to nice restaurants had become pretty rare . . . that going to the movies had totally become a thing of the past.

I remember finally figuring it out near the end of my freshman year, four or five months after Mom had died.

"Do you think I should get a job?" I asked.

"That might be a good idea," he said. Which scared the crap out of me, to be honest. Then he added, "But only during the summer. Your job during school is school."

I ended up getting a job at Vista Grande Screens, the giant multiplex out by Costco. It paid minimum wage and the manager was a total jerk who hated teenagers, but I could eat from concessions on shift and I could get Ollie into all the movies she wanted for free, so overall it was still pretty cool. I worked there all that summer and all last summer—and hopefully next summer, too—and whatever I save has to last me through the school year, unless I pick up some hours over winter break. So I've learned to budget my spending wisely. Which isn't as hard as it seems, because I really don't have much to spend it on . . . like doing stuff with friends or going out on dates or whatever.

Until now.

I had everything bundled up by Sunday morning. I was going to bring it with me the next day and give it to Kennedy at school, but I was looking through the book (for like the thousandth time) and I guess I was a little excited about it.

hey, I texted, are you going to be home? i have something to bring by

Fifteen minutes later I heard back. give me an hour

I looked at the time—10:15. cool. see you then

My first thought had been to put it in a box, like the kind you put fancy shirts in. Maybe even wrapped. Then I realized that was stupid—it wasn't a birthday present or something. But mostly I didn't box it because I wanted her to look at it right there, in front of me. I settled on a nice bag I found in the closet—probably something my mom had gotten at a dress shop.

I puttered around until it was time to head out, then at the last minute I decided to put on a real shirt, with buttons and a collar and stuff. It's not like I wore a suit and tie or anything—I rolled up the sleeves and left it untucked—but for some reason I thought I should wear something nicer than a T-shirt. Don't judge.

I got there and knocked. Nada. Then I pushed the doorbell and I could hear something back in the house that sounded like church chimes playing a song.

Before the song was over, the door opened. Her dad. He didn't look real happy to see me.

"Hi, is Kennedy here?"

He kind of half nodded. "Lemme see . . ." Then he closed the door and went away, leaving me standing on the porch. After a few minutes the door opened again and it was Kennedy, and she didn't seem much happier to see me than her dad.

"Uh . . . hi," I said.

"Hi." She looked pretty burnt, maybe hungover or something? She also looked like she'd slept in her clothes and was still wearing last night's makeup. But you know what? Even with the whole scraggly bedhead thing going on, she was still hot.

"I've got something for you." I held out the bag. "I worked on it all week, and I hope you like it . . ."

She took the bag. "Thanks." She didn't even look inside it. "Um, I have to . . ." She pointed back into the house. "I have some things to do."

"Oh . . . sure. I mean, fine. It's just that I knew you were really looking forward to seeing the portfolio, and . . ." She just stood there. "I sent you the files too, so you can submit the pics electronically, and . . ." I ran out of gas. "Anyway, there you go."

She sort of nodded. "Okay. See ya."

"See ya." By the time I got the *ya* out, the door was closed.

Wow. That was absolutely awesome, wasn't it?

"So what else can influence the impact of a work?" Ms. Montinello asked the next morning. "Is completing the rhetorical triangle enough, or is there more?"

I'd already spoken up once or twice so I kept my hand down. And besides, I was in the middle of replaying yesterday's scene on Kennedy's porch. Then I realized someone was talking behind me.

". . . and it's not really a triangle anyway." I recognized the voice. AK. "I think it's a square. Or at least a quadrilateral."

"Explain," Ms. Montinello said.

"It's not like things happen in a vacuum. You have to consider the times of the work. Like those civil rights speeches we read. They were groundbreaking in the 1960s. But the same thing would probably get you thrown in jail back in the 1930s and burned at the stake three hundred years ago. But today, most people would just say *duh*."

Ms. Montinello nodded slowly. "Interesting perspective." She looked around. "Comments?" No one said anything. Probably because lunch started in a few minutes and everyone was hoping the discussion would fade and she'd cut us loose. Then she looked directly at me. "Jamison?"

Why me? "Well . . ." *C'mon . . . engage brain . . . open mouth . . .* I closed the mental image of Kennedy with bedhead. "Hard to say." *Stall . . . humor . . .* "Aristotle didn't exactly post the rules on his Twitter feed . . ." A couple of people laughed. *Pick a position . . . defend it . . .* "But I'd say historical context might still fall under the broader definition of *audience,* as readers are a product of their times." Ms. Montinello nodded and was going to say something—probably *Class dismissed*—but for some reason my mouth kept going. "But you know, she makes a great point." *What?* "Two thousand years ago context changed a lot slower, so maybe it wasn't really considered."

"So perhaps Aristotle missed an aspect of the elements of rhetoric?"

I shrugged. "Maybe. But still . . . three out of four ain't bad."

Ms. Montinello smiled. "No, it's not." She looked up at the class. "Have a nice lunch."

As we were leaving I caught AK looking at me. I'm sure she was pissed off about something, but I didn't stick around to find out. I put my hands in my pockets and kept on moving.

"So, how come you didn't sit with us at lunch?" Ollie asked. "Are you too good for us?"

I was driving her home after school. "You must be Beal Wilson's long-lost soul mate after all—he asked me the exact same question a few days ago."

Her reply was to ignore me and put her nose in her phone. Actually, I'd been waiting for Kennedy to come up and tell me how much she loved the portfolio. I mean, she had to have looked at it by now. I saw her in the hall on the way to lunch—and I was pretty sure she saw me—but she acted busy and didn't say anything. Plus AK sat near the 7-Ups and I didn't want to deal with whatever bug was up her butt either, so I'd eaten in my usual spot.

Finally Ollie got bored with the standoff. "Well, it's too bad, because your model portfolio was a hit."

I turned. "What?"

"Kennedy had it with her and showed it around at lunch. She's been bragging about trying to be a model and everyone's been doing eye rolls, but that book shut them up." She looked up from her phone. "You really did an awesome job, J. Seriously. Everyone loved it—they thought it was real professional."

"Oh, *great*."

"What's the matter?"

"Now they're all going to want me to do one. Do you know how much work that was?"

She stared at me for a long time with a funny look on her face. I couldn't tell if she was sad or mad or what. But there was no crinkle in sight.

"What?" I finally asked.

"They won't be asking you."

"Huh?"

"Kennedy never even mentioned your name."

CHAPTER 10

*... it came to me that what I had to do was take
pictures and concentrate on people, only people,
all kinds of people ... people who paid me
and people who didn't.*
—Dorothea Lange

SOMETIMES YOU HAVE TO FOCUS ON THE IMPORTANT
stuff. Like, I spent most of fourth period the next morning trying to decide where I was going to sit at lunch. On the one hand,
it would be nice to actually get some love for all the work I did on
Kennedy's portfolio. But maybe she hadn't brought up the fact
that I did it because she wanted the others to think it was done
by a real pro, not just some guy at school? Which I guess I could
understand. Sort of.

I'd decided to just eat at my usual spot and avoid any
drama when I heard the teacher reply to someone reading from

their paper. It's funny, but even in the middle of deep boy-girl thoughts, some part of your brain can hear the tiniest trace of an edge in someone's voice. Especially when they're trying not to let it show. "Isn't that a little subjective for a critical piece, Ms. Knudsen?" Ms. Montinello asked.

Knudsen? Who was Knudsen?

"I agree that it's subjective," AK said. "But I disagree that it's necessarily a bad thing."

Oh, of course. *Her.*

"The idea is to present your thoughts as clearly as possible," Ms. Montinello said.

"I agree. But unless we're talking about something like geometry or chemistry, there's subjectivity in just about everything anyone writes. Maybe it even helps."

Ms. Montinello looked around. "Interesting theory. So, does anyone have an opinion—subjective or otherwise"—she gave a tight smile—"about this idea?"

The digits 3 and 4 popped into my head. Blue-ish and orange-ish, respectively. As in third period and fourth period. As in math and art.

A guy behind me coughed up a direct quote from the syllabus. "An effective essay is supposed to have soundly supported critical interpretations."

A side effect of my synesthesia has to do with problem solving. The frustrating part is sometimes I can "see" the solution right in front of me, but I can't always explain it . . . at least not in any sort of normal language. Like at the moment, my brain was deep into considering the primary difference between mathematics and literature, because somehow that's how it shaped the argument around this thing. But instead of recalling the lessons from the textbook in some sort of logical fashion—like most of the other students were probably trying to do—my brain was working away at solving the problem . . . with *little dancing figures,* of all things.

And oh crap, it was getting away from me . . .

"And . . . ?" Ms. Montinello asked.

It was a ballet involving numbers and letters . . .

"And . . . And I guess that doesn't leave much room for subjectivity," the guy said.

And they were on totally different sides of the stage . . .

"Anyone else?"

And no matter how much I tried to make them do the same dance, they worked best when you played to their differences . . .

"Jamison?"

Huh? My hand wasn't up. "Au contraire," I said.

She folded her arms. "Explain, s'il vous plaît . . ."

How? It was such a huge, nebulous concept . . .

Suddenly I saw a thin, bookish woman with dark eyes. Holding a cigarette and staring at the camera. In black-and-white, of course. Sure, why not? "Here's a brief quote from Joan Didion's essay 'Why I Write,'" I said. "I, I, I."

I could tell she got it, so I dropped the mic and left the stage. See what I mean?

* * *

"That's an eight, for sure." Riley and Tris nodded, then Beal looked down my way. "J, you're gonna have to give up your man card pretty soon—why don't you ever weigh in?"

I don't know . . . maybe because the whole thing's so damn reductive, like you really think people can be summed up as a number? Or maybe because it just seems really mean and stupid, like you're going to say "Hey, baby, I think you're a solid eight" and somehow she's going to find that attractive? Or—when you get right down to it—maybe because seven is actually a far more interesting number than eight?

But I didn't say any of those, because that would just be pissing into the wind. Instead I said, "Your system has a fatal flaw—you're using a quantitative methodology to assign value to qualitative concepts." Which I suppose was also pretty pointless, considering.

He just stared at me, then pulled a face. "Man, you're *beyond* weird."

For some reason I tried to push through it. "No, what's *weird* is thinking you can take something as complex as a human being and boil it all down to a number. It's wack. If you took all your so-called eights and followed them for twenty years, you'd probably find that some of them end up as complete losers and some of them might discover a cure for cancer, or . . ."

I stopped because I could tell I was losing the battle. I glanced at Seth, who shook his head like *Give it up—they're never going to get it.*

Just then Kennedy came into the room and started walking toward the 7-Ups. We all watched. Even me. So I guess I got to keep my man card for another day.

Beal cleared his throat. "You know . . . ," he said. "I had a little taste of that once."

I'd had enough. I swiveled to face him. "Really? Tell me about her tattoo." He was clearly stumped so I helped him out with a little more fiction. "I heard it was a butterfly or something. Right on her flawless ass."

"Well, actually, it's a dragonfly." He held his thumb and finger a couple of inches apart. "About this big. Green and purple." He pointed to his left butt cheek. "Right here."

"Wow. Dude, that's incredible." Seth gave me a funny look but I ignored him because my phone was buzzing. It was Ollie. don't be a dork—get over here

I looked for her. She was sitting a few spaces away from Kennedy, who somehow had landed right in the middle of the table. It hit me that the only times Kennedy and I'd really been alone together were business-type things—taking pics or talking about her portfolio or whatever. I suddenly had an idea that scared the crap out of me—it might be cool to see if she wanted to get together just for fun. I don't know . . . maybe coffee or something to start with?

I knew it was a stretch, and the thought of asking her made my gut twist up. But on the other hand, she *had* been pretty friendly with me lately. Maybe I could just play it by ear and see how it went . . . ?

I mentally shrugged, then got up and clapped Beal on the shoulder as I walked by. "I mean it, man—you're incredible. Literally."

I walked over and plopped down next to Ollie, near the end of the table. She was a little more hipsterish this week—the wet-head raccoon was gone and in its place she had a little pork-pie hat on top of fluffy hair, with a bow tie and suspenders over an oversize white dress shirt (that I recognized as one of my movie theater work shirts) and a pair of baggy slacks with old Chucks that she almost certainly got at the thrift store. It was a strange mash-up of hipster and vintage, but somehow it worked. It hit me that maybe there actually *is* some sort of talent to the art of choosing clothes.

I started eating and was about to ask Ollie how she decided what to wear each morning, when I suddenly stopped.

Stopped talking, stopped chewing, stopped *breathing.*

Because in the midst of all the conversations going on around me, my brain picked out the sound of Kennedy's voice and zoomed in on it to the exclusion of everything else.

"... so just don't ask me any questions about Saturday night," she was saying.

Sofia—sitting next to her—laughed. "Sounds like a good time was had by all."

I couldn't see because I was consciously staring at my food and not her, but I could hear the grin in her voice. "I *think* so. From what I can recall. But man, I sure paid the price the next morning."

Sofia laughed. "I'll bet!"

I suddenly had this weird, totally fucked-up feeling in my gut. Like, I didn't exactly want to do whatever she'd done that night—especially considering how she'd seemed the next day when I'd given her the portfolio—but I also had a wicked case of FOMO. Was this what jealousy felt like? I didn't know. All I knew was, it went down like a cold shit cocktail.

I took a deep breath and made myself focus on my pizza, even though the thought of food made me want to gag.

I spent the rest of lunch staring down at my plate until everyone else at the table left the cafeteria. I was seriously considering sitting there clear through history when I heard someone come up behind me.

"How come you're backing me up in AP lang again?"

I didn't even turn around. "I'm not backing anyone up. I just have this problem—I say what I think. Trust me, it's got nothing to do with you."

There was no reply. By the time I finally looked up, she was gone. Fine by me.

I went to history—and sixth-period chem, too—on complete autopilot. When I got home I went into my room—to lie on my back and examine the ceiling.

After a while Ollie knocked on my door. Whatever she wanted, I wasn't in the mood. "Go away—there's nobody home."

She came in and read from her phone. "*Three to four hours of location shooting, including three changes of clothing. Selection and editing. Photo processing. Ten 8x10 color prints in a presentation book.* Does this sound like what you did for Kennedy?"

"Yeah, pretty much. So what?"

She held up her phone to me. "So you 'pretty much' gave

away a thousand dollars' worth of work. To someone with zero gratitude."

I took it and looked closer. It was a local photo studio's ad, promoting their "portfolio special." "It's only nine ninety-nine." I pointed to it. "See? It's on sale this month."

She snatched her phone back. "Don't be a fucking door-mat, J." She paused on her way out, then added without turning around, "You're better than that."

CHAPTER 11

To know ahead of time what you're looking for means
you're then only photographing your own preconceptions,
which is very limiting . . . and often false.
—Dorothea Lange

I WORRY ABOUT MY DAD. BESIDES THE OBVIOUS. LIKE, YOU might *expect* someone whose wife died suddenly of cancer to be totally depressed and maybe freak out and cry at unexpected times and drink too much and stay home in bed all day and fall apart. But—luckily for me and Ollie—that's not my dad. Because—other than something like being depressed on her birthday—he doesn't really do any of those things. At least not where we can see it. Which is why I'm a little worried. Where does he put his grief? He sure doesn't talk to us about it . . .

I finished up my homework after dinner and went to the garage. Sure enough, he was out there, still working on that prehistoric machine. The spring-driven motor—like a giant windup clock mechanism—was laid out in pieces on his workbench. At the other end of the bench was the wooden cabinet, where he'd been stripping off the old finish. It looked like a construction worker's lunch bucket, complete with a rounded lid and a carry handle on top. If the construction worker were the Hulk and his lunch pail were made out of solid oak.

I watched him sitting on a stool hunched over his workbench and just shook my head. He'd spent *hours* on that stupid thing, and there was still a long way to go before it was even close to working. And for what? Some ancient precursor to a record player that would undoubtedly sound like complete crap if it even worked at all?

Then I glanced at the vintage bike poster up on the wall, only this time I thought about the photo session behind it, and all the work it took to get the bike and the girl looking that good, and the lighting and the backdrop and the camera and the film and the processing, and all the time the photographer put into it.

And I wondered if there was any chance in hell it had been done for free.

He finally noticed me standing there and turned around. "Hey, J. What's going on?"

I shrugged. "Not much . . . did my homework . . . studied for my chem test tomorrow. Just kind of hanging out." I nodded at the metal parts he was cleaning. "I don't really get why you're doing all that."

"What do you mean?"

"No offense, but . . ." I paused. "But what's the point? I mean, you're going to spend a ton of time fixing that old thing up, and end up with something that probably doesn't sound half as good as my phone and a pair of earbuds."

"No offense taken. You're right. As far as it goes."

"As far as what goes?"

He held up a rusty old crank with a wooden handle and slowly spun it in his hand as he spoke. "If all you care about is fidelity, you're right—go listen to your phone. But remember, there was a day when a cylinder phonograph like this was the absolute best music player available. And they were made by hand, by crafts- men who took pride in their work. And bought by families who must have really valued music, because they weren't cheap. This cost thirty bucks back when it was made, in 1903. That'd be a thousand dollars today. How many people do you know who'd pay that much just to listen to music?"

He was so intense about the whole thing. I had no response that wasn't snarky so I just shrugged.

"I know it just looks like a pile of greasy parts and some splin- tery old wood right now," he said. "I don't blame you for think- ing it's a stupid project, because there's no way you can see the potential here." He paused. "Look, someone put their heart into making this over a century ago, but now it's ready for the trash heap. And no one's going to make another one. Ever. But if I can step in and bring it back to what it once was, when it was new, then I sort of feel like I should do it." He looked at the pile of parts. "And it feels good, to be bringing something back to life . . ."

It hit me. He'd had no control over what had happened to Mom, but this was something he could actually fix . . . actually make whole again.

"*Plus*," he suddenly added, all excited, "it doesn't need electricity. Just think how awesome this thing would be if the zombie apocalypse happened!"

See what I mean?

I looked up at the poster again. I mean, if you were going to waste your time fixing up old machinery . . .

I pointed at it. "When are you going to finally break down and get one of those?"

He glanced up. "She's a little young for me."

I folded my arms and glared at him, like I was the dad and he was the smartass kid.

"There was a time when I really wanted one," he finally admitted. "But that was before . . . you know. And they're not free."

A dozen thoughts went through my head but I couldn't seem to put any of them into words. Finally I said, "You know, it'd be okay with us if you had a little fun occasionally."

After talking with my dad I felt like I needed to be alone for a while. Which was kind of ironic after *me* lecturing *him* about having fun.

Around nine o'clock I found myself down at Fig and Gardena with my camera. Waiting. I know one of the main points of the project is to avoid filtering, but you can't help hoping you get at least a little character in your subjects, like rocky road swirl with sprinkles on top. I'm starting to realize you usually get vanilla, but I'm learning to go with it and do my best.

But this time, not only *didn't* I get the leather-clad nun with the pet rhesus monkey or the crusty old guy with high-waters who looked like Mr. Krabs crawling out of rehab a week early, I didn't even get the plain old Mom & Dad & Two Kids menagerie. It was worse.

Way worse.

When my alarm buzzed I looked down the street and saw two guy-girl couples about my age, laughing loudly as they walked toward me. I wasn't thrilled, but I got my camera ready just the same. When they got closer I could see it was Kennedy Brooks and another girl from La Montaña High. With a couple of dudes that were at least nineteen or twenty.

It was a total punch in the gut. Yeah, I knew—in theory— that I was pretty clearly in the friend zone. And I also knew—in theory—that Kennedy never expressly said she *didn't* have a boyfriend, and that she could go out with whoever she wanted to. But having it suddenly go from the theoretical to the actual right in front of me was like a sledgehammer to the solar plexus. I mean, here they were—falling all over each other, laughing the laugh of the highly intoxicated—and you just *knew* what they were going to do once they got wherever they were going.

I wanted to drop my camera and run, or at least bend over and tie my shoe until they'd gone by. But it was too late—there they were, on the corner at 9:09, completely unplanned. I had to take a photo, or at least make an effort.

As I got ready to ask them, it hit me that Kennedy would get the situation and let me off the hook. I mean, she wasn't stupid—she had to know there was a good chance I felt something for her, so maybe she'd cut me some slack and say, *We'd love to, J, but we have to be somewhere.* Then maybe we could get together later and talk about it.

Yeah, *right.* When monkeys grow furry little wings and fly through the sky.

Instead, she saw me and sort of did a double take, taking a second to place me. "Oh . . . hey! How's it going, uh . . . Jamison?" I explained to her what I was doing (the "school project" version) and she turned to the others. "Hey, this is J, from school. He's a photographer and he wants to take our picture for a class project." Only it came out slurred, and she called me a *photo*-grapher.

The others were all for it, and as they were getting situated I heard Kennedy whisper to the other girl, "This is the guy I was telling you about." She was trying to keep it down, but it came out in the loud, overprecise version of "keeping it down" that people use when they're hammered.

The other girl glanced at me as I was getting my camera ready, and her whispering wasn't much better. "Him? Huh. He *is* kinda cute . . ."

Kennedy turned to the guys and raised her voice to drunken cheerleader level. "C'mon, let's do this!"

They all crammed together, the girls in front and the guys behind, and I started shooting. They were laughing and leaning on each other—mostly to keep from falling over—when the dude behind Kennedy reached around and grabbed her boobs and said, "Woo-hoo!" He was clearly looking for me to snap a pic, so I pointed the camera, then nodded, like *Got it.* But I didn't trip the shutter.

He let go and I took a few more frames, then basically said, "Thanks guys, I'm good." Before they took off I got near Kennedy and said quietly, "Hey, I saw that guy grab you. Are you okay? Do you want me to get you a ride home?"

She just laughed at me. "Are you kidding me? I'm great!" Then she turned and joined her friends as they staggered and laughed their way down the sidewalk. I just stood there for a minute, then slowly put away my camera and did the same.

Minus the staggering.

And the laughing.

When I got home I loaded the evening's pics into my computer but I couldn't bring myself to review them—I felt bad enough without ripping off that particular Band-Aid again. Plus I knew there was nothing there worth putting up on my page. So instead I went to check out my usual sites, starting with Street Shooters Anonymous.

The main discussion at the moment seemed to be whether you should know ahead of time if the final image is going to be monochrome—and shoot accordingly—or wait until you're done and decide after you've seen them both ways. I probably wasted half an hour on that thread before I bailed and went to my own site to see if there was any activity.

When I first put up the site, the only one going there was me. And I know that because—once Seth showed me how it worked—I checked the site's stats like once a day, at least for the first week. And there were still lots of days when no one went there. I complained to Seth about it being a ghost town and he reminded me I was doing this for my mom. "If all you care about are clicks," he said, "you should have built a porn site like I'd originally suggested. Otherwise, suck it up, buttercup." *Thanks for the sympathy, dude.*

Tonight there was a new comment. Someone wrote I like your style, straddling the line between spontaneous and considered. Some really nice stuff here. Keep at it! That got my attention. And so did the sig underneath the comment: AndréSSA. Who happened to be the moderator at Street Shooters Anonymous. Wow. The good mood lasted for all of sixty seconds, then it evaporated and I closed my computer and sat there in the dark. So some guy who maybe knows something—or maybe not—says he likes my photos. So what? That's great but it isn't going to bring my mom back or make me any friends or even buy me a cup of coffee at Finch.

Or make a girl like me when it's screamingly obvious she doesn't really care if I'm alive or not.

Finally I did what I knew I was going to do all along—I started reviewing the photos I'd just taken. And yeah, seeing her with that no-longer-theoretical dude made my gut hurt all over again.

And what made it worse was that it was pretty clear I'd never even been in the running.

I mean, *she* sure didn't spend much time thinking about *me*. She didn't hate me, either—which would have been better than nothing. It was more like I wasn't even a tiny blip on her radar screen.

She totally doesn't give a shit, dude, so just get over it. I told myself that, over and over, like a mantra. I mean, it was pretty clearly true, and made perfect sense.

So why wasn't it working? I mean, I sure didn't *feel* over it. But either way, with her new college guy and everything, I doubted I'd ever have to deal with her again.

CHAPTER 12

Art is a by-product of an act of total attention.

—Dorothea Lange

". . . SO DID THE AUTHOR'S TECHNIQUES CONVEY AN authentic experience, or were there still unanswered questions by the end of the story?"

I sat on my hands. Hard. And avoided eye contact with Ms. Montinello. It helped that half my brain was still stuck on the corner of Fig and Gardena watching my fantasy have a high-speed collision with reality, but even with that playing in the background I had the bizarre urge to reply. Which is never a good sign.

Turns out someone did it for me.

"Yes." There were a few snickers.

"Care to extrapolate, Ms. Knudsen?"

I looked over (uh, since when did Ms. Automatic Kalashnikov

sit off to my side instead of behind?) and it was pretty clear she didn't, but she gave it a shot.

"It was authentic for me because it worked—it felt real and I was emotionally invested in the story. And yes, there were some unanswered questions, but that didn't detract from the experience."

"Why not? Don't we need a clear resolution?"

"Well . . ." AK glanced at me—just for a split second—but it was enough to totally throw me. Because it wasn't her usual hardass look. It was more of a wide-eyed *Hey! A little help here?* While I was trying to sort this out, she continued. ". . . Some things were wrapped up but some weren't. And I was okay with that, because it lets you project where things might go instead of spoon-feeding it to you."

"But isn't that the writer's responsibility, to tell you where things are going? Isn't it lazy not to?"

I had this sudden image of a bunch of brightly colored birthday presents, wrapped way too fancy, with miles of ribbon around them.

"Maybe some people are allergic to bows," some idiot spouted.

"What does *that* mean?" Ms. Montinello asked. Why was she looking at me? Oh yeah—I was the idiot.

"In real life, things are never perfectly buttoned up. So fiction seems less real if everything's wrapped up with a big bow, like a Hollywood ending. If we get a vague idea of where things might go, sometimes that's better than happily-ever-after." Then I totally cheated. "Way more verisimilitude that way." (That was a calculated risk. She'd used that word in a lecture a couple of weeks ago. If it'd been yesterday she might have remembered and thought I was mocking her, but as it was she might buy it.)

Ms. Montinello nodded thoughtfully. "Good point." *(Whew.)* She looked at AK and raised her eyebrows.

AK nodded. "Exactly. And it seems like talking down to us, to spell everything out. It works better if the author gives the reader some credit."

A textbook appeared in my mind, but all the sample questions at the back of the chapter had answers instead of just the odd-numbered ones.

"What if there were a math book that had the answers to *all* of the questions at the back of each chapter, instead of just half of them?" I said. "Would the student learn more or less that way?" Okay, so I totally plagiarized my own synesthesia. Tough shit—it was all I had at the moment.

Ms. Montinello held up her hands. "I give up." She looked up at the clock. "And . . . it's lunch."

On the way out I saw something I'd only seen once before in my life: a hint of a smile on the face of Ms. Letter-Letter/ Number-Number. And yeah, it got my attention.

I was eating in the vicinity of the usual losers. Partly because I actually found myself looking forward to hanging with Seth and partly because I was in Kennedy-avoidance mode. This tactic worked well. For all of ten minutes.

Beal and Riley and Tristan were sitting there deciding which girls were worthy of their attention (duh) while Seth and I were at the other end of the table, riffing on weird old guys and the weird old crap they liked. I'd done a thing on record players and Seth had fired back with "Oh yeah? Well, when *I* was a kid we stood in the kitchen and talked to our friends. On the *telephone.* Tied to the *wall.* With a *cord.* In front of our *parents.* Beat that, Instagramma . . ." when someone put a hand on my shoulder.

I turned.

Kennedy.

I took in a shaky breath. "Hey," I said. With zero enthusiasm. The awful feeling of last night came flooding back, and the taste of it in the back of my throat just about made me sick.

She kind of tilted her head sideways at that. "Uh . . . hey." Then she recovered and turned on her smile, which raised the ambient temperature of the room at least ten degrees. She squatted so she was level with me, keeping her hand on my arm. God, she smelled great. "So, do you think we could do another shoot? I thought it might be good to have some photos in winter clothing."

I shrugged. "Maybe."

"Okay! How about this Saturday, same park as last time?"

I swallowed. This was harder than I'd thought. But I reminded myself that she didn't actually give a rat's ass about me. "Um, I think I'm busy. Maybe some other time . . ."

She let go, stood up, and stared at me for a second. Then walked away. The ambient temperature had dropped by twenty degrees.

Beal looked down our way and broke the silence. "You," he said slowly, "are a total moron." He sneered. "In fact, you might be the stupidest dude I've ever met . . . if you even *are* a dude." Riley and Tristan snickered along with him, like some kind of little hater-boy fan club.

"And you," I replied, "can kiss the nonexistent tat which you never fucking saw on her gorgeous ass." I turned away—he was too stupid to waste words on.

"I don't know what the hell you just did," Seth said quietly, "but whatever it was, it totally took balls. And I'm sure you had a good reason. So, congratulations." He looked at me for a second, then slowly shook his head. "And I'm *so* sorry . . ."

I had to move. Anywhere. I looked across the room. Ollie was at the 7-Up table. And more important, Kennedy wasn't. I turned to Seth and jerked my head in that direction. "C'mon."

"Uh . . ." I didn't wait for him. He caught up when I was halfway across the room. "Man, I don't know if this is my crowd . . ."

"Like those losers are?" I said, jerking my thumb behind us. "If nothing else, there's some good comedy material here. You'll see."

When we got there Ollie was all *Hey, guys, what's up? Have a seat!* She was sitting near Chloe and Sofia, who seemed fine with us being there too. As the girls moved to make room for us, Seth leaned over and said quietly, "Okay, so tell me once again why you waited so long to drag me over here?"

"Have you heard about Sofia's party?" Ollie asked us.

"Nope," I said, without much enthusiasm. "Is it a Halloween

thing?" I had visions of dorky costumes and cheesy games. No thanks.

She shook her head. "No, the day after, on Saturday. It's a Día de los Muertos party."

Seth looked around the cafeteria. "Every day is Día de los Muertos around here." I nodded—he'd nailed that one.

Ollie suddenly turned to Sofia, all excited. "Hey, do you mind if my brother"—she shot a micro-glance at Seth—"and his friend come to your place Saturday night?"

Sofia smiled. "No, that'd be awesome. As long as they're into it. Nothing worse than a Debbie Downer to kill your Day of the Dead."

Ollie laughed. "Thanks." She turned to me. "So, assuming you're going, can I get a ride?"

She saw my hesitation and I saw where she was going. "If you use the puppy-dog look, the answer's definitely no." She dropped it. I rationalized it by thinking I could "watch out for her." Whatever *that* meant. "Okay."

I was just hanging out on my computer, wearing my usual whatever clothes, when Ollie popped into my room about an hour before the party on Saturday and said, "So you're going like that?"

I did a face palm. "*You said* no costume. *You said* this wasn't some cheesy thing."

"It's not. And you don't *need* a costume—it's not a Halloween party."

"So what's wrong with what I'm wearing?" I had on jeans, a T-shirt, and an old hoodie.

She spoke to the sky. "Where do I begin?" Then back at me. "Nothing. But this isn't Day of the *Living*." She looked at my blank stare. "Okay, come with me." As I followed her into her room she said, "You know how when you have a new idea for a head shot you always tell me 'Trust me'?"

"Yeah . . . ?" Where was this going?

"And I usually do and it usually works out pretty well?"

"Uh, yeah . . . ?" I didn't think I liked the sound of this.

She pushed me into a chair in front of the little vanity-table thing she had in the corner of her room. "Well, trust me." I *definitely* didn't like the sound of this.

She spun me in the chair. "Don't look at the mirror—look over here."

Then she got to work. She did a bunch of stuff to my face with makeup and brushes and pencils and pens and God-knows-what. Then she put some crap in my hair and brushed it, then she sprayed some different crap on it, then she shot it with a *third* type of toxic-smelling stuff and said, "Don't move for a minute." She did a few more things to my face, then spun me back around so I could look in the mirror. "There. Done."

My hair had wild spikes on top—with black tips—and it glistened like it was wet, only it wasn't. It was hard, like it was glued in place. And the face that looked back at me was a weird piratey/vampire mash-up, like Captain Jack Sparrow meets the Crow. Or maybe that dude from *Rocky Horror*. Only more subtle—mostly shades of black, white, and gray. I had to admit, it looked good. Really good.

I just sat there, checking out my reflection. Finally Ollie couldn't take it any longer. *"Well?"*

I shrugged. "I don't know. It's okay, I guess."

"Huh . . ." She tried to act cool, but I could tell she was crushed.

I looked at her for a second, then busted up. "Just kidding." I pointed to my face. "This right here? This is *amazing.* I almost can't believe it's me."

"It's not. It's a much better-looking, creepier-yet-cooler alternate version of you. As a dead guy." She pointed toward the door. "Now get out of here! I wasted so much time on your ugly face I don't even have time for myself . . ."

CHAPTER 13

Surefire things are deadening to the human spirit.
—Dorothea Lange

BELIEVE ME, SHE MADE THE TIME.

If anything, her makeup was even more elaborate than mine—it was a stylized take on the classic Day of the Dead face paint. Her face was pale and her nose was dark—like a cat face—but her eyes were surrounded by big blue circles. She'd put blue flowers on her chin, too, and dark blue lines—almost purple—across her lips, representing a skeleton's teeth. Instead of flowers or a spiderweb on her forehead she'd drawn a black heart right in the center.

She was wearing some sort of red corset thing—which she kept hidden under her jacket until we were out of the house—and long black fingerless gloves. Red roses were pinned in her hair, which was sprayed as black as mine.

It took us a while to get there—it was on the mesa a couple

miles east of Vista Grande, one of those big houses on acreage out by the vineyards—and by the time we arrived it was absolutely raging.

As we walked in I had a couple of thoughts . . .

1. No, this is *not* your typical Halloween party.
2. There is no fucking way Sofia's parents are home. (It was a good thing it wasn't in town. If this had been in my neighborhood, the cops would have already shut it down.)

And shortly thereafter . . .

3. These dudes are already paying way too much attention to my little sister.

Most of the guys looked like how I'd looked before Ollie came to my rescue. A few of them maybe had eyeliner on, but that was it. Mostly they were just standing around drinking and checking out the girls. And the girls . . . It seemed like their dress code must have said "Wear frightening makeup—and not much else."

Sofia was near the front door as we entered. "Wow, you guys look awesome!" she shouted over the noise. "Glad you could make it!" She gave me a hug and said in my ear, "Damn, J—you're looking muy caliente!" That caught me off guard. I just smiled and looked around. I'd heard her dad owned a construction company, and it showed—the place was sprawling. Sofia pantomimed drinking, then pointed out toward the back. I grinned and gave her a thumbs-up, then headed in that direction.

For once, Ollie actually went with me. On the rare occasions when she and I go somewhere together, she usually says, "Thanks, see ya!" the minute we get out of the car, and I don't see her again until it's time to leave. Maybe it was the dudes loitering in the front room leering at her, but she hung near me as I made my way to the backyard, close enough that anyone who didn't know us might think I was with her instead of just her ride.

That ended when we got to the backyard. It was packed—there were a hundred people out there, easy. An old wooden bar sat off to the side of the patio where some guy in a skeleton costume was pouring drinks in plastic cups. Across the patio from the bar a band was playing. Or I guess they were more of a banda . . . instead of electric guitars and drums they had two dudes with acoustic guitars, a guy on one of those big acoustic bass guitars, a woman singing and playing hand percussion, someone on trumpet, and a dude playing cajon . . . a box drum that he sat on as he slapped the front with his hands. They didn't only play traditional music, either—these guys were cranked up through some type of sound system, and they *rocked*.

In between the band and the bar, the patio was being used as a dance floor. Hanging over the whole thing were strings of colored lights in the shape of little skulls, giving the scene an eerie-yet-festive vibe, like *The Walking Dead Go to Disneyland*.

Ollie and I stood there for a minute, looking around, and then she suddenly grinned and waved at someone across the patio, kind of bouncing up and down. I followed her glance. Seth.

We walked over to him, but besides a quick "Hey, how's it goin', J?" the conversation was all Ollie and Seth. After standing there for a few minutes feeling like the third hydrogen atom on a water molecule, I said, "Hey, see you guys later." Seth glanced up and nodded, then went back to listening to Ollie, who didn't even bother looking up.

I wandered off, hands in my pockets. I couldn't really get pissed at Seth. He hadn't done anything wrong, and as far as I knew he'd even kept that stupid deal. And Ollie, well . . . I'm not her mom. And she could do a lot worse than Seth. Heck, she could end up with the male equivalent of Kennedy Brooks or something, and—

I stopped, because at that moment I could swear I caught a glimpse of Kennedy heading through the crowd toward the house. I moved to get a better look but there was no one even close to resembling her. Man, was I losing it over her or what?

It hit me that part of what put me in a shitty mood was the fact that I've had like zero friends for the past couple of years and it takes me forever to find one dude I can even stand to hang out with, but within a few weeks of starting high school Ollie has a whole table of friends, and now she's over there chatting up that one friend like she's known him for years.

How does she *do* that?

"Hola, amigo! Qué quieres?" I looked up. I was standing in front of the funky little bar and the skeleton was talking to me. I looked at the bottles behind him and he must have sensed my confusion. I didn't know much about booze—all I'd ever really had to drink was beer. "What ails you, amigo?" he asked.

I surprised myself by saying, "Uh, how about loneliness?" Wow . . . is this what they mean about bartenders being therapists?

"Ah!" He raised a bony finger. "Tequila."

I laughed. "What if I'd said anger?"

He reached for a bottle behind him. "Tequila."

"Or jealousy?"

He grabbed a cup and poured a big shot of golden liquid into it. "*Definitely* tequila . . ." He handed it over.

I took a sip. *Whew.* He must have been watching my face because he took it back, added a handful of ice, then topped it with something that looked like lemonade. I took another drink. He watched, then gave me a toothy grin. "Vaya con dios, amigo."

I held up my cup in salute. "Muy bien! Muchas gracias!"

I made my way across the patio, feeling awkward and weirdly alone in a place packed with people. I finally left the crowd and walked across the grass toward the rear corner of the big yard. There wasn't much light back there, but I could make out a tall plaster structure over in the corner. As I got closer I saw it was a kiva fireplace, with a fire going in the rounded opening. I walked up to it and stood there for a minute—it seemed like a great place to just hang for a while. Then I flinched as I realized I wasn't the only one with that thought—there was someone sitting on the little built-in bench near the hearth. I hadn't noticed her at first because she was wrapped in a black shawl, with a black hood over her head. I felt extra awkward and was about to go back to the party when she looked up and patted the bench beside her.

The skeleton bartender must have known his stuff because instead of making an excuse and leaving, I mentally shrugged and thought *Why not?* I sat down and turned to thank her, then stopped. Her face was painted entirely black on one side and completely white on the other, with a sharp line dividing the two. No flowers, no spiderwebs, no designs of any kind. In the firelight it was like looking at half a face, floating in front of me.

"Thanks," I said. "I didn't mean to interrupt. It's sort of a zoo back there and . . . uh, it seems really peaceful and quiet here and . . . I mean, I was just looking for somewhere to sit and . . . I don't know . . . just be quiet for a while." I paused for a second as that sank in. "Uh, which is a little ironic, isn't it?"

She nodded slightly. "Are you always this stupid?"

Huh?

"I mean, you seem pretty bright in class, but now . . ." She gave an exaggerated shrug. "I'm not so sure . . ."

I looked closer. It was AK. And she was trying hard not to bust up. I stood up. "Look, I am *not* stalking you. I didn't even know it was you. I was just looking for a place to—"

"—to sit and be quiet for a while. I know. I heard you say so. Several times."

"Sorry. Didn't mean to bug you . . . I'll just . . ." God, I felt stupid. "See ya," I mumbled, then turned to walk away.

"Hey." I turned back. She patted the bench next to her. "Sit down and enjoy the quiet." She grinned. "If you can."

I could.

So we just sat there, side by side, and you know what? It was nice. I took a drink and felt the tequila warm my throat as I considered Día de los Muertos. It was a time to honor the dead . . . to celebrate the dead. Really, you were supposed to *party* with the dead, which I guess was the whole point of the evening. But I really only knew one dead person. I raised my glass and looked up toward the sky. "Miss you," I said quietly, and took a big swallow.

"Who?" she whispered. She'd said it so faintly I wasn't sure if I'd actually heard it or just felt her think it.

I sat there for a minute, then I finally replied, just as quietly. "My mom."

She nodded, then took my glass, looked up and mouthed something too soft to make out, and took a drink.

We both sat there silently after that, side by side, sharing my drink and breathing in the air of the dead.

After several minutes she turned to me. "How's your photography going?"

I wasn't expecting that, but she seemed sincere. "I honestly don't know." She raised an eyebrow. "I mean, sometimes I think I can take a halfway-decent photo, and sometimes I feel like I'm faking it . . . like I don't have a clue."

She nodded. "I'm not a photographer, but I totally understand that feeling." She pointed at a bush next to the fence. "If both of us took a picture of that hibiscus—from here, without moving—I bet they'd look pretty similar. Yours might be a little better—maybe you'd zoom in more or whatever—but not that different."

"Other than I don't really know what a hibiscus is, you're probably right. So . . . ?"

"So I'm thinking what makes your stuff unique is probably more about your vision—your way of looking at the world—than about standing in a certain spot and pushing a button."

I wasn't expecting that, either. I nodded slowly. "Huh." Which I hoped came across as *That was really meaningful and thank you for the insight,* and not just *Huh.*

"Speaking of looking at the world a certain way," I said, "I thought what you said in class the other day about leaving things unanswered was really interesting."

She actually smiled at that. For a second I wished I had my Nikon because something about her smile was . . . I don't know. But she was already responding. ". . . and I have this theory that a story doesn't necessarily end on the last page. It ends somewhere down the road, in the reader's mind, when they think about it and how it might unfold *after* the last page. Which is why I don't think everything needs to be completely resolved, because . . ."

We were off and running. It was like the best day ever in AP lang, only without a teacher or other students to get in the way. We didn't always agree, but somehow it was easier to talk to her than just about anyone I'd ever met.

We'd been yakking away for quite a while when I said, "How's your writing going?"

"It's going." She looked at her phone and seemed surprised,

then stood up. "Speaking of going, I have to get, uh . . . going."
Now she seemed like the awkward one. "Which I suppose is
redundant."

"Not at all. And sorry again for interrupting your quiet time."

"No, I'm really glad you interrupted." She smiled. "This was
nice."

I smiled back. "Yeah, it was."

And then she was gone.

After she left I sat there for a minute, thinking about my
mom.

Mostly.

Okay, maybe a little.

I made my way back through the thick of the party to the
patio, where I found Sofia hanging out with Chloe and some
other friends from school. "You know how to throw a great
party," I said.

"Thanks, but it's really my brothers—they make it happen.
The music . . . the food . . ." She nodded toward the BBQ pit,
where two college-age guys were grilling big chunks of meat over
tall flames. "They do it every year, but this was the first time
they've let me invite my friends."

"Well, I'm glad they did."

She smiled. "Me too." She pointed toward the dance floor.
"Looks like she's glad too."

I glanced over. It was Ollie, hopping and bopping with Seth.
I'm a crappy dancer so I hardly ever dance. And honestly, Seth
wasn't much better. But no one cared, and he and Ollie seemed
to be having a blast.

Just thinking about jumping around like that made me realize I really had to pee. "Um, where's the bathroom?" I asked.

"On the right, just past the family room." She waved toward the house. "Can't miss it."

"Thanks."

On the way through their family room I saw the ofrenda Sofia's family had set up. It was decorated with flowers and candles and sugar skulls, along with a bottle of wine, a glass of water, a plate of tamales, and a mug of hot chocolate. And photos. *Lots* of photos. Many of them were old—some in faded black-and-white—but a few of them looked recent.

It suddenly hit me that their family altar, with all its memories and connections, was what I was trying to do with my photos and my mom. And thinking about that gave me an idea for something else I could do for my family—including my mom—but that idea would have to wait because the idea foremost on my mind at the moment was finding the restroom.

Sofia wasn't kidding with her *Can't miss it* comment—the bathroom turned out to be a popular place. The door wasn't locked so I walked in. Oops. There were at least four people inside—in various stages of un-costume—acting out scenes from *Night of the Horny Dead.* They didn't even look up as I left.

I swear, I'm not the kind of guy who goes nosing around other people's homes, but at this point I *really* had to go. It was too populated out back to use the bushes so I went upstairs and searched for another bathroom. The second door I checked led to a bedroom, but before I backed out I spied an open door in the far corner leading to a bathroom. Aha!

I went in and did my thing, then came out of the bathroom . . . and walked straight into Kennedy Brooks. She was standing next to the bed, her "costume" consisting of that see-through jungle scarf thing she'd worn during our outdoor photo shoot and a pair of clip-on cat ears. And as far as I could tell, not much else. Wow.

I also had the distinct impression she'd been drinking.

I was about to ask what she was doing there when she smiled shyly and said, "Hi, J." She did that eye thing. "I saw you walk in here and I really needed to talk to you. Alone."

"The last time I saw you, you treated me like shit because I wouldn't do another photo shoot."

She gave me her version of the puppy-dog look. Which she's probably been perfecting since she was three. "I wasn't mad, I was just disappointed . . ."

My bullshit detector was going off but part of me still wanted to believe her. "And the time before *that*," I added, mostly as a reminder to myself, "you could barely remember my name."

And you broke my fucking heart . . .

She sat on the bed and indicated I should sit next to her. I sat but kept some distance between us. "It . . . it was a bad night. And I'd been drinking." She paused. "We were friends, J. And I miss that. I had such a great time working with you before, and I can't wait to do it again." She moved closer and put her hand on my shoulder. "What's so wrong with that?"

I had the impression there was an answer to that, but I couldn't think of it at the moment.

Just then the door opened and a girl and a guy started to

come in. They looked vaguely familiar—probably from school—and they were laughing as they stumbled into the room, until they saw us on the bed. "Oh. Uh, sorry!" They backed out, laughing even harder.

I turned to face her. "Look, I don't mind being your friend." Well, I *sort* of believed that. "But I mind you pretending to be *my* friend to get me to do something for you."

She shook her head at that. "Fuck, J . . ." She brushed her hair out of her face and said something really quiet—almost to herself—that got my attention. I was about to ask her to repeat it when the door opened again.

Jesus—what now? I glanced over. There was some girl in really cool Día de los Muertos makeup standing in the doorway. She saw us but she made no move to leave. Then I recognized her.

"I'm leaving with Seth," Ollie announced, like we were just having a random conversation at lunch. "He's pretty hammered, but don't worry—I'll drive. Just to his house. So can you stop by on the way home and pick me up?"

Kennedy didn't even look toward the door. "Get out, bitch," she snapped. "Can't you see we're busy?"

I turned back to Kennedy. She had the look of someone who's used to getting exactly what she wants.

I heard the door shut as Ollie left.

Kennedy's hand was on the back of my neck and she was saying something into my ear but all I could think was *Ollie's not quite fifteen . . . no license . . . I've let her drive the car exactly twice in her life while I gave directions . . . she wasn't very good either time.*

Shit!

I pulled away from Kennedy. "I have to go."

Her eyes flashed death beams. "What the *fuck* . . . ?"

I made my way downstairs and found Ollie in the front room near the door. "Let's go," I snapped.

She could tell I wasn't exactly happy. As we were walking to the car she said, "You know, you don't have to do this."

I snorted. "I promised Mom I'd look after you. Whatever the fuck that means."

She gave me a funny look but didn't say a thing.

CHAPTER 14

Every image the photographer sees, every photograph
he takes, becomes in a sense a self-portrait.
—Dorothea Lange

WE WERE IN THE CAR AND I WAS READY TO TURN THE KEY when I suddenly stopped and slammed the steering wheel. "I have to go back—I can't let Seth drive home drunk."

"He's fine, actually," Ollie said quietly.

"What the hell are you talking about? I thought he was hammered."

She shook her head, then turned in her seat to face me and sighed. "Look, J. Mom had me make the same promise." She paused. "About you."

I thought about Kennedy Brooks and how I felt as she was trying to apologize or make up with me or whatever that was. "I hate you." Then I thought about the fact that Ollie was leaving with me instead of hanging at the party with Seth, in an effort to keep *her* promise to Mom. The irony wasn't lost on me. "Okay, and I kind of love you too."

"Same here," she said with a straight face. "But mostly hate."

I just shook my head. God, what a night. I suddenly realized that between the Tequila Skeleton, talking with AK, and that weird thing with Kennedy, I hadn't had a chance to get any food at the party. Man, I was starving.

I was going to offer to take her to Happy Jack's, then I realized it wouldn't be necessary. Besides, it was still Día de los Muertos, right?

"So, you down for some Tacos de?" I asked. "I'm buying."

Full crinkle this time. "Hell yes!"

On the way there I thought about that whole stupid promise thing. Like, what does it really mean, and would I actually do anything different if Mom *hadn't* talked to me about watching out for Ollie? I don't know. Maybe the whole thing was Mom's way of saying *I'm not going to be around, so I want you to do some of the things I'd do if I were here.* I guess I can get that, but it doesn't really work for me because I'm *not* Mom. Like, I'm not forty, I've never had kids, and I'm not Ollie's parent—I can't make her do shit, and I can't even play the experience card with her.

Maybe being an older brother is somewhere in the gray area between being a friend and being a dad. I don't know, but whatever it is, it's pretty clear I'm not the boss of her. I thought about her busting into Sofia's bedroom on a mission to save me from Kennedy's wily ways with that wild story about Seth being hammered and driving him home and stuff, and I started laughing.

"What's so funny?"

"Absolutely nothing."

When we got there I gave Ollie some money and sent her to the counter to order so I could stay at the table and work at being a better big brother.

hey seth, so right now i'm at tacos de with an annoying blond . . .

quit bragging. i heard something bout u and kb up in sofia's room. don't know if I'd call her annoying tho

wrong blond, dude. this one's currently a brunette . . . get your ass down here

He showed up before the food did.

Ollie lit up when he walked in. "Hey, what brings you here?"

"A little bird." He glanced at me as he slid into the booth next to her. "Apparently a very confused little bird with a very sad story to tell . . . ?"

Just then our food arrived. I guess we'd picked the right place on the right night to wear our Día de los Muertos faces, because along with our tacos they threw in some free horchatas and some pan de muertos, with a bunch of little sugar skulls scattered all over the tray. As we dug in, Seth got back on topic. "Uh, sad story . . . ?"

"Right. Well, the bottom line is Kennedy Brooks wanted me to do another photo shoot for her and probably make her a new portfolio."

Seth nodded. "I was impressed by you not rolling over in the cafeteria when she asked," he said. "Any other dude would have been a total lapdog." Ollie shot him a sideways glance but didn't say anything.

"Yeah, and I thought that was the end of it. Plus I ran into her downtown the other night with some of her friends, and she acted like she barely knew me."

Ollie just shook her head slowly.

"So . . . ?" Seth asked. "Tonight? Upstairs? I heard you two were looking pretty friendly."

"It's not what you think. We were just talking."

"Right."

"Seriously. She hit me up again to do another shoot for her, and I was standing my ground until she, uh . . . started getting friendly."

Ollie snorted. "You make it sound like she smiled and offered to get you a drink. It looked more like you guys were about to turn gametes into zygotes."

I ignored her and spoke to Seth. "I guess she was playing nice with me either to thank me for doing the first shoot, or maybe to make me feel guilty so I'd do it again."

Seth had his mouth full of food so he just shrugged, then nodded, like *I guess so.*

Ollie snapped. "Stop! For supposedly smart guys, you're *so fucking stupid.*"

We both just stared at her.

"This doesn't have shit to do with *thanking* you or *guilting* you or whatever."

We continued to stare, wide-eyed, like dogs who don't understand what they've done wrong.

She sighed. "Look. The whole point is to get you hooked. *Duh.* She knows you used to have a major crush on her, she comes on to you, gives you a little attention, gets you all infatuated—which you'd probably mistake for love—and then she can get you to do whatever she wants. *Hello! Paging Mister Lapdog . . .*" She shook her head in disgust, although I'm not sure if it was aimed at Kennedy or us. "Guys fall for it all the time."

Seth raised his eyebrows. "Witchcraft, I say!"

"No, it's just Mean Girl 101," she said. "Basic, fundamental, first-year stuff."

Even though it came from my kid sister, it had the smell of truth about it. "Maybe so," I admitted. "So, um . . . thanks. I guess."

She nodded and mouthed *Remember this moment.*

I nodded back.

"If it's so basic, why do supposedly smart guys fall for it?" Seth asked.

"Because you're thinking with the wrong, uh, *thinker* . . ." (Wow. I'd never seen Ollie blush before. It was really subtle, like her crinkle, but I noticed it despite her makeup.)

When we were done eating Ollie went to use the restroom and Seth and I had one of those guy moments—the kind you see in buddy movies more than in real life. He just looked at me, raised his eyebrows, and said, *"So?"*

I shrugged. "Pretty much what I just said." I paused. "Well . . . somewhere between the first interruption and the second one, she might have mumbled something about maybe we should get together or whatever. I couldn't quite hear it all, but—"

"*Get together*?" he interrupted. "Holy crap, dude. Maybe she's more interested in you than you thought?"

I shrugged. "Hard to say. There may have been alcohol involved." I let it go, but to tell the truth, when I played back the recording in my mind, maybe what I heard wasn't "*get* together." Maybe it was "*be* together." As in, *"Fuck, J . . . We should be together."*

Maybe.

Amazing what a difference a little verb can make.

A few minutes later we were all in the parking lot, heading out. As Seth was walking toward his car I watched Ollie watching him. I tilted my head toward her. "You know, it's cool if you want to ride with him," I said quietly. "Well, as long as *he* drives."

"You're *such* a big brother," she said, getting into my car.

"Shut up."

"You shut up."

The next morning I started cruising through my recent photos to see if there was anything worthwhile. I'd been getting a little feedback on my site and I hadn't posted anything new in a while, but as I started looking through my latest pics I wasn't super inspired, and I reminded myself of my rule when I'd been putting Kennedy's portfolio together: no filler. I was about to close my computer when I went to the photos of Kennedy and her friends from the other night.

Yeah, maybe I was heading there all along. So what . . . don't judge. And yeah, maybe there was a weird, painful attraction to checking out the pics of her and her friends, leaning on each other and joking and laughing. Something about it made me feel totally depressed and left out, but I had a hard time not looking.

One shot I'd bypassed before caught my eye. It must have been after Mister College Guy had grabbed her from behind and I'd passed on taking the pic. The photo showed Kennedy standing next to her friends, like most of the others, but in this one she was looking away. The whole manic/drunk/fun/party mood was still there in her friends. But not in her. She had her head turned away from them, and for an instant she looked, well . . . totally alone and wanting to be somewhere else. Anywhere else. It must have been over quickly, but looking at the pic on the screen in front of me there was clearly a vibe of not belonging, or maybe *wishing* she didn't belong. Then the next pic was back to *woo-hoo* for everyone, including her.

Maybe what surprised me about it was I'd pegged Kennedy as one of those uber-popular people who're always at the center of whatever's happening, and happy to be there. I mean, she was probably the most socially successful person I knew, and I usually thought of her as whatever the opposite of lonely was. But seeing this, it was like *she* looked like *I* usually felt.

I don't know. Maybe I was making too much of this particular 1/100th of a second, but the thought of her feeling like that made me feel like I understood her a little . . . like, if nothing else, at least we shared that.

I'm not sure exactly what was going on, but I definitely felt a connection to the image and I decided to see what I could do with it. I cropped in until she was on the left side of the picture—and looking out of the frame, away from her friends—and they were on the right. The gap between her and her friends was only a couple of feet, but I made the photo wider than it was tall, almost like a pano, so in the image the gap seemed significant. This ended up with all of them being shown from the waist up, so it was almost a pair of portraits on a single page instead of a group shot. One of her, one of her friends.

I rendered it in black-and-white but with a subtle bluish tone . . . cool instead of warm. Then I jacked the contrast so it felt gritty and I brought her friends down a little to make her stand out. Finally I faded it toward black near the outside of the frame—so it seemed like they were hovering in a field of darkness.

As I looked at it, it hit me that there was more to her than met the eye. Not that the stuff that *did* meet the eye wasn't outstanding but . . . Okay, I know it's weird, but looking at that photo of her—and what it seemed to show—somehow made me feel more connected to her on some level than all those gorgeous fashion poses of her I'd worked on.

In spite of what Ollie'd said.

I tweaked things a tiny bit more until it seemed complete. *Happy* is the wrong word for how I felt, but I was finally satisfied with the image. I uploaded it to my site fast, before I could change my mind.

CHAPTER 15

Photography takes an instant out of time,
altering life by holding it still.
—Dorothea Lange

MS. MONTINELLO PACED BACK AND FORTH IN FRONT OF the class. "So can you all see the value in describing something so completely that it brings it to life for the reader?"

No. What *I* saw were several little cartoon dudes, and each had a thought bubble above their head with a photograph in it. All different versions of the same scene, but all really detailed.

I shook my head. "With description sometimes less really is more," I said.

"How so?"

All the photos in the thought bubbles were replaced with identical cartoon drawings.

"No matter how much you describe something, you're not

going to paint a more realistic picture than something that's already in the reader's mind." I thought of Tacos de Ensenada. "So you could go on for pages about a specific restaurant and the reader might or might not get the same picture the writer has in her head. Assuming they don't fall asleep first." A few people snickered—most of the class didn't share Ms. Montinello's passion for descriptive passages. "Or you could mention that the setting's 'a little family-run Mexican diner,' and the reader'll call up a detailed setting, with all the sights and sounds and smells they associate with it. Probably a more authentic picture than anything the author could describe in a hundred words."

"Maybe," Ms. Montinello said. "Or maybe it's just rationalization for lazy writing." She looked around the class. "I noticed some of our last essays were a little short on description." She acted like it was a general comment but I could tell it was directed at me. I glanced over at AK, hoping for some backup. After all, we'd had a pretty good talk the night before. She saw me, then looked away, but ended up raising her hand.

Yes!

"Ms. Knudsen?"

"I agree with you," she said to Ms. Montinello.

Huh?

"It's lazy," she continued. "Otherwise you're just leaving your setting or character up to the reader's preconceptions."

No!

"In what way?" Ms. Montinello asked.

"The reader may have stereotypical tastes."

"So . . . ?"

"So let's assume instead of making the effort to describe a unique, interesting female character, the author just says 'she was a beautiful girl.' And the reader is a typical straight white guy and immediately envisions the typical blond hair/blue eyes/big boobs/Barbie-doll bimbo."

Ms. Montinello didn't say anything for a second, then nodded slowly. "I see. Very well stated." She kept a straight face, but I swear I saw the tiniest hint of a smile. Which I didn't find the least bit funny. "With extra points for alliteration."

Shit.

I stopped inside the cafeteria and tried to take in the whole "who was sitting where" thing without making it obvious, but my quick glance was enough to steer me away from the 7-Ups and over toward my usual spot. Kennedy was holding court with the fashionistas and AK was sitting one table over, and there was no way I was going anywhere near either of them. Apparently one of them hates me and the other one fucking hates me. I'm just not sure which is which.

I grabbed some food and pulled up near Seth at the end of the UL table just in time to be greeted by Beal Wilson. "Hey, if it ain't the man of the hour! Someone said you hit on Kennedy Brooks at a party and she told you to go fuck yourself." Riley and Tristan laughed, right on cue.

"Yeah, and someone said you were smart. Can't believe everything you hear, dude."

"So why're you sitting here with us instead of over there?" He nodded toward the 7-Up table. "Huh?"

He's the kind of low-imagination guy who'll hound you until you give him some sort of answer. "Let's see . . . I have food. I need to sit somewhere so I can eat it. I actually like Seth, and having a place to eat where I can talk to him is worth sitting near the rest of you guys. None of which has shit to do with me supposedly hitting on someone."

"So she didn't tell you to go fuck yourself?"

"Oh, she probably did. But not because I hit on her."

"So, uh . . . ?"

"It's a complicated story, involving intellectual property and uncompensated labor."

I've read about people screwing up their face, but this was the first time I'd actually seen it. *"Huh?"*

"I said it was complicated. Let's just leave it at that."

He looked at me like I was a moron. "So you don't think she's hot."

"Oh, she's undeniably hot. Assuming you're talking about outward appearance."

That made him screw up his face even harder. "We're talking hot—what else is there?"

"I don't know why you don't just tell him to fuck off," Seth muttered to me.

"This is more fun."

Just then Ollie walked across the room and parked herself at the 7-Up table, away from Kennedy and closer to AK. The guys turned and watched. Of course. "I know someone else who's 'undeniably hot,'" Riley said, mimicking me.

"What about her?" Beal said, turning back to me. "If that little hottie isn't your type either, then you're *definitely* a moron." Tristan and Riley thought that was hilarious. Big surprise.

Seth started to tense up, which was stupid—Beal had fifty pounds on him, easy. I put my hand on his shoulder and pushed down. "I got this," I said quietly. I looked at Beal. "Nope. Not my type either." Before he could flap his lips I said, "I don't know much about your family history, Bubba, but where I come from they frown on you dating your siblings."

It took him a second. "So you're saying what . . . ? That little hot pocket is your *sister*?"

"Congratulations, genius. You broke the code."

His next thought only took him half a second. "That's awesome! So you can, like, set me up, and—"

I held up my hand to stop him. "Never gonna happen. Ever."

"Screw you. I don't need some moron's help. I can do what I want. And if I decide I want to go after that little hot pocket, then I will."

Again with the hand on Seth's shoulder. Harder this time. And again with my other hand in Beal's ugly mug. "You know, in some cultures spreading lies about someone's girlfriend is considered a capital offense."

"What are you talking about?" He jerked his thumb toward where Ollie was sitting. "I ain't said shit about her."

I shook my head. "You have, but I'm not talking about her. I'm talking about your little comment—in front of four witnesses and everyone else within twenty feet—that you had a 'little taste' of Kennedy Brooks. Which I happen to know for a fact is complete bullshit." I let that sink in, then continued conversationally. "Hey, have you met her new boyfriend? Plays football, in college. Like a tackle or a guard or something. Huge guy, believe me." I shuddered. "So what I'm saying is, you really need to think before you talk, dude." I paused. "Got it?"

He stared at me. I didn't look away, and he finally dipped his head a fraction of an inch.

I turned to Seth as I grabbed my food and stood up. "I'm outta here—I am *so* done with these assholes. I'd rather go eat out on the fucking curb than anywhere near them."

He stood up too. "What took you so long?"

That night, as I stood on the corner and waited for the appointed time, I thought about my mom and how we'd understood each other. I don't mean I could have talked to her about things like drinking tequila and being in hurt with someone and girls who hate you. I mean, I can't even talk to my dad about stuff like that, and for those things he'd be easier than my mom.

But I could have told my mom all about how I sometimes get the correct answer in class from little multicolored letters and numbers, and she would have totally gotten it. If I told anyone else about that I'd get a *What the . . . ?* look at best, and have to launch into a frustrating explanation of the weird way synesthesia helps me access my thoughts. No thanks.

Some days I really, really miss my mom, and this was one of them.

My alarm went off as an older couple came shuffling down Fig toward me. Damn. Not that I hate old people or anything, but even when they agreed to be photographed they were always so formal. They usually just stood there, side by side, staring at the camera like it was a solemn event. Oh well, it was 9:09 and there they were, so . . .

As they got closer I realized they weren't both old. The man was middle-aged, but he was walking slowly because he was helping the woman along.

"Hi," I said when they finally reached the corner. "I'm doing a project for school, documenting people in Vista Grande. I was wondering if I could take your picture?" I held up my camera. To be honest, part of me hoped they'd pass. And it looked like the guy was leaning that way.

He hesitated. "Um, no thanks. We have to get—"

"Now, Michael . . . ," the old woman said.

"Mom, I need to get you home."

"We can take a minute to help this young man with his schoolwork."

The guy looked at me and shook his head, but he was grinning. "When she gets like this, I've learned not to argue."

So they let me photograph them, and they were awesome. He joked about her wild hair, but he made sure she looked good—he put her collar down and he held her purse while she straightened her coat. And the whole time he was kidding with her, telling her how lucky she was to have him helping her out, and she'd roll her eyes dramatically and say, "Lucky? Ha! Who's helping who?" Then he put one arm around her and gave her a smooch on the cheek, and they both ended up laughing.

"You *are* lucky" was all I could manage to say when I was done.

She must have thought I was referring to her. "I really am," she said. "I give him a hard time, but he's a great son—I'm lucky to have him."

I nodded. "I'm sure." I lost my voice for a second and they both stared at me until I found it back. "But I was talking about him."

They left and I stood there on the corner, unable to move. It had finally hit me, the full weight of how much I'd lost. I mean, here was this guy, maybe fifty, and he still had his mom in his life.

Every minute I would ever have with *my* mom was already behind me.

It was like a dam burst open. I looked up into the streetlights and found myself staring into an abstract painting, out of focus, full of drips and streaks and runs. And stars.

CHAPTER 16

The portrait is made more meaningful by an
intimacy shared not only by the photographer with
his subject, but by the audience.
—Dorothea Lange

". . . SO, WHAT IS SHE TRYING TO SAY IN HER ESSAY?"
Ms. Montinello asked, looking directly at me.

"I guess I don't understand the question." If I'd had a pair of
brain cells to rub together I would have shut up right then and
there, but the mood from last night was definitely still with me.
"I mean, this is an essay. In English. Why do we have to interpret
what she 'really meant' when her words are right there on the
page, in black and white?"

Before Ms. Montinello could answer, AK put up a hand and
started talking without waiting to be called on. "Sometimes writers use metaphors or allegories that aren't always obvious, and
if you want more than just a surface understanding you might

actually have to put out the effort to dig a little deeper." She paused. "If we're going to take this seriously, that is."

Before I could fire back Ms. Montinello put her hand up. "I enjoy a spirited discussion as much as anyone, but this is all academic because we *are* going to dig into the intent behind the words, regardless." As she turned toward the whiteboard I heard her muttering something about "trouble in paradise."

After that I zoned out for the rest of the class, and for once Ms. Montinello didn't call me on it.

I found a random empty spot by myself at lunch, and as I ate, I glanced over at the fashionistas. Going from one end to the other, there were a few girls I didn't know, then the girl that was with Kennedy downtown the other night, then Kennedy in the middle, then Chloe, then Sofia, then Ollie, then AK. It reminded me of those kids in a band lining up to be photographed, only there wasn't any jockeying for position going on. Instead there was a gap between Kennedy and Chloe/Sofia/Ollie, and then another little gap between Ollie and AK, who was at the next table. Although I looked over once and saw Ollie and AK with their heads together. Which worried me a little.

Okay, it terrified the crap out of me.

On the way home I was thinking of bringing it up when Ollie preempted with the news that she'd overheard Kennedy "getting out ahead of the story."

"Ahead of what story?" I asked.

"The party thing. She's going with the 'J was hitting on me and I had to be firm with him' line."

"So *I* come off looking like a jerk or a creeper or whatever? Screw that! I need to do something . . ."

She turned to face me. "No, you *don't*. Trust me, the best thing is to just let it fade away. It's not that big of a story, it was just a slow news day—something'll happen soon and bury it." She shook her head. "And it's not like you'd be the only one who ever hit on her, believe me."

I looked over at her, then back at the road. "You sound like a news analyst on CNN or something . . ."

Growing up, I was considered the "smart one" at school— which was complete bullshit, let me tell you—probably because of the whole memory and connections thing. (I don't know how many times Ollie came home after the first day of school with a story about her teacher saying she was "expecting great things from Jamison Deever's little sister.") But she was so far ahead of me when it came to actually making connections with people and other social stuff that I felt like a complete idiot. I mean, how do you learn that stuff?

After dinner I started on some homework—mostly assigned reading for AP lang—but I bailed after ten minutes because I had zero interest. So instead I went with my usual default and vegged out online.

I don't visit the SSA site every day—especially now that I'm doing more of my own stuff—but I swing by once or twice a week to see if there's anything worth checking out, like cool new techniques or interesting images. They have a thing they call Pic of the Week where they feature a street photo each week that they think is noteworthy. They're usually pretty cool shots, so I check to see if there's a new one whenever I visit the site. I clicked on that tab and stopped cold, because I suddenly found myself faced with a photo I knew intimately.

What struck me even more than seeing a small rendering of the street shot I'd taken of Kennedy—and the link to the full-size version on my site—was the write-up that accompanied it, and the realization that it was about something *I'd* done.

> We were really taken with this image. Monochrome is sometimes used as a gimmick to up the artiness of an otherwise mundane work but in this case the decision was inspired. Loneliness is often depicted by use of a single person in the photo, frequently off in the distance. This week's pic uses neither of these traditional techniques, with the subject both close to the camera and close to others in the frame. Yet it manages to convey the concept of "cold isolation" better than anything we've seen in quite a while. Kudos to our photographer, who from the statement on their site wishes to remain anonymous. Whoever you are, keep up the good work.
>
> (PS: Thanks to @mygodmsod for the heads-up.)

Wow. Just wow.

Just for grins I checked my site to see if the SSA mention

had resulted in anyone going there. And for the second time in ten minutes, I was surprised. For the past day or so—since SSA had featured my pic, apparently—my traffic was several times normal. And the comments had gone up too. There were maybe a dozen of them on that one image alone, and a lot of them were pretty positive. Not to be redundant, but wow.

As I sat there reading the latest comments, it hit me that people didn't just like to look at work they enjoyed. They liked to be part of the conversation. And not just to say *I like it* or *I don't like it,* but to throw their thoughts into the mix too. Then I thought about the recent visitors to my site, and how some of them might actually come back and check it later, but for them to become regulars they needed a reason to return. Maybe new images, but maybe something more.

Then I flashed on what typically ran through *my* mind when I looked at images I connected with. And way more than *What techniques did the photographer use?*, the question that usually popped up was some version of *What's the story here . . . the human story?*

And what came to mind was my talk with AK the other night, along with a couple of other conversations we'd had. I mean, she had this way of saying something that packed a lot of meaning into a few words. At least for me. Like when she'd said that maybe what made my work different was my way of looking at the world more than just knowing which button to push . . .

I've only seen the world through my own eyes so I can't say for sure, but I could agree with her that maybe there were times when vision was more important than technique, which was an eye-opener.

So maybe there was a way to get other viewers' takes on what *they* saw when they looked at a specific image . . . ?

I thought about it some more, then I dug out the notes Seth had left me on adding a new page to the site. I'm sure he could make it look better than I could—and I'd probably ask him to spruce it up later—but right now I needed to get this thing going while I still felt obsessed.

It took me a couple of hours, but in the end I was happy. The heading across the top of the new page was:

Do You See What I See?

I would show an image, and below that:

> I see a story here. And hopefully, so do you. But are they the same? Enter your version of the story behind this image, and then you'll see mine.

There was a blank text box where the user could enter their thoughts about what sort of backstory the photo evoked in them. Once they did this and pressed Enter, my take on the picture would pop up. And below this would be all the replies that had already come in about that particular photograph.

The first image I put up was one I'd taken a while back of a woman with long, dark hair, holding a sleeping baby. She completely ignored the camera—she just gazed down at her baby with this expression of, I don't know . . . adoration? Devotion? My take on it was corny and Ms. Montinello would have hammered me for my "lack of objectivity," but it summed up the vibe I'd gotten right after I'd taken it: *This woman is a wandering, uncanonized saint. Her baby will grow up to be an amazing person, because it's the most loved baby in the world.*

I let the new page go live, then I tried to do some reading for school before I went to bed, but it was tough going. I was about to nod off when my computer chimed. I looked over. I'd gotten a notification that someone had entered something on my DYSWIS page . . .

> This image perfectly illustrates a line from one of my favorite songs. "I once saw a picture of a lady with a baby, and the lady had a very, very special smile." Gorgeous.

I was still thinking about that when my computer chimed again . . .

> In my mind, the young woman had to work late. She's just picked up her child from daycare on her way home, and she's overjoyed to see him. This is the absolute high point of her day. Lovely.

And again . . .

> This woman is the great-great-great-great-
> granddaughter of Mona Lisa.

And yet again . . .

I finally shut off my computer and tried to sleep, but I spent another hour just lying there thinking. Mostly about the fact that my mom would have loved the new page. Because she usually saw what I saw.

I felt sad and proud at the same time.

When my alarm went off I could have used another couple of hours of sleep, but the buzzy feeling of the previous night carried me through the morning. All the way to fourth period.

I was reasonably alert for my first few classes and even aced a popper in math, but when I got to language I planted my butt in my seat and stared straight ahead, trying to project a vibe of invisibility. And it worked pretty well. Right up until Ms. Montinello said, "But what about an exigency? A social pressure . . . a demand? Don't we need one as a requirement for a good essay?" My eyes flicked to hers and I immediately pulled them back to the whiteboard, but apparently not fast enough.

"Mr. Deever?"

Damn.

I saw the rhetorical web in front of me (in brown, of course) with half a dozen different elements—including exigence (in green, of course)—and I was going to spout out the textbook answer just to get her off my back, when I stopped. Screw that. I mean, what was the "exigency" for my photo project? And was my work complete crap if I didn't have one? At least not one I could name?

She was waiting. "Um . . . Mr. Deever?"

"Yeah, no."

"That's certainly succinct, but could you perhaps expound a bit?"

"The author needs whatever motivation it takes for them to write the piece. That's all. Beyond that, whether or not it's effective should be up to the reader, right? So it's probably more honest to judge the work on its actual merits than whether or not the author had some lofty reason for writing it."

"Interesting. Anyone else have any input here?"

"Yes." I didn't even turn. I knew the voice, so I mentally prepared for the stick-and-twist routine of a knife in the back. "In the beginning of *Les Misérables,* before getting on with the story, Hugo gives us the social background of the town where the theft takes place and the economic conditions of the time and everything else." Yup, that was the stick.

Ms. Montinello nodded for her to continue. Stand by for the twist . . .

"So what would you think if you found out maybe he didn't do it only out of social consciousness," AK said, "but because back then novelists were usually paid by the word and routinely padded their stories? Would this somehow change the value of the work?"

What the . . . ?

For some reason Ms. Montinello seemed to find this amusing. "Well done." She looked out at the class. "But what *I* think isn't germane. So, who else has an opinion about this . . . ?"

Seth was busy during lunch so I managed to find a spot with the Unaffiliateds to sit and eat by myself. I was halfway done when I felt someone sit down next to me. You know how your brain can think a bunch of different thoughts in half a second, like between the time you see the mayonnaise jar leave the counter and the time it explodes on the floor? As I was turning my head I thought *It's probably Seth . . . or maybe Ollie with the latest news update . . . or maybe even Kennedy, explaining how it was all a misunderstanding and would I please-please-PLEASE shoot her new portfolio?* But instead it was the one person I least expected.

"Hi," she said quietly. I would have called it shy, except it was nothing like most girls' version of shy. (Like, Kennedy's take on shy is, *Aren't I adorable when I act shy like this?*)

"Hi," I said.

"I thought you made a good point in class."

I nodded and thought about leaving it at that, but that would have cost me points for dickishness and I didn't know how many I had left. "Thanks." *C'mon, dude—you can do better.* "Um, your comment about Victor Hugo was great—thanks for the backup."

"I'm not backing up anyone," she said like she was reciting a line. "I just have this problem—I say what I think. Trust me, it's got nothing to do with you."

She said it with a straight face but I looked close. She didn't have the give-away crinkle like Ollie but her eyes had this tiny twinkle, like they each had an extra milligram of water in them. I took that as a sign so I nodded and laughed, like *Good one—you got me!*

She actually—sort of—grinned back.

"Whoa!" I said. "That's the third time I've seen you smile this year."

"How do you know it's not four?"

"Because I count like a crow—one, two, three, and many. And there's no way you've made it to *many*." I paused. "So, was I really that much of a dick when I said it?"

"Oh yeah."

"Ouch. Sorry." I thought about it. "But isn't this different? I mean, you weren't exactly thanking me for backing you up when *I* said it. You were pissed."

"No I wasn't. I was just checking your motives . . ."

". . . which are always pure."

She snorted and raised an eyebrow. "I highly doubt that."

"You sound like you've been talking to my sister."

"Actually, I have. She told me a little about your photo project."

My smile disappeared. "She what?"

She held up her hands. "Hey, if you don't want to talk about it, don't."

I shook my head. "Not your fault. It's just that Ollie knows it's private, and . . ." I stopped. I never talked about it. Not in any detail. I mean, the only person I'd mentioned it to besides Ollie was Seth, and that was only because I had to. And that one time I tried to talk about it at Finch was a total fail. But the look on her face was so sincere, and I was still amped about what had happened with the site last night, so . . .

"You promise not to laugh?" I asked.

She nodded, solemnly.

"Okay." I took a breath. "I call it the 9:09 Project, and . . ."

So I told her about it. Not in uber-detail, but I covered the basics about why I was doing it. Meaning the words ". . . because that was what time it was when my mom died" came out of my mouth.

When I was done she looked at me for a second. "You continue to surprise me. Thank you for telling me that . . . I'm guessing it's something you don't talk about much."

I nodded. "Um, yeah. Like, ever."

"Well, I think it's a beautiful idea. And I'm glad you trusted me enough to explain it."

"Thanks. So, uh . . . does this mean no more shooting me down in flames?"

How can someone put their hands on their hips without moving? "I agree with you when you're smart, and disagree when you're stupid." She pursed her lips and shook her head slowly. "If there's any shooting going on, you're doing it to yourself."

I wasn't exactly sure what she meant, but I definitely had the feeling I'd rather have her on my side than not. "*Okaaay* . . . So I guess I'll try to be smart from now on."

She nodded. "Good idea." Again, I had to look for it, but that little gleam was back.

I looked up and noticed Kennedy Brooks walking down the

aisle in our direction, and just as I saw her, she saw us. She paused for like half a second, then kept going like we weren't even there.

AK's eyes followed her. "Hmm," she said when she'd passed us. "Sure is cold in here."

"Yeah," I said. "I guess some people are more endothermic than others."

She stood. "If by that you mean she takes in way more attention than she gives out, then you're right."

I just looked at her and something inside me sort of clicked. *Remember this fucking moment.*

CHAPTER 17

We see not only with our eyes, but with all that we are and all that our culture is.
—Dorothea Lange

I CHECKED MY SITE'S NUMBERS THAT EVENING AND IF anything they were even better, so I decided to put up another *Do You See What I See?* post. For this one I used the best of the shots I'd made of the middle-aged man and his mother. I'd been directly in front of them while taking it but neither of them was looking at the camera. In the photo the man is next to his mom with one arm around her shoulder, pulling her toward him as he bends over and plants a kiss on her cheek. She, on the other hand, is looking skyward and rolling her eyes. I'd cropped in fairly close, so you could clearly see both their faces. To me the whole point of the image was the juxtaposition of their expressions, which seem opposite on the surface but are really the same. Like the 9:09 images, I'd rendered it in black-and-white, but much warmer in tone than the one I'd taken of Kennedy.

What it said to me was *This is a lucky, lucky man. And part of his good fortune is that he gets to repay a fraction of what he owes his mother. She acts like she doesn't want or need the attention, but underneath it all she loves it. And him.*

By the time I was done putting up the post—and wiping my eyes—it was after eight-thirty, so I grabbed my Nikon and headed for Fig and Gardena.

It was cold out and there wasn't much foot traffic downtown. As I went by Finch I was tempted to bail on the shoot and just curl up with a hot cup of chai, but I made myself go to the corner and wait. I'd been standing there for several minutes with no one in sight, when right before 9:09 someone came around the corner up ahead and started walking toward me. Something about her walk seemed familiar—fast, with a purpose—and as she got closer I recognized her. The girl who previously fucking hated me.

When she got to my corner I held out my camera, then made a show of putting it behind my back. "We've got to stop meeting like this. And don't worry, there's no way I'm going to take your picture."

"But I want you to—that's why I'm here."

"You're kidding me."

She folded her arms. "Do I look like I'm kidding? I'm not here freezing my ass off for nothing."

"Um, that's not really how it works . . ."

"Hey, I like your idea and I want to be part of it." Her arms were still folded. "What's so wrong with that?"

I flashed to the last time a girl asked me that, then tried to push that image far, far away. Just then a guy with two little kids started crossing the street toward us. "Uh, nothing. Can you give me a minute, and then I'll explain . . ."

I told the guy about my "school project," and to my surprise he agreed. "As long as you hurry," he said. "We've got a date with some hot chocolate."

"Wouldn't want to stand between these guys and some cocoa," I said, indicating the kids. He was in his thirties, and the kids were both boys, maybe three and five. They'd been walking with the man in the middle, holding his hands, and that's how they stood as I photographed them.

"Hey, guys," I said to the kids as I started snapping. "Is this your dad?"

"Yeah!" they both said at the same time.

"Is he a good dad?"

"Yeah!"

"So what's your favorite thing about him?"

"Ice cream!" the little one shouted.

"Huh-uh, cookies!" the other one said.

"Huh-uh, ice cream!"

"Huh-uh, cookies . . . !"

The dad was grinning the whole time.

"Okay, okay. I think you're both right," I said. "Enjoy your cocoa." I turned to the dad. "Thanks." He nodded and they took off, the boys still shouting back and forth.

I turned to AK. "Um, you got time for a cup of coffee? I mean, it's pretty cold to stand out here and talk . . ."

"I don't know," she said. "I heard you were a real player, getting handsy with Kennedy Brooks at that party and everything . . ."

I did a face palm, shaking my head back and forth.

She let me suffer for about three seconds, then laughed. "Just kidding. Ollie told me the real story."

I made a mental note to thank Ollie. Which did *not* happen every day, believe me. "So, uh . . ." I nodded toward Finch. "Warmth? Caffeine? Indoor plumbing?"

I got a chai, and an espresso for her—which she insisted on paying for—and brought them to the booth she'd found near the back. She pointed to the man with the two boys I'd photographed, sitting up at the front counter. The guy had a coffee and the boys had their hot chocolates on either side of him, swinging their legs as they sat on the tall stools, still yakking away. "You were really good with them," she said.

"Thanks."

"And it was fun seeing the 9:09 Project in action. So, why can't I be part of it?"

"Selection bias."

"Excuse me?"

I explained about using time as a way of ensuring I got a more diverse cross-section and didn't end up only choosing the kind of subjects *I* found interesting, forcing me to make the best out of whatever the universe provided, blah blah blah . . .

". . . so I can't use your picture from tonight in the 9:09 Project, because you knew about it and came here specifically at that time for that reason." I suddenly realized how nerdy that must have sounded. "I hope that makes sense . . . ?"

She nodded. "Totally. I corrupted the randomness of the selection process."

I couldn't help smiling. "Exactly!" But I also couldn't resist a dig. "You know, you *could* have been part of it—"

"Back when I blew you off," she interrupted.

"Yup. Well, the second time, at least. The first attempt was too early in the day."

She grinned, remembering. "Oh yeah—that time in the cafeteria when you were lining up girls for photo shoots."

I mimicked swinging a bat, then said in an announcer's voice, *"Annnnd . . . it's a swing and a miss. Strike one!"* We both laughed and I almost went into a routine where she was on the mound throwing fastballs at me, when I realized I didn't know what to call her. Awkward. Finally I asked, "So, um . . . what's up with your nickname?"

She winced. "AK-47?"

"That's pretty much all I've heard people call you."

She nodded. "I know. I'm half Lebanese, so people assume I must be Muslim. Which they somehow equate with being a terrorist. So they morph my initials into AK-47, a terrorist's weapon named after a Russian named Kalashnikov. So yeah, who *wouldn't* want to be called that?"

"Ouch. That'd be like if my dad's parents were German or something . . ."

"... which they equate with being a Nazi ..."

"... so they called me Swastika or whatever," I added.

She shrugged. "Something like that."

"So, what should I call you? I mean, I know your initials are AK, and I've heard the teacher call on you as Ms. Knudsen."

"Ms. Knudsen . . ." She nodded like she was considering it. "Yeah, I like the sound of that. From now on you can call me Ms. Knudsen."

It was my turn to fold my arms and stare.

"Assi," she finally said. Like *ah-SEE*. "My mother's Lebanese, and she told my dad—who was Norwegian—that since he determined my last name, she got to pick my first one."

"Assi," I said. "What a cool name. So why let people call you AK-47?"

She shrugged. "You don't always get a choice. And when your real name has the word *ass* in it, there are worse options ..."

Looking at her, something suddenly occurred to me. "You know, I'd still like to take your photo sometime. Outside of the whole 9:09 thing, I mean."

She was quiet for a second, then nodded. "How about right now?"

I looked around. "Here?"

"Sure. Why not?"

I had a hundred reasons—lighting, background, distance ... Then I saw she was serious. "All right. Give me a minute."

I took out my Nikon and thought for a second. I could handhold it, like I do outside, but camera motion is worse than subject motion and I wanted a portrait, not just a casual snap. I took out the little tabletop tripod I keep in my bag and sat it on the edge of the table, with my camera mounted on top.

"Okay," I said when I was ready. "Look over here and we'll give it a shot."

As far as I could tell she didn't have any practice doing the whole "give them your look" routine, like Ollie and Kennedy did. And she certainly didn't pull the usual duck-face selfie pose. She just looked at me with zero artifice. It was intense. Almost like she was looking through me. I didn't wait around—I tripped the shutter.

I started to take another when she held her hand up. "That was it."

"Uh, I usually take a few, just in case . . ." Her hand didn't budge. "Really?"

She nodded. "Really."

I put the camera away. "Okay. Uh . . . speaking of photography, you really gave me something to think about at the party the other night."

"About not always being so stupid?" She said it with a straight face but I could see the smile behind the mask.

"Well, yeah, there *is* that." I snorted and shook my head. "And here I was trying to pay you a compliment and all you can do is—"

She propped her head in her hands and batted her eyes. "A *compliment*? From *you*? I'm all ears!"

"More like all mouth," I muttered. But she dropped the routine so I tried again. "I was trying to figure out how to frame an idea for my website and I remembered you saying something about it being more about how someone looks at the world than their technical know-how, and that really hit home." I told her how that had inspired the DYSWIS page on my site, and how people seemed to like the idea of comparing their vision of what was behind a photo with the photographer's vision of it. "So thanks. Seriously."

She didn't bat her lashes or glance at me, then quickly down at the table, or any other "shy" stuff. She just looked directly at me, sort of like when I'd taken her picture. "I appreciate it. But I really didn't say much."

"I know, but there was a lot in what you said. Quality is way more important than quantity." It was my turn to hold her gaze. "I just wanted you to know that."

She swallowed, then nodded. "I'm really glad it helped."

When I got home I did something I don't normally do—I went to work on the photo I'd just taken, the one of Assi. Usually I like to separate the two, because they take different mind-sets. Ms. Montinello talks about "leaving some breathing room between taking off the writer's hat and putting on the editor's hat," but this was different. I'd gotten a certain vibe when I'd taken the picture and I wanted to make sure the final image had that same mood, so I decided to work on it while the feeling was fresh.

I'd reviewed the pic a couple of times on my camera on the way home, but I couldn't see much. So when I transferred the file to my computer and opened it on the bigger screen I was nervous. But there it was. Even in the raw, with the funky lighting and everything, the mood I remembered was definitely there. Now my job was basically to take away everything that detracted from it.

Sometimes you can take an image and just start messing with it—more brightness, less contrast, jacked-up color, whatever—and you might stumble on something that works. But for this one, I had a pretty good idea of what I wanted from the start. Realistic, but without the edgy hyperrealism of overdone digital. Maybe more like a good analog photo from fifty years ago.

I knew I wanted monochrome—along with the right vibe, it would also eliminate the issue of the weird lighting color. But not strictly neutral . . . more like sepia. I made the lighter tones creamy instead of cold white, and the darker ones leaning more toward chocolate than gray. So even though it was "black-and-white," her eyes ended up the same deep liquid brown in the image as they were in real life. As I worked on it, I was glad I'd taken the trouble to set up the tripod—I'd opened the lens up and there was almost no depth of field behind her, but her eyes were absolutely sharp. And when I looked close I could see that little gleam in them, like she was sharing a private joke.

As far as I could tell she didn't have a lot of makeup on, but looking at her face I didn't feel any desire to zoom way in and try to micromanage anything. I burned down everything near the edge of the frame so your eye was drawn to her face, but rather than crank up the brightness, I left the skin tones right where they were—smooth and warm.

When I was done I sat back and looked at it for a minute. What I saw made me feel the way I'd felt when I'd taken it. Like she could see right into me . . . like she *knew* me. And that was all I could ask for.

I shut everything down and got into bed but I had a hard time falling asleep. And when I finally did drop off, my brain kept taking random clips from the past week and zipping through them in no particular order—until it finally resolved into an endless loop of Kennedy and Assi, each saying *What's so wrong with that?*

At some point I woke up, threw off my covers, stumbled to my desk, and opened up my computer. I had no idea what time it was . . . two or three in the morning? I brought up the head shot of Assi again and looked at it.

Okay, I wasn't really observing the image on the screen as much as how it made me *feel* when I looked at it.

And man, there was something there that just . . .

Wow.

I don't know.

I just don't know.

CHAPTER 18

Whatever I photograph, I try to show as having its position in the past or in the present.
—Dorothea Lange

". . . WHICH IS WHY WE CARE ABOUT THE DEPTH AND breadth of your lexicon, Ms. Knudsen," Ms. Montinello said. "Vocabulary and syntax are tools, and I want you to have a full toolbox. The example you gave seems somewhat limited."

"If you're trying to authentically portray a certain culture," Assi said, "then as long as you're respectful, what's wrong with using terms familiar to that culture?"

Sorry, but my synesthesia was still stuck on *Lexicon*. I mean, just *look* at it, with that black *X* in the middle, bordered with faded red—almost rose—on the left and pale blue-green on the right. And the *i-c-o-n* on the end was also pretty rare, bringing up similar words . . .

"Those who've crossed the Rubicon have little need for lexicon . . ."

Ms. Montinello stopped in midsentence and spun on me. *"What . . . ?"*

"Dead men tell no tales, right?" I glanced at Assi, then back to Ms. Montinello. "Which better reflects the true meaning, being jargon of the times . . . don't you think?"

She just glared at me, expressionless except for her tongue working against the inside of her cheek. Finally she turned back to the class.

"I think that's enough for today. Remember, tomorrow you need to bring a hard copy of your Big Day essay."

The bell rang, and as everyone got up to leave she said, "J? A word?"

I knew I'd gone too far.

"I'm sorry" was all I said as I approached her desk. There was no way I could explain the attractive nuisance of a word like *Lexicon* to someone who didn't see what I saw.

"You're bright, and you're a verbal thinker," she said. "And that can be a curse as well as a blessing. For example, I'm fairly certain not all of your classmates admire that."

You're not kidding, I thought. But I just nodded.

"Not that I want you to hide your light," she went on. "Not for a second. And trust me, I'm glad that two of my students seem to have reached a working symbiosis rather than continuing to use my classroom as a Battleship game board. But along with power comes responsibility." She literally pulled her glasses down her nose and looked at me over the top of them. "So choose wisely."

*   *   *

I stopped by the Unaffiliateds table and nudged Seth. "Let's move."

"Uh, what's changed?"

I looked across the room and started counting off reasons on my fingers. "The girl who hates me isn't there, although the girl who likes you is—which is almost as annoying—but at least she's hanging with a couple of girls who're usually pretty nice to us. And the girl who fucking hates me is apparently okay with me for the moment . . ."

He stood up. "Clearly, you're good at math."

We sat with Ollie and Chloe and Sofia. I parked myself between Sofia and the end of the table, and after a couple of minutes a voice from the next table said, "Nice to see your butt is still convex instead of concave."

"Nice to see someone noticed," I said as I turned.

"I appreciate the support," Assi said, "but you don't have to throw yourself in front of a moving train for me."

"That's kinda what Ms. Montinello said, except there was a little more superhero metaphor in her version."

"Death by locomotive isn't heroic enough for you?" She tilted her head. "And where did that Rubicon/lexicon thing come from?"

"Genetic, from my mother's side."

"What?"

"It's hard to explain."

She looked at me for a second, then shrugged. "Okay. But thanks, regardless. I think Ms. M got the point."

I nodded, and she turned back to talk to the girl next to her. I wanted to say something about her photo but I didn't want to come across as a creeper. Like, *Hey—I got up at two a.m. and looked at your picture.* Pretty much the definition of creepy, right?

I spent the rest of lunch talking with Seth and Ollie and Chloe and Sofia, and you know what? My initial job of selling it to Seth turned out to be correct—it was all good.

Ollie must have thought so too, because she brought it up on the way home. "You know, it was nice hanging with you and Seth at lunch today . . ."

I nodded as I slowed for a red light.

"And you know," she said, "it might be fun if there was a fourth . . ."

I just shrugged without looking at her.

"I just meant for Tacos de and stuff," she added quickly. "To keep Dad happy. No big deal."

I nodded again. Dad had decided that Ollie could "go out" as long as it was with a group. I drove another block before responding. "Okay," I finally said. "I think Kennedy would be down for that."

She bent over and pantomimed putting her finger down her throat, then paused. "Actually . . ."

I gave it a second. "Actually . . . ?"

"Actually, I was thinking of Sofia."

I shrugged. "Hmm."

She turned toward me, eyes flashing. "What's the matter—didn't your loser friends rate her high enough? She's funny, she's nice, and she's totally hot regardless of whatever Butt-Face Beal said." She paused. "And I happen to think there's a pretty good chance she'd say yes."

This was my cue to show some interest, to ask how she knew.

But for some reason I just watched the road and drove.

. . . and although it seems counterintuitive, there were no surprises for us on the big day. Nothing stunning, nothing unexpected. Which was the whole problem—the unexpected would have been a welcome miracle. Instead what happened was something we'd been expecting for months . . .

The assignment was to write an "effective, engaging essay" about a big day in our lives. I really didn't want to relive that day—and I'm not sure *big* describes it—but it was definitely the most impactful day of my life. Besides, what else was I going to write about? *The Day Kennedy Brooks Kissed Me* probably wasn't going to cut it.

"So," Ms. Montinello said as she walked around the room handing out papers at the end of class the next day, "I've taken your essays and divided them into pairs, at random. You have someone's essay, and they have yours. The next part of the assignment is to take your critique partner's essay home, read it, and generate constructive commentary based on the list of attributes I've given you. Then we'll regroup and discuss them on Monday."

She dropped some stapled pages on my desk as she passed. I shoved them in my backpack and headed out.

When I got home I went to my website for a quick peek at the stats. The viewership was actually a little higher than right after that blurb from Street Shooters Anonymous, instead of slowly falling off like I'd expected. And the 9:09 stuff was getting at least as many hits as the *Do You See What I See?* posts, with lots of people saying they loved the idea of the project. I had to give Seth credit—most of the people who commented on it seemed to be into the idea of doing a project in honor of someone who'd passed away as much as they were into the photos themselves.

I was cruising through the photos in my file, looking for something new to post, when I found myself looking at Assi's head shot. After everything I'd said to her I sure couldn't use it as a 9:09 post, and I didn't really want to use it as a DYSWIS image because . . . well, because I'd have to say what I thought about it, and I wasn't sure I knew. Then another image came to mind—her walking across the cafeteria—and I knew *exactly* what I thought about that one.

I pulled out my phone and scrolled until I found it, then sent it to my computer. I cropped the top down and the bottom up but left it full width so you saw the large room spread horizontally across the frame, but nothing really below her feet or above her head. The background was a blur as I'd moved the camera to follow her pace—her hands and feet were also blurry due to their motion—but her face was sharp and her determined expression was apparent. Instead of moody black-and-white like the 9:09 pics, I left it bright and colorful because I wanted a modern, active vibe.

For my take on the image I entered: This girl is definitely going somewhere. From the look on her face it's clear she'd make a great guide if you were heading toward an unknown destination . . .

After I posted the pic I looked around for something to do. Something fun, I mean. I had no intention of reviewing the essay of my "critique partner" until sometime Sunday afternoon. Like maybe 8:00 p.m. Sunday afternoon. Because how excited could I get about reading someone's paper describing the day their little brother was born or they won the city-wide Little League championship or the Little Miss Vista Grande contest or whatfuckingever?

That was my state of mind as I pushed my books aside, making room on my desk for more important activities—like cruising the internet. I guess I pushed too hard because the stack slid off my desk and hit the floor. I bent to pick them up and saw the essay I was supposed to read, flopped to the first page where I could see the name. And the title. Holy shit.

There wasn't a Little League game or Little Miss contest anywhere in sight . . .

    . . . *because humans seem generally well programmed for knowing what to do during a traumatic emergency. If you wake up and the house is on fire, you don't stand around thinking about it—you wake everyone else up and get out. If a vehicle drives by and bullets fly, you don't debate the politics of it—you get on the ground.*

Because it still matters.

Because you can still affect the outcome.

But if the traumatic emergency has no variables left, if you can no longer change the outcome, then your actions no longer matter. And therefore you have no idea what to do. Because humans aren't programmed for the after-emergency. We get PTSD, not TSD. So you vacillate wildly from one false start to another, trying unsuccessfully to decide which course of action is more important, until you finally realize nothing is important. Because nothing can bring back the dead.

On the day my father was killed I probably burned more calories than on any other day in my life. And I probably accomplished less than on any other day in my life . . .

"Ollie!"

She came running into my room. "Jesus, I could hear you through the wall. What's the matter?"

"I need a phone number." To her credit she just gave it to me without a lot of questions. I sent a quick text.

hey, it's j. do you have time for coffee?

The reply came back almost immediately. sure. when?

any time after 9:09

CHAPTER 19

*I do not molest what I photograph, I do not meddle
and I do not arrange.*
—Dorothea Lange

SHE WAS IN THE SAME BOOTH WE'D USED EARLIER, IN THE
back. With an espresso and a chai waiting. I unslung my camera
bag and put it on the seat next to me. "Thanks," I said, picking
up my drink.

She pointed to my gear. "Did you get anything?"

Good question. "I'm not sure . . . maybe . . . I don't know . . .
I hope—"

She held up her hand. "You did."

She didn't say anything more so I got to why I'd texted her
in the first place. "I read your essay this evening, and I loved it."

"And I loved yours."

I thought she was just being nice. "No, I mean I *really* fucking
loved it."

"And I really loved yours. Let's stop—this isn't a competition."

"Okay." I paused. When I'd read her essay all these things came to my mind that I wanted to tell her. But now, with her sitting across the table, the words bailed on me. "Um . . . and I also wanted to say how sorry I was to hear about your dad."

"Thanks. It's coming up on five years . . ."

So she'd been about the same age Ollie'd been when our mom died. "It's been almost two years for me, and I still miss her like crazy. Does it get any easier?" I looked at her face. "Sorry. Stupid question."

"No, it's not. But I can only answer for me."

"And . . . ?"

"Yes. And no. The worst part is when I forget. When I see something and think 'I can't wait to tell my dad about this!' And then it all comes rushing back."

I nodded. "Sometimes I have that first thing in the morning: I wake up and everything's fine. Nothing amazing, just another ordinary day. Then suddenly I remember and it's like getting run over by a truck. Again."

She took a sip of her espresso. I could smell it from across the table, dark and roasty. "I checked out your site. It's amazing, and . . ." She blinked for a couple of seconds, and I was surprised to see she was tearing up. "Sorry—I hate it when I do this!" She kind of fanned her hand at her eyes. "What you're doing—for your mom, for anyone who's lost someone—it's wonderful. And the photographs . . ." She paused. "It's like your eyes are older than the rest of you."

I felt uncomfortable. But maybe I liked it a little, too. Coming from her, I mean. Heck, I don't know. "You don't see all the crappy ones where I miss."

"Sure, but you still have to decide which ones say what you want to say, and that takes vision, too." She raised an eyebrow. "I even liked the one of Kennedy Brooks. I thought it did a great job of telling the story behind the story."

"Thanks."

"So . . . what do you think of her?"

Danger, Will Robinson! I decided to punt. "I asked Ollie that same question, and she said Kennedy acts like someone who's really popular." I studiously avoided any mention of the word *hot.* "And I guess I'd agree with that."

She nodded slowly. I wasn't sure if it was in agreement or more like *Good answer, dude,* but I wasn't asking any questions. "I *also* saw the picture of me that you put up . . ."

She didn't seem real happy about it. "I hope you don't mind. I just thought it was kind of cool. I mean, with the way you were walking fast and looking focused and, uh . . ."

She waved all that aside. "Can you see how it might be considered a little, um . . . *stalkerish*?" I started to say something— probably something defensive—when she continued. "The people you photograph at 9:09 on the corner, they agree to it, right?"

"Yeah, sure."

"So not only do you have their permission, you have their cooperation. They're a partner . . . a *contributing* partner . . . in your project. And I think that makes a connection. One you can see in the results." She sort of cocked her head. "Does that make sense?"

Does it ever. But I didn't say that, I just nodded slowly.

"Look," she said, "I get why you're putting the photos up—especially the 9:09 ones—but what are you trying to get *from* it, in return?"

"You're really coming with the hard ones tonight, aren't you?"

That eyebrow went up again. Nothing else.

"Wow. Okay . . ." I tried to get my thoughts together. "It makes me feel better . . . about my mom, I guess. She encouraged me to pursue my photography, so when I'm doing that, I feel like . . ." What *did* I feel like? "I feel like I'm sort of doing the project *with* her. If that doesn't sound too stupid?" I shrugged. "I sure hope that's enough for you, because beyond that, I got nothing."

She swallowed, then bobbed her head. "No, that's enough. Thanks."

I sat there for a second, just looking at her. Hmm. I wasn't planning on showing it to her, but . . .

I took out my phone and found it—the final version of the one I'd taken of her the other night. "Here's the head shot I took of you. I'll send it to you, because it looks better on a bigger screen, but . . ." I showed it to her.

She took the phone and looked at it for quite a while, then zoomed in a little, then back out. She finally glanced up at me, still holding the phone. "Is this how you see me?"

Oh crap. Was I in trouble or something? There was no one left to punt to. "Uh, if you don't like it, no worries. I haven't posted it or anything. I can delete it, or—"

She handed my phone back. "You made me look beautiful."

"*I* didn't. That's just how you looked. All I did was take away everything that was distracting from you." I reached for my bag and dragged out my Nikon. "Wait, I'll show you . . ." I called up the original shot and zoomed in until it was the same magnification as the finished image. "See? That's you. I just cleaned it up a little and rendered it in black-and-white . . ."

She barely glanced at the image on the back of the Nikon. "You know, you never answered my question." She looked at the time on her phone and started to gather her things. "I have to get going."

"Uh, sure." I stopped, suddenly feeling awkward. "Let me at least pay for the coffees."

She kept a straight face and maybe I imagined it, but for a second I thought I saw that little gleam. "Maybe next time."

As she walked away I thought about her question. *Yes. Exactly.*

Photographs are a strange thing—they can either describe or evoke. They can either point directly at something and say *Look right here!!! At this!!!* or they can hint at a certain vibe, a certain feeling. Tonight for some reason I'd been out for the second kind, but I had no clue if I'd captured it.

I sent this evening's images to my computer and started

going through them. The subjects were a pair of middle-aged women who'd been walking down Gardena. It turned out they were sisters, which you'd think might be interesting, but the first half dozen left me flat. *No. No. Not quite. NFW. Maybe, but . . . no. And no.* Okay, they weren't terrible, but somehow they felt like a beer left open on the counter all night. Same taste, no sparkle. They just didn't make me feel anything.

I was about to give up when one of the shots in the final group of pics had it. In the first batch they were just standing there side by side—looking at me—but in this shot, one of them must have said something funny because the woman on the right was smiling and the woman on the left was laughing out loud. And they were looking at each other, not the camera. Somehow in that fraction of a second you could see all fifty years of their relationship . . . all the memories and jokes and experiences they'd shared, all the laughing, all the crying.

Boom—there it was.

This is going to sound ridiculous—because there's no real correlation between a teenage girl and two older women—but as I started to work on the image it hit me. What I was looking for in those photos had something in common with the feeling I had when I talked with Assi. And whatever that was, I'd found it in the image of the two women sharing a laugh without regard for the camera.

I sat there for a minute, staring at the wall, then suddenly got up and went to Ollie's room. She was sitting on her bed, tapping away at her phone. I had to wave to get her attention. She pulled the earbuds and I could hear music spilling out. "What's going on?"

I sat on the edge of the bed. "I was talking with Assi tonight . . ."

She scrunched up her face. "Who?"

"You know, AK."

She pressed a button and the music stopped. "You were, huh?" Full crinkle. "Like texting, or like actually talking on the phone?"

"Like *talking* talking. Like you and me, right now." I ignored her grin and continued. "What I wanted to say was, well . . . she was twelve when she lost her father."

Ollie's smile vanished. "She was?"

"Yeah. He died in an accident." I paused. "Look. I know you never talk about Mom, but if you were looking for someone who . . . I don't know . . . maybe understood a little, then maybe you might want to talk to her?" I shrugged. "Or not. I don't know. Maybe it's a goofy thought . . ."

She shut off her phone and set it down, blinking at me for a second. "No, it's a good thought, J. Really." There was no crinkle now, but she gave me a little of the vibe those sisters had in the photo. "Thanks."

". . . so let's pair up and go over each other's critique sheets," Ms. Montinello said in class on Monday. She had to raise her voice as students started moving around the room. "And remember, people—be kind! The goal is to *motivate,* not *decimate.*"

As I found a seat next to Assi I thought she might ask about my weekend or make small talk or whatever but she got right down to business, so I mentally shrugged and did the same. The critique sheets had a few basic questions about the piece under review, like *Did it engage the reader?*, *Did it employ figurative language?*, and *Did it achieve the desired effect?* Then we were supposed to list the pros and cons of the piece.

My issue was that I had no real cons for her essay. The other questions were easy (yes, yes, and hell yes) and I could gush about the quality and the poignancy of her writing at length (and I did) but I was having a hard time with constructive commentary. I finally summed up my critique sheet at the bottom with: *The positive—this was a powerful, emotional, very well-written essay about the impact the death of a loved one had on the author and her family. The negative—I cried like a baby.*

I pushed my paper over to her and she read it, then smiled. She finished hers and handed it over without a word. It had lots of nice comments in the body of the report, followed by her plus/delta at the end. *In summation, the best thing about this essay was the visceral way in which the author made the passing of his mother a real event not only in his life, but in ours. This left me with a transferred sense of loss that rendered me absolutely bereft and emotionally drained. The negative aspect of the essay: see above.*

Wow. What do you say to that?

"Wow," I said. See how clever I am? I cleared my throat. "I didn't mean to make you feel bad or sad or bereft, even."

"Of course not—you didn't even know I was going to read

it when you wrote it. And—" She stopped and snuck a glance at Ms. Montinello. "So . . . just how 'random' do you think all this was?"

I looked at Ms. Montinello, then back at Assi. "I'm definitely thinking what you're thinking."

Just then Ms. Montinello said, "Okay, class, hand your worksheets in. Tomorrow we can discuss today's interactions."

After she collected the papers and dismissed the class, I called out, "Ms. Montinello? A word?"

She walked over toward us. If I didn't know better I'd say she knew exactly what was on our minds. "Yes?"

"We beg to differ with your understanding of the word *random*."

She shrugged. "Coincidences happen." Then she smiled. "What are the odds?"

The math was trivial. $1/(n\text{-}1)$ expressed as a decimal, then convert it to a percentage, then subtract that from a hundred. I looked around the room and roughly counted seats. High twenties . . . call it twenty-seven. Close enough. "*The odds* say there's a ninety-six percent chance it wasn't random at all . . ."

She did that looking-over-her-glasses thing at us. "From the master: *Sometimes the smaller falsehood supports the larger truth.*"

Assi looked confused. "I don't know that quote. Who's the master?"

Ms. Montinello cocked an eyebrow. "Me."

* * *

". . . and I'm getting more daily visitors with some comments on the 9:09 pics, plus feedback on the DYSWIS posts, and—"

Seth scrunched up his face. "*Dish wish?* Is that like a death wish? Only with tableware somehow involved?"

"You know—the *Do You See What I See?* stuff." We were talking at lunch. And yeah, we were eating at the Unaffiliateds table. (Kennedy was front and center at the 7-Up table—call me chicken-shit but I didn't want the drama.)

"Dude, that's awesome. You need to add Like and Share buttons."

"Why?"

He sighed, like I was the dumbest kid in Social Media 101. Which I might be. "To help spread the word. In theory if someone likes your site they can post the URL on their Twitter or Instagram or whatever. But people are lazy, so they don't. But if all they have to do is click a button, they'll do it."

"Do you think you could help me with that sometime?"

He took out his phone. "Give me admin privileges and I'll do it right now."

So I gave him the password and sure enough, in about two minutes the site was updated with all those little bird and thumb and camera icons at the bottom of the home page.

"Thanks," I said when he was done.

"No problem. Hope that helps your site."

Just then Assi walked by with her food. To eat near the 7-Up table, no doubt, but outside the radius of total distain. "Hey" was all she said as she passed.

I nodded. "Hey."

Seth doesn't miss much. "What's up with that?" he mumbled after she was out of earshot, still playing with his phone. "Other than she flips your Che switch, as I recall."

Like I said . . .

By some unspoken agreement we didn't talk about girls. Okay, we talked about girls all the time, but only in general terms. Never specifics. Never how we actually felt about them. But if not him, then who . . . ?

"Um . . . I think she's smart. At least, way smarter than I am."

"So does that make you feel, like, threatened or something?" he asked.

"That's the funny part." I lowered my voice and looked around, like I was confessing to some totally perverted thought. "I fucking *like it,* man . . ."

After Seth left I was just sitting there for a minute, thinking about what I'd said, when someone plopped down next to me. I glanced over. Kennedy. You could have knocked me over with a fart. I was expecting her to either give me shit about the way I'd treated her at Sophie's party or maybe apologize for how she'd spun it afterward. I was wrong on both counts.

"You have AP history with LaRue, right?"

I sure wasn't expecting *that.* "Uh . . . yeah?"

"How's it going for you?"

I was pulling an A but for some reason I didn't feel like

bragging about it. "Okay, I guess. Except for the minor detail that he seems to hate me." I laughed. "He must've had a son that looked like me who ran away from home or something, because that dude does *not* like me."

She didn't even crack a smile. "I have him third period. God, I'm dying in there . . . barely hanging on."

"Didn't you used to love history? I remember back in seventh grade—you were the annoying girl who always had her hand up."

She gave me a sad sort of smile. "I was, wasn't I?" She looked down at the table for a moment. "Where did she go?" she said so quietly I almost missed it.

Wow. This conversation was *not* going the way I expected. I shrugged. "Maybe you just had other priorities?"

It was her turn to shrug. "Maybe." She brushed her hair out of her face and just looked at me for a second, and I got the impression this wasn't easy for her. "So . . . do you think you might find the time to come by this afternoon and give me your top ten tips for surviving AP history?"

She seemed sincere enough, but I've seen that movie before. I think what did it for me was she didn't attempt to use the eye thing or the puppy-dog look or any of that stuff. Not once. And of course, she was already going out with that college dude. So . . .

"Okay. But I don't have ten tips . . . more like my top two or three."

She seemed relieved. "That's fine . . . I'd be happy with one."

Just then the bell rang and she left.

Like that whole party thing had never happened.

* * *

"Remember when everyone was oohing and aahing over the awesome portfolio you did for your little blond bestie-with-the-breasties, only she didn't give you any credit for it?"

Ollie's definitely been hanging with Seth too much. I glanced at her as I drove us home from school. "Ignoring your total humor fail . . . yeah, what about it?"

"The same thing's going on now, with your site."

"What do you mean?"

"People at school are talking about it. Somebody saw it and recognized that some of the shots were taken on campus or wherever. They're all saying how awesome it is."

"So?"

"So you ought to take credit for it, that's all."

No, I thought, *but I should be more careful taking pics from now on.* But I didn't say that. I just shrugged. "I'll think about it." Which is universal for *Yeah, no.*

I did think about it, though, and when I got home I checked the stats. Not only were the page views up but the number of unique visitors was also up, which meant that besides people going back to look at other pages on my site, there were new people going there too.

And something else . . . In one of the comments someone asked if I'd mind if they started their own 9:09-type project, in honor of their brother who was killed in Afghanistan. I almost never replied to comments, but I thought about it for a minute, then said sure (how do you say no to that?), as long as he gave my site credit and a linkback. But I left the sig under my reply as *Admin,* because I still felt weird about having my name on something that seemed so private. I mean, I didn't start all this for some kind of ego-fest.

I started this because I miss my mom.

Here's how different I felt from the last time I went to her house—I just wore the same old whatever clothes I'd worn to school.

Okay, I sort of regretted my fashion choice when she answered my knock. She'd clearly changed clothes . . . she had something on that looked like a robe, but nicer. Silkier. Like a Japanese kimono, maybe? She smelled great, too.

I was feeling kind of self-conscious but she gave me a big smile and said, "Hi, J! Come on in." As she led me back to her room we walked by the family room where her dad was watching a football game. He didn't even look up.

And yeah, once we were inside I'll admit my first thought was *Holy crap—I'm in Kennedy Brooks's bedroom!* It was probably twice the size of my room, and done up in muted colors like beige or taupe or whatever—I'm sure Ollie could give you the official names—but to me it just looked *designed.* Like out of a magazine. And up against one wall was a four-poster king-size bed with some kind of leopard-print thing draped across it. Wow . . .

I forced myself to look around and focus on why I was there. There was a desk against the opposite wall, so I set my backpack down and took out some quick notes I'd made.

"Um, so I'm guessing you guys are where we are in class—late 1800s, second industrial revolution and all that stuff?" She nodded and I looked at my notes. "Okay, here are some of the main things LaRue really seems to care about, and I'm guessing the test'll focus on these . . ."

We went over the high points and she seemed to get what I was saying. After fifteen minutes I sort of wound down and stood to put my stuff away.

"So," she said, standing also, "do you happen to have your camera with you?"

I did, but I didn't tell her that. "Why?"

"I was thinking . . ." She took a step toward me. "That maybe . . ." Another step. "We could do a little photography session . . ."

"A photo shoot?" I looked around the room. "Here?"

She nodded. "Right here. Right now. A glamour shoot."

"Glamour?"

By now she was right in front of me. "Uh-huh. You know what I mean." She did the eye thing, then looked down to finger the thin material of her kimono. "Wouldn't you like to see what's under this?"

Man, the brain can think of weird shit at times like these. First was *Is that a rhetorical question?* Then *I'm a single, straight seventeen-year-old dude . . . what do you think???* Followed immediately by an image of Assi. Which sort of freaked me out, to tell the truth. But I didn't say any of that. "What are you getting at?"

"What do you mean? I'm just asking if you'd be interested in doing a glamour shoot with me. That's all."

That's *all* . . . ? Like that was the *norm*? Like, first you study for a history exam, then *of course* you immediately follow it up with the obligatory nude photo session? This was starting to feel like when she got me to do that whole portfolio thing. I shook my head. "I don't know . . ."

She took a step backward and it got noticeably cooler. "I didn't expect it to be a big deal." She squinted at me. "Like, are you a real photographer or not?"

Wow. I picked up my backpack. "Kennedy, what the fuck do you *want* from me?"

Another step back, another ten degrees cooler. "I want you to leave."

"Guess what? We both want the same thing for once." I pulled on my pack and opened her bedroom door, then stopped and turned. "You're welcome."

CHAPTER 20

*This benefit of seeing can only come if you pause a while,
extricate yourself from the maddening mob of quick
impressions ceaselessly battering our lives, and look
thoughtfully at a quiet image.*
—Dorothea Lange

I WAS STILL IN A SHIT MOOD AS I HEADED DOWNTOWN
later that evening. And the universe was right there with me. The
only people around at 9:09 were a pair of wasted college guys
who were either leaving or going to a frat house . . . they seemed
unclear on the details. I took a couple of obligatory snaps and
gave up, then walked down to Finch.

I got a chai and sat in that booth near the back for some
reason, even though the place was pretty empty and I could have
any seat I wanted. And I looked up whenever I heard the little
bell over the door ring, for some reason. And I also looked up

occasionally even if the door *hadn't* opened. Like approximately every forty-seven seconds.

For some reason.

After doing my so-called work (reviewing the uninspired photos, which took all of two minutes . . . or three looking-up-toward-the-door sequences) I finished my chai and left.

On the way home I thought about my mom, and my essay about her. And Assi's essay about her dad. And talking to Ollie about talking to Assi. And I realized there was another important player in this drama.

When I got home I went straight to the garage and told my dad about writing the essay for language class, and sort of paraphrased it for him. I even told him about the really nice things "someone" had said about the paper. Then I heard myself ask, "So how are *you* doing? About Mom, I mean . . ." In the almost two years since the original 9:09 I'd never asked.

Not once.

The question just hung there, floating in the air. Finally he got up from his stool, walked over to the little mini-fridge next to his tool cabinet, and took out two beers. (Coors Light—he's *such* a dad.) He cracked them both open, handed one to me, and said, "Fuck if I know."

Wow. This was a first, on a couple of levels. It felt like I was in strange new territory, without a map. Was this part of that whole promotion thing?

I took the beer and said, "I'm just asking because I've been thinking about her even more lately, maybe because of this project I'm doing, and that essay." I took a drink and set the can on the bench. "I think about what she would say if I told her stuff about school or friends or Ollie or whatever."

"I know you miss her. And I know you two could talk, even about the weirdest things." He smiled. "You guys used to go on about what color different numbers were. And . . . well, I can't do that. To me, numbers are numbers."

I nodded. "Believe me, most of the world sees it your way." I paused, trying to put my thoughts about my mom into words. "The funny thing is, it's like she's still here. Like I can totally see her and hear her in my mind. And she can still tell me things. Just nothing new, nothing she hasn't told me before. It's like watching your favorite show, except it's all reruns." I suddenly stopped and picked up my beer and took another swig, mostly so I'd have something to do with my hands. "I don't know . . . does any of that make sense?"

He looked really sad, yet sort of happy at the same time. "All of that makes sense, J. Every word of it. I feel exactly the same." He was silent for a second. "But along with all that, she was also my best friend in the whole world and the singular love of my life, so . . ." He stopped, then coughed like he had something in his throat. "So that's how I'm doing." He held up his can. "Cheers."

Ms. Montinello stood in front of the whiteboard. "So, what did we learn yesterday during our paired-off critique sessions?"

Boy, *that* was a loaded question. I sat on my hands while she fielded responses. One girl said, "It's easier to give than to receive." Several people laughed.

"Aha! Explain, please."

"Well, it's not that hard to find something wrong with someone else's writing and point it out," the girl said. "But when it's your writing that's being picked apart, it's a little tougher."

Ms. Montinello nodded. "Okay, and why is that?"

"When you write you're putting yourself on the page. So it's way more personal, and criticism of the work feels like criticism of you."

"Fair enough," Ms. Montinello said. "And yet my job is to criticize your work, among other things. So keep this in mind: Critique of your work is not a critique of *you*. It doesn't mean you're bad, or even that your work is bad. It might mean there's another way to present it that's more effective. Or I could simply be wrong." She looked over her glasses at the class. "As unlikely as that is." She picked up a marker. "Anyone learn anything else, before we move on . . . ?"

"Never doubt the master," I said.

She didn't even blink. "That goes without saying." She wrote *Metonymy* on the whiteboard. "Now, who can expound on this?"

What a cool, pastel-blue word, with the *M* and the *N* and the *M*. "Not me," I said. "I leave that sort of stuff to the suits, up in their ivory tower."

"Two points," she said. "Anyone else?"

"That was a bit of an easy free throw," Assi said. "As Shakespeare said, *Doublet and hose ought to show itself courageous to petticoat.*"

Ms. Montinello kept a straight face. "She shoots . . . she scores."

That evening I put my computer in my backpack along with my Nikon, and after I took a 9:09 photo I actually got some work done at Finch. It probably didn't hurt that I finally quit looking up whenever the bell rang, either—that had proven to be a losing game. I was in the middle of writing a paper for my psych class when I realized someone was standing next to me.

"You know that's *my* thing," Assi said, holding up her computer bag. "Coming down here to work, I mean."

"I didn't know you had a lock on it."

"Yeah, well . . . sometimes I just need to get away from the unwashed masses—which would be my little brother and sister—to do some homework or whatever."

"Or whatever." I pointed to the other side of the booth. "Have a seat."

"I didn't mean to interrupt your work . . ." I studied her face. There was zero sign of sarcasm.

"Doublet and hose are petitioning petticoat to rest her tired bones upon thy yonder, uh . . . booth. Milady."

She sat. "*Milady?* Hmm . . . I think I like that even better than *Ms. Knudsen.* Yeah, you can call me milady from now on. Knave."

I made a show of turning back to my computer and starting to type. "You're like three seconds away from going back to AK . . ."

". . . or Assi will do just fine," she added quickly.

I grinned and closed my computer.

"You know, you definitely see the world through a different lens," she said. My smile must have disappeared, because she added, "Hey, that's a *good* thing."

"Uh . . . I do, actually. See the world differently, I mean."

"Oh." She was quiet for a second. "So are you color-blind? Is that why you like black-and-white?"

"That's a good guess," I said, "but it's the opposite—I see color where I shouldn't."

"Huh?"

I explained to her about synesthesia. Which I normally hate doing, but she seemed genuinely interested, plus she'd heard a little about it so I didn't have to go through the whole "guess what—letters have colors" thing. I ended mostly talking about my mom, and how she'd been the only one who really understood the way my brain worked. Firsthand, at least.

"Wow," she said when I was finished. "That's so terrible." Then she got an *oops* look on her face. "About losing your mom, I mean! Not the synesthesia."

I nodded. "I knew what you meant."

She was quiet for a long time. "My mother is an immigrant," she finally said. "She speaks French and Arabic . . . and some English, of course." She smiled. "Otherwise I probably wouldn't be here, as my dad spoke only Norwegian and English. But she doesn't really like to read in English. My dad, on the other hand, *loved* to read English-language novels—he'd bring new books home once a week. I remember us both reading all the Harry Potter books and talking about them . . ." She blinked, then did that fanning-her-eyes thing. "We were our own little book club."

I just sat there for a minute, thinking *Remember this moment.* "I'm guessing he's the reason you wanted to be a writer?" I said.

She nodded. "He got me started, for sure."

"Then I want you to do me a favor."

She looked at me, all serious. "What?"

"Let me read some of your stuff."

"You already have—that essay."

"Yeah, and it was amazing. But I'm talking about something you're writing for *you.* Your novel, or whatever writing project you're working on."

She did that virtual hands-on-hip thing. "What makes you think I'm writing a novel?"

"Tell me I'm wrong."

Silence.

She glanced over at her backpack and stared at it for a minute, then pulled out a thick stack of pages—stapled into smaller groups—and picked up the first few sections. "Do you have time?"

Are you kidding me? I shrugged like it was no big deal. "Sure."

She held up the pages and looked at me like she was trying to decide something. I must have passed the test, because she finally handed them over. It hit me that this was the first time I'd ever seen her look this vulnerable.

And *then* it hit me that I recognized that look—I had it myself whenever I showed my stuff to anyone else. You put your heart and soul and a big chunk of your life into something and all some people can come up with is a list of what they think's wrong with it? Like that's somehow equal to creating the work in the first place?

So yeah, I totally got why she had reservations about showing her writing to anyone.

I placed the pages on the table in front of me, took a sip of my chai, and started reading. After a couple of minutes she got up to go do something but I didn't even look up.

It was titled *A Flick of the Switch*. After she'd mentioned reading Harry Potter with her dad I thought it might be a fantasy novel, but it was a contemporary story. The main character is a French girl named Astrid. The first few chapters did a great job of laying out her situation . . .

Astrid's mother is a diplomat and she and Astrid's father are going to spend a year in Bulgaria on assignment, but Astrid won't be going with them. Instead she has to leave her home and friends in Orléans, France, and attend an honors academy in Edinburgh, Scotland. On her first night there she ends up with a kitchen knife in her hand as she confronts a strange girl who's climbing in the window. The girl turns out be one of her new roommates—coming home drunk from a party without her keys—and Astrid ends up with the nickname Switchblade, soon shortened to Switch. (Synonymous with *broom* locally, slang for *witch*. It's not a compliment.) She has a hard time fitting in: most of the other students are from somewhere in Great Britain and her accent seems funny to them, as well as her clothes and everything else about her.

Scattered among the chapters were short entries from Astrid's journal. I thought Astrid's description of struggling to fit in with her peers was interesting . . .

Astrid's Journal (entry IV)

My roommates actually asked me to join them for lunch. (Well, Emma and Clover asked Poppy, and—oops, too late!—they realized I'd heard.) But on any account, I went along—it was a Saturday and I was happy to get out of the flat and see a bit of the city. It being a rare warm fall day in Edinburgh, I dressed accordingly. Or perhaps accordingly for Orléans, but there you are. I wore a sleeveless blouse and capris, and brought along a light sweater just in case.

We ended up in a little walled-in pub patio, warmed by the sun and really quite nice. After we'd ordered Emma started complaining about the sun (she's a ginger) so I went to put the umbrella up. As I stood and reached overhead to finish raising it, out of the corner of my eye I noticed the ever-so-sly nudges and subtle head tosses. I wanted to yell at them to grow up and stop being so damned provincial, but instead I sat down like nothing had happened. And pulled my sweater on.

On the way home I decided I'd shave during my morning shower. After all, the goal was to fit in here, correct? But later that evening I overheard them whispering in excited tones in the kitchen:

Did you see? I mean, did you fecking SEE...?

Of course I saw! How could you miss...?

She has pits like a sweaty mechanic...!

And even her legs...

So do you think...you know...?

How the feck do I know?

I couldn't believe it—they were in there discussing me like a bunch of old hens. And I was worried about fitting in with this? I went back to my room, grabbed my books, and ran off for the library with one thought on my mind: fuck them and their "sweaty mechanic."

The undertaker can shave me when I'm cold and dead. Until then—fur is fine.

When I looked up from the end of the chapter, Assi was back in her seat across from me. Not studying, not on her phone, just sitting. I didn't say a word—I just reached for her backpack and started to unzip it. She stopped me. "Well . . . ?" she said.

"I want to see the other chapters. How much more is there?" I pulled at the backpack.

She took the pack away and set it on the seat next to her. "So, you liked it?"

"Not really." I watched her face for several seconds until I was about to lose it. "I *loved* it."

"God, you're such a shit!" She sat up straighter. "Okay. Serious assessment, s'il vous plaît."

"I meant it—I loved it. I was totally sucked in by it, and I can't wait to read more. I loved Astrid's voice . . . she's sort of like you, but not."

"But not, definitely. That's why they call it fiction."

I shrugged. "All I know is, I really liked it. The voice, the characters, the plot . . . it's all super well done. And the subject matter—who hasn't felt at some point like they didn't fit in? That's a universal thing, and you describe the feeling so well . . ."

As she smiled down at the table, something occurred to me. "Speaking of that, what's it like being . . . well, being *you,* in a city that's half Hispanic and half white and not much else?"

"You mean being of Middle Eastern descent?"

I nodded.

"Well . . . yeah, sometimes it's a little, uh, *different.* Not because of Vista Grande . . . half the people here think I might be Latina—if they think about it at all—and the other half doesn't seem to really care." She paused. "Or maybe it's 49/49 instead of 50/50, because there *is* that two percent that look at me and somehow think my dad was in ISIS or something." She shook her head, remembering. "I can't believe I actually had a guy say that to me once. So I brought up a photo of my dad on my phone and said, 'Oh, you mean him?' and he just looked confused and angry. Or the people who say, 'Where're you from?' and I say, 'I live in Vista Grande,' and they say, 'No, where're you *from*?' and I say, 'Well, I was born in Missouri but my mom got a job in California after my dad died, then we moved to Vista Grande over the summer when she got promoted,' and they have a hard time with that, too."

"So you're saying it's a bundle of laughs, then?"

"It has its moments. But then I try to imagine coming here from outside the US *today*, maybe not speaking much English, maybe with an accent, maybe wearing traditional clothing, maybe practicing a non-Christian religion, and I realize it could be *way* worse."

"I'm sure you're right, but you convey that outsider vibe so well in your writing."

"Maybe that's part of why I want to write. Because really, we're all outsiders on one level or another."

I just nodded, but inside I was thinking, *Man, this girl is like fifty times wiser than I will ever be.* "Hey, do you keep a journal, like Astrid?" Now *that* would be interesting.

Her eyes flashed. "We're not going there. Not in a million years."

I held up my hands. "Sorry—just asking." Her backpack was still sitting there. "When can I read more?"

"When I'm ready."

"So when will that be?"

She shrugged. "We'll see . . ."

By the time I got home she'd sent me something. At first I thought it might be more of her novel, but it was an essay. **Here you go,** her message said, this is a little something I wrote for myself.

> Think of a loved one. Someone you really care about—parent, child, partner, sibling, friend— who is alive but not physically with you right now. They could be across town, across the country, or across the world. They're away but they're not gone. Not forgotten. When you think of them, everything they mean to you comes right back into focus. They're away, but they're still inside you. They influence you, even though they're not next to you. In stressful times you imagine what they might do in your situation. Just the act of picturing them makes you smile. Or laugh. Or cry. Regardless, they're alive in you. You carry them with you as you go about your life, whether you're aware of it at any particular moment or not. Now think of a loved one who is no longer living. All of the above can still exist if you keep them alive inside. They are away, like any other loved one who is not with you. But they are not necessarily gone.

There was more, but that was the core of it. It was late by the time I finished but I wrote back. Not to be redundant but this is great. Would you mind if I used it on the main page of my website? This says exactly what I want to say about why I'm doing what I'm doing. I paused for a second, then surprised myself by adding You're pretty amazing, you know that?

I heard back within a few minutes: Thanks J. Really glad you liked it. It's fine if you want to put it on your site. And . . . you're not too shabby yourself. All that was good, but it was what came next that I never expected to see in a message from Miss AK-47: ☺

Before I went to bed I added her writing to the home page of my website (I titled it *"The Difference Between Gone and Away,"* *contributed by Milady A. Knudsen*). It was after midnight by the time I finally finished posting it. But as I got in bed and lay there in the dark, I didn't feel the least bit tired.

I felt . . . something else. I don't know.

CHAPTER 21

*I am trying here to say something about the
despised, the defeated, the alienated. About death
and disaster, about the wounded, the crippled, the
helpless, the rootless, the dislocated.
About finality.
About the last ditch.*
—Dorothea Lange

PROBABLY THE LESS SAID ABOUT TURKEY DAY THE BETTER. This was our first real Thanksgiving without Mom, because we basically skipped the whole thing last year by unanimous agreement. And I thought we might do the same this year. But no, Dad had other plans. Plans involving food.

He spent most of the day in the kitchen, working away. Besides roasting a turkey he made stuffing and mashed potatoes and gravy and yams and green beans. And my mom's favorite—pecan pie. Almost like he thought if we had all the stuff we used to have, it'd be the same as it used to be.

It wasn't. Not even close. My mother was more present by her absence than if she were still here, and we did everything we could to make sure the conversation never came close to mentioning her. In the end, we didn't even cut into the pecan pie— everyone said they were too full, but it didn't take a genius to figure it out. Finally my dad put his fork down and pushed back from the table. "Well, I think I've done all the damage I can do here."

"That was really great, Dad," Ollie said.

"Thanks."

My mind was somewhere else until Ollie gave me a fierce look that was a virtual kick in the shins. "Yeah, um . . . that was really awesome, Dad. Great job with the turkey and, uh, everything." I looked at the mess around us. "I'll clean up, it's the least I can do." I turned to Ollie. "You too—I got this."

I didn't have to say it twice. She took off for wherever and my dad helped me clear the table, then left too. Usually I listen to music when I clean the kitchen and do the dishes but this time I worked in silence. It took me quite a while, too, but when I was done I found myself wishing it had taken longer. I had feelings I was trying to make sense out of. By the time I had the kitchen clean I wasn't anywhere close . . . my brain was still stuck somewhere on the corner of *Remember This Moment* and *What's So Wrong with That?*

I thought it might help to get out of the house so I grabbed my camera bag, but on the way out I decided to swing by the garage. I opened the door and sure enough my dad was in there, messing around with that old phonograph. I was going to say something when I stopped. He had the radio on and hadn't noticed me, and there was something about the way he looked, hunched over his bench and illuminated by the lamp as he worked. I slowly set my bag down and retrieved my camera, zooming in close and snapping a few frames before he finally looked up.

"Oh, hi, J. What's up?"

I moved closer. "Ignore me—keep working."

He did, and I was able to get right in front of him, looking down at his head, shoulders, and hands as he installed impossibly small screws in a metal cylinder. I managed three or four good frames before he moved and the composition was gone.

When we were kids we used to watch all those old Disney movies, and for a minute he'd looked like Geppetto working on Pinocchio. "So, is it a real boy yet?" I asked.

He laughed. "Not quite. I'll let you know when it starts talking."

"Hey, I just wanted to say you did an awesome job with Thanksgiving dinner." I paused. "Mom would have loved it."

He nodded, then quickly looked back down at his work.

I was an idiot to bother coming down to the corner. At least that was my first thought. Because it was totally deserted. I'm talking like full pandemic lockdown deserted—when my alarm went off there was *no one* around. I waited a few minutes, but still nada. I was about to pack it up when I realized that *this*—absolutely nothing—was what was happening at this particular time on this particular evening in this particular corner of the world, and that was as valid as anything else. I took out my tabletop tripod and used it to park my camera on a planter box. I made sure it was level, then took four frames—rotating the camera between each one—to show as much of the corner as possible. I checked them on the monitor—yup, the whole scene was there in all its glorious nothingness—then packed up and decided to see if Finch was open.

To my surprise, it was.

I ordered a chai and grabbed a little table near the front window. It wasn't like the place was packed, but it was busier than I'd expected. Then I realized they were mostly college-age, probably students who didn't go home for Thanksgiving. I was on my phone just cruising around when I heard a voice next to me.

"So, how was your Thanksgiving?"

As I turned I found myself surprised. Not by who it was, but by how happy I was to see her. We'd been on break and hadn't seen each other for a few days.

"Kind of weird, to be honest."

She laughed. "Sounds just like mine."

"How come?"

She sat across from me. "Well, my mom isn't big on Thanksgiving—she hates turkey."

"Yeah, that might put a damper on the whole thing."

"You think? But we got lucky. Lebanon's Independence Day is November twenty-second, and my mom loves to celebrate it because of the food. So we made a deal—we told her either we could have mezze and kibbeh on Thanksgiving, or roast a big fat turkey on the twenty-second. She went with the first choice, so we do a weird mash-up holiday on Thanksgiving."

"That sounds like fun. What are mezze and, uh . . ."

"Kibbeh? It's a lamb and wheat thing." She shrugged, like she could take it or leave it. "You can bake it or fry it up in balls like falafel. My little brother loves it. But mezze . . ." She brightened. "Mezze is like tapas, on steroids. Like a little miniature feast, with a couple dozen different foods all spread out at once. Then baklava, with ahweh."

"Ahweh . . . ?"

"Really strong, sweet Turkish coffee." She nodded toward where the barista was making a drink. "Sort of like espresso. But different." She shook her head, like she was sorry for me. "You've been missing out."

"I guess so. That all sounds awesome."

"It is. You should try it sometime . . ."

"I'd love to."

She glanced up at me for a second, then back down. "So, what was weird about *your* Thanksgiving . . . ?"

I almost brushed it off with *You know—the usual* or something equally meaningless, but I stopped. She seemed honestly interested. And—out of everyone I knew—she actually had the best chance of understanding.

"Well, it was our first real Thanksgiving as a family without my mom." She looked up at that but didn't say anything. "So of course all I thought about was my mom. And I'm guessing it was the same for Ollie and my dad." She nodded. "So here's what's weird. When I'm by myself, I miss her, sure. But when it's the three of us, in some ways it's worse. And when it's the three of us at some sort of official 'family function' thing—like Thanksgiving—it's *way* worse. Because it has this whole 'What's wrong with this picture?' vibe to it."

She nodded. "Oh, yeah . . ."

I told her about the uneaten pecan pie and how we never went to my mom's favorite restaurant anymore and a bunch of other stuff. "So . . ." I shrugged. "Any advice here? I'm wide open."

"Well . . . everyone's different," she said. "And every family's different."

"Uh-huh. And . . . ?"

She just looked at me for a second. "And we talked about it," she finally said.

"What do you mean?"

"At some point my mom had the four of us sit down and we all talked about how my dad was gone but"—her voice quavered—"but we still carried him, *here*." She placed her hand over her heart, then fanned at her eyes, and I thought of her last essay and realized where its power came from. "Then my mom told us there would be times when we would feel sad about Dad, but that was okay . . . it was a sign of how much we loved him, and how much he loved us. And I told my little brother and sister it was okay to talk about him—because they didn't say a word about him for a long time after he'd died—and if something came up that reminded them of him, it was good to share it." She sort of shrugged, then blinked. "I don't know. Stuff like that."

"And it helped?"

She nodded. "Yeah. A lot."

"Well, thank you. Because you've helped me. A lot . . ."

What was really weird about my Thanksgiving, I thought later that night, was that for some reason I spent a couple of hours of it hanging out in a coffee shop, talking with a girl who used to fucking hate me. And even weirder, in some ways it was one of my best Thanksgivings ever . . .

I was in my room just killing time. I'd gone to the SSA site and cruised around, trying to get inspired. They had a big banner across their home page proclaiming *Don't forget—the Streeties are announced next week!* Great, but I was looking for inspiration, not spam. And tonight I sure wasn't finding it in other people's work. So I made myself close the site and open my last session— the shots I'd taken of my dad.

I examined the best one on my monitor. Usually "people at work" shots feel cold and sterile, like a scientist in a lab or a technician in a factory. But that was the opposite of the feeling I got when I hung out in the garage watching my dad tinker. I was shooting for something more like the image I'd imagined earlier: Geppetto in his workshop. So I played with the tone until the light spilling from the work lamp gave everything a golden glow, and brought down the midtones a little to make it more gritty and organic . . . I wanted the viewer to be able to feel the sawdust on the bench. Lowering the color made it seem . . . I don't know. Not necessarily old-fashioned. Just not modern. Maybe timeless? Not sure of the words here, but the image did what it needed to do.

I was ready to post it on the *Do You See What I See?* page. But what *did* I see when I looked at it? I knew what I felt, sitting there in my bedroom, but I had a hard time putting it into words. Then I remembered something Ms. Montinello said when we were talking about stimulating creativity—*At times like these, a change of venue may be in order.*

Why not? I grabbed my laptop and went out to the garage. Quietly—it was after midnight. I turned on the lamp, set my computer on my dad's workbench, cracked open one of his beers, and perched on his stool. I sat there with my eyes closed for quite a while, trying to channel the feeling I got when I watched him work on stuff, especially after my mom died. Then I tried to channel my dad himself . . . What went through his head as he worked on these old, forgotten machines? Or maybe, what went through his *heart*?

With all this filling my brain, what did I see when I looked at the image of him?

I took a deep breath and started to write. It took me a

while—I'd write a little and then delete and then write some more. But eventually I had something. Maybe not perfect, and it might seem stupid tomorrow, but tonight it felt right.

> I see . . . a man trying to fix himself.
> When life goes horribly, unexpectedly wrong, you stop everything for a while. Then after some time you try to get back into life where you left. But that river has gone by. You're in a different spot than you were when you left and there's no going back. You either move forward or drown. Sometimes the way forward might be to build, to plant, to grow. To renew, to repair. To fix things. Things other than yourself. And by doing this, you just might begin to fix yourself.
> That's what I see.
> Do you see what I see?

CHAPTER 22

Seeing is more than a physiological phenomenon.
—Dorothea Lange

AT LUNCH ON MONDAY I GOT A TEXT FROM OLLIE. **HEY loser, we talked about a fourth, for tacos de? remember???**

Seth and I were eating semi-with the fashionistas, like we'd done a few times before. Kennedy was at the center of the long table, like usual, but we sat down near the end and she ignored me, like usual. Next to her was some other girl, then Sofia/Chloe/Ollie/Seth, and then me at the end.

kennedy looks busy right now, I replied. I meant it as a joke, but as soon as I sent it I remembered really wanting to ask her out for coffee awhile back . . . and how well *that* had gone.

ha-ha very funny. dork

when?

She looked over at me, wide-eyed, and shrugged. It was pretty clear she was winging it. **uh . . . today?**

time? after school or later?

dunno. 6???

sounds good

Maybe it was because I'd just gotten out of class with her—where we'd done our verbal tag-team thing once again—but it actually felt semi-normal as I moved across the aisle next to Assi.

She noticed me and looked up. "Hey."

"Hey." I nodded back toward the other table. "So, Ollie and Seth and I are going for tacos tonight. You want to go with us?"

She looked at me with an unreadable expression. After a couple of seconds of nothing I held my hands together over my shoulder like I was cocking a bat. "There's the windup, *aaannnnd* the pitch . . ."

She finally cracked a smile. "What time?"

I shrugged, like no big deal. "I don't know . . . how about six?"

She shrugged back—like she didn't really care either—but I thought I saw that little twinkle. "Okay. Might be fun."

"Cool. We'll swing by on the way."

"Great. I'll text you my address."

"Awesome."

I went back to the other table and texted Ollie. done. i'll drive

Dad was fine with it once Ollie explained that I was going, too. And he became downright mom-like when Ollie told him another girl was going with us. "Dad!" I finally said. "It's not like a big date thing—we're just going for tacos with some friends, okay?"

He nodded. "Okay." But as I was leaving the room I heard him asking Ollie about "the other girl." Oh my God, get me out of here . . .

A couple of hours later when we went to pick up Assi I wondered if my dad had called her mom and told her to play the mom card too. When we got there I texted Assi. we're out front

can you come to the door? all 3 of you, i mean

???

it's a mom thing

um . . . ok sure

So we went up and knocked. Assi opened the door and pulled a face before saying, "Hi. Come on in." Behind her were a girl and a boy—maybe ten and twelve—curiously checking us out. "Hey, guys," Assi said to them, "why don't you go play in your rooms?" They took off down the hall as we walked into the living room, where a woman stood to greet us. I'm not sure what I was thinking but from the way Assi had talked I was expecting someone a little more old-school. She was maybe forty and dressed like Ms. Farina, my math teacher, and I could totally see where Assi got her eyes. "This is my mom. Mom, this is J, Ollie, and Seth."

We all kind of nodded and mumbled *Hi,* but she opened her arms and invited us in like we were old friends. "Come in, come in! What can I get for you?"

We gave her a chorus of *Nothing, thanks* and *We're good,* but she said "Nonsense! You're our guests. I insist. Now, what would you like?"

We all basically looked at our shoes, but a sentence popped into my head—*You've been missing out.* "Um, Assi mentioned you make great ahweh . . ."

She smiled and slapped her hands on her hips. "Perfect, but of course!" Waving at the couch and chairs, she said, "Have a seat," and hurried out of the room.

Assi looked at me and rolled her eyes. I grimaced, like *What was I supposed to say?,* and she mouthed *Sorry!* She had us pull up seats around a big square coffee table with a tiled top. I wasn't sure why until her mom came back carrying a tray full of stuff.

She unloaded a little propane burner, a small copper pot with a long handle that looked more like a scoop than anything else, and five tiny cups about the size of shot glasses. She lit the burner, put on the copper pot with some water in it, and scooped in several heaping spoonfuls of sugar. When the water started to boil she added five spoons of ground coffee, then held it by the handle, watching it while she talked. It was clear from the way she worked that she'd done this a thousand times. "So," she said, briefly glancing at Ollie and me, "you two are siblings, no?"

I nodded. "No. I mean, *yes,* we're brother and sister."

She smiled. "That's nice. I hope Assi and her siblings do things together when they're—" She stopped, because the liquid in the pot suddenly began to foam and boil. She immediately lifted it and it subsided. Then she put it back on and it boiled again—and again she lifted it—and then a third time. She turned off the burner and sat the pot on the tabletop, placed one of the dollhouse-size cups on a saucer in front of each of us, then carefully poured a steaming shot into each one, making sure every cup got a little foam on top.

She looked at us and raised her cup, smiling. "Santé."

We all tried to say that back, then took a sip. Wow. I *had* been missing out. It was dark and strong like espresso, but with a totally different vibe. I took another sip and held it up. "Wow. Assi was right. This is really different."

Assi's mom shrugged, like *No big deal.* "It is ahweh. Like always." But then her eyebrows went up and she said, "You like?"

I shook my head and waited a moment—while she just stared at me—then said, "I *love.*"

She laughed and turned to Assi. "These friends of yours, they are okay." She paused, then added with a straight face, "Not like you said."

Assi put her cup down with a loud clink. "Mom!" She looked over at us. "I didn't say anything. She just—" But it was too late—we were all cracking up.

We drank our coffee and joked around for a few more minutes. When we'd finished, Assi's mom turned her empty cup upside down on the little saucer, then looked expectantly at the rest of us.

Assi pulled a face. "Oh, Mom, no."

Her mother shrugged. "It is tradition."

When in Rome . . . I turned my cup over, then glanced at Ollie and Seth, who did the same. Assi looked at me and shook her head. "You don't know what you're doing." Then she turned hers over too, but not before saying to her mom, "But no love-life stuff. Promise?"

Her mom gave a single nod. "Career only." She turned our cups back over and studied the coffee grounds in the bottom of them. She looked at Ollie first. "You will have a new position soon . . . and possibly a new title." She glanced at Seth. "I see something similar for you. Perhaps you will work together?" Seth looked skeptical and Ollie kept a straight face but I could see the hint of a crinkle. She turned to Assi. "Your good work will gain you even better work." Then me. "You have recently been promoted. But there are more steps yet to climb." Wow. I was still thinking about that when she looked into my cup again, then glanced from me to Assi, then back to my cup. She looked up at us and smiled. "You must be hungry. I think it is time for you to get tacos, no?"

We all stood and headed for the door. When we got there I turned and said, "Thanks for the coffee. It really was great."

She shrugged. "You really have to try it with baklava. After mezze, of course . . ."

Assi interrupted. "Mom!" Only it came out as three syllables. She looked at us. "She's always trying to feed the world."

Assi's mom put her hands on her hips. "And what's so wrong with that?"

The weird thing about us going to Tacos de was that it wasn't weird. It didn't feel like a date. There was no gut-twisting nervousness like when I was sitting near Kennedy, and there was no awkwardness like when one couple gets all kissy-feely while the other couple has to sit there feeling totally out of place. In fact it wasn't like there were couples at all. Just the four of us. Okay, I'd be lying if I said I wasn't aware of Assi the whole time, and I'd also be lying if I said I didn't find something about her totally cool.

We ended up mostly talking about school and people we knew and stuff, just like at lunch. Only not.

It turned out Assi and her family had never been to Tacos de, so before we left I went up and ordered a container to go and put it in a bag. When we got to her house I handed it to her. "Here. Don't say I never gave you anything."

"You never gave me anything." She hefted it. "What is it?"

"Pollo colorado. Probably the best thing they make. I figured your mom and your brother and sister might like to check it out. That way they won't have to hear you say *You've been missing out!*"

She smiled. "Thanks. That's nice of you." She looked back at her house for a second. "And I'm sorry about my mom. I mean, the whole deal with her having to meet you guys, and then reading the coffee grounds, and—"

I waved her off. "Are you kidding? She was great."

She looked dubious. "Yeah, well . . . thanks."

We stood there staring at each other for a second while my brain struggled to find something to say.

Then she turned and was gone.

✴   ✴   ✴

Later, when I was working on some photographs in my room, Ollie came by.

"Hey, I just wanted to say thanks for making that happen. It was fun." She paused. "Although I about choked when you asked Assi in the cafeteria. I wasn't actually expecting you to do that."

"Half the fun of asking her was watching you crap your pants. And I knew you really wanted to go, so . . ."

"So you asking Assi was just about doing me a favor, then?"

I nodded. "Yup. And it looks like now you owe me one."

She ignored that. "So, if we were in the drive-thru at Happy Jack's right now, would you give me the same answer?" I was sitting there trying to think of a clever reply when she said, "Exactly."

She walked out of my room and I got back to work.

I was dealing with the photographs I'd taken on Thanksgiving night of the totally empty corner, stitching them together into one wide panoramic image. I loaded them into my computer and did the initial stitch, then I brought in the sides until it felt right . . . showing the whole scene without that inch-high/foot-wide filmstrip effect.

I ended up with an image about four times as wide as it was high, which looked pretty natural as the scene itself was horizontal in nature. Then I converted it to monochrome. No warmth, just stone-cold black-and-white. I played with the contrast and brightness until the image on the screen made me feel the way I felt that evening, standing on the desolate corner, thinking about my mom. I ended up with a dark, cold, lonely atmosphere, but somehow different than the vibe I got from the image of Kennedy and her friends from that same corner. Emptier.

I leaned back and studied it. Man, I felt lonely just looking at it. For some reason I wanted to put a spotlight on it, like I'd done with the one of my dad in the garage where I'd written more than usual. Which made no sense, because it really had no subject. In fact, the subject was the *absence* of anything.

A cartoon image suddenly popped into my head, of a gray room with little black-and-white creatures running around in it. Occasionally one of them would leave the room, and when they left, they never came back. Eventually they'd all left, and the only thing remaining was the empty gray room.

This gave me an idea. Or two. Maybe three, to tell the truth.

I sent the picture to Assi, with a message:

Hey, I have a favor to ask. I have this photo, which I took on the corner at 9:09 on Thanksgiving. I went there thinking about my mom, and when the time came there was absolutely nothing to photograph. So I made this image to commemorate that. I call it *The Empty Set.* (An homage to nothing . . .) But something about it reminds me of the feeling I got when I read your essay for AP lang, and especially the piece you wrote about loved ones being away but not gone.

I want to feature this image on my site—with some words to accompany it—but nothing I could write would capture the feeling as well as you. SO . . .

Would you be interested in writing a short piece about this general concept/vibe/feeling, to go along with the image? By way of payment I can offer you 50% of the total proceeds from the image, which would equal . . . absolutely nada. Or I can buy you more tacos. (Which was really fun, by the way!)

If you don't have time or whatever, no worries. I feel bad even asking you—I'm sure you already have enough on your plate—but I know you could hit it out of the park.

I sent it but didn't get a reply.

The next day she came up to me in language before class started.

"Two things. First"—she handed me a page with text on it—"here. This is for your photo. Which is amazing. I almost can't believe that level of visual sophistication can come from a happy boy like you."

"*Happy boy?*"

"Yeah, that's what my mom called you. *I think he is a nice boy,* she said. *He seems so happy.*" I was in the middle of thinking *What's up with that?* when she went on. "Which is the second thing—you were a big hit with my mom."

"Huh?"

"In Lebanon, people drop in on their friends all the time. Like, every day. And coffee is always served, no matter what time. So when you asked for ahweh . . . bingo! Also, she approves of you and Ollie going out in a group together. And finally, you thinking to bring back some food from Tacos de . . . ?" She cocked her hands like she was swinging a bat. "Home run."

I was still stuck on the "happy boy" thing, but this was too good to ignore. "So your mom likes me, huh?"

She shrugged, straight-faced. "I guess. Although God knows why . . ."

CHAPTER 23

*I've never not been sure that I was a photographer
any more than you would not be sure you were
yourself. I was a photographer, or wanting
to be a photographer, or beginning—
but some phase of photographer
I've always been.*
—Dorothea Lange

SOMETIMES YOU ASK A FAVOR OF SOMEONE AND THEY DO a good job of it (which is probably why you asked them). And sometimes . . . not so much. But once in a while you ask someone for something and they do a job that's not only more than you expected, but different than you expected. In a unique and wonderful way.

Combating the Empty Set
by A. Knudsen

The Empty Set. That's the title mathematicians use to represent a set having no elements. Represented by the symbol Ø, or just brackets with nothing inside: { }. It's important to recognize that the empty set isn't the same thing as zero. The set containing zero has one element in it {0}, while the empty set has nothing. Not even zero.

It not only has nothing in it, it has no hope of ever having anything in it. Life may sometimes feel like it holds nothing, but even at its worst it contains the possibility of having something—no matter how small or how distant—at some point in the future. And sometimes having possibilities is enough. You don't think so, in the moment, but looking back you realize that having at least the potential of happiness or freedom or love is not a full life in itself, but it is a seed.

The interesting thing about seeds is that when you plant one, you know that—at best—it's going to grow into a replication of the original plant. You don't plant a turnip seed and get a strawberry. Or a kitten. Or a happy, healthy, loving person. But with hope, with belief, with possibility, you can plant a seed within someone's heart—even your own—and the potential outcomes are unlimited.

You may know someone—may love someone—may need someone—whose life no longer contains any possibilities. Because they are no longer among the living. They may appear to personify the empty set. A pair of brackets—a birth date and a death date—with nothing else between them. { }. And you yourself may feel empty because of this. But between their brackets exists not nothing, but the meaningful sum of their entire existence. The opposite of the empty set. Not { }, but {LIFE}. Keep this in mind as you go forward, trying to fill the emptiness within your own brackets.

Plant a seed, no matter how small. Of hope. Of potential. Of possibility. And the outcome may surpass even your wildest imaginings.

I worked on posting the photo when I got home from school. When I was done, the horizontal image ran near the top of the home page, with Assi's words set in a box in the middle of the screen. Afterward, as I sat there looking at it, I remembered something she'd said about my eyes being older than the rest of me. I'm not sure about that, but the way *she* looks at things is . . . well, not necessarily older, but really different.

In a way I really love, if I'm being completely honest.

Later that night I went to my site to see if there was any feedback on the image or Assi's essay on it.

There was. Like, a *lot*.

But even more than that, there were tons of general comments. Most of them saying good things about the site and the images. But as I began skimming them, I saw about half had some sort of congratulations included, and I started to see the word *Streety* appear. Holy crap.

I went to Street Shooters Anonymous and clicked on the tab for *Tenth Annual Streety Awards Results,* right between the *Pic of the Week* tab and the *Check Out Our Books* tab. An award overview said the Streety was the award given to "those individuals, organizations, and companies that best exemplify the ethos, philosophy, and artistic excellence of contemporary street photography." They had a bunch of different categories, like *Best Professional Street Photographer, Best Amateur Street Photographer, Best Image (Color), Best Image (Black-and-White), Best Print Publication, Best Online Publication, Best Website,* etc. It was the last one that got my attention.

When I clicked on it, it said that the winner was the 9:09 site. The text said, Our judges would have given this person an individual award, but we weren't sure if he or she is a pro or an amateur, or even if all the work was done by a single individual. Same for a Best Image award, even though some of these are certainly contenders. So we decided on this award, as it seemed like the best fit given our lack of data. But regardless, get thee over to this site posthaste, where you'll see one of the best new voices currently working in street photography. As well, some of the essays accompanying the images are incredibly thought-provoking. And beyond the photography itself, this site is a boon for anyone looking for help in dealing with loss. What a wonderful way to transform grief into art.

A good photograph will remind you of something familiar, but a great one will make you nostalgic for something you've never seen. These tend to do the latter.

"Holy shit!" Seth lowered his phone and stared at me. We were talking right before first period the next morning.

"That's what *I* said. Crazy, right?"

"What's really crazy is this." He zipped over to my site's admin page and pulled up the stats. "You've had over ten thousand viewers already today. And it's not even eight a.m." He paused. "Well, it's eleven o'clock on the East Coast. But still . . ."

Then I had someone come up to me between my morning classes and say "Great photos, man!" I remembered Ollie saying people were talking about the site, but other than her and Seth and Assi, no one knew it was mine, or what it was about. Had someone seen me taking snaps and broken the code, or what?

I put it out of my mind until lunch, when two people said something to me before I could even find a seat near the 7-Ups. First, Brett Legrande—a guy in my history class I barely knew— came up to me and said, "Hey, man . . . sorry to hear."

"What are you talking about?"

He shrugged. "Uh . . . someone said your mom died or something. I'm just saying sorry."

What the . . . ? But he seemed sincere so I just mumbled, "Thanks."

Then some senior I didn't know got right in my face. "Are you Jamison Deever?" He didn't seem nearly as sympathetic as Brett, either.

"Uh . . . yeah?"

"So you're the creepy dude that's going around taking pics of people at school and posting 'em on some website?"

How do you answer that? "Not exactly. Well, I have a photography site, but—"

He didn't wait to hear the rest. "I don't give a shit *who* died. You post any pics of me and my friends, we're gonna fuck you up good. Got it?" Apparently his final question was rhetorical, because he turned and left.

Wow.

After I got some food and sat down, I pulled out my phone and went to the site to see if someone had given me up in the comments or something.

Nope. It was worse. Right there on the front page—before even the *Empty Set* pic and essay—was a little head shot of me, and next to it the words *All Photography by Jamison Deever, Vista Grande, CA.*

Holy crap.

It wasn't hard to figure out—there was only one other person besides me with the access to do this. And here he came now . . .

"Why the hell did you do that?" I demanded as he sat down.

"What the fuck are you talking about?"

"Don't play dumb. My site . . . my name . . . my photo . . ."

"What the fuck are you talking about?"

"You *knew* I wanted to stay anonymous . . ."

"I need one of those little sampler toys, where every time I push the button it says *What the fuck are you talking about?* in a deep voice, because this is getting old."

And *I* was getting pissed. "Dude!" I showed him my phone. "Look. Right here." I pointed. "My home page. My face. My name. You're the only one with admin privileges. Do the math."

He suddenly laughed out loud. "I just did."

"What the fuck are you talking about?"

"That's my line. But I think you'd be better off looking in your own backyard, genetically speaking."

"What the . . ." I took a breath. "Seth. Someone put my name and my picture on my website. You're the only one with the password to get in and do that. If you didn't do it, then who did?"

Ollie plopped down next to Seth. "I did."

"Which was my guess," Seth said to me, "once I figured out what you were talking about. She hit me up for the password a couple of days ago." He shrugged. "I didn't think it was a big deal—she's your sister and all . . ."

I looked at Ollie. *"Why?"*

"Honestly? I'm looking out for you. Just like I promised."

I swear, I almost reverted to *What the fuck???* but I held my tongue. "That doesn't make it okay to out me," I finally said. "The road to hell is paved with bullshit like this."

"Look. You have a site—an amazing site that honors Mom—which a lot of people apparently really like. And which also shows off your photography. So I let everyone know about it. What's so wrong with that?"

I was *so* sick of hearing that question. I was also sick of her sticking her nose into my business. "How about *everything*? It ought to be *my* choice, right? Hey, here's a wild idea—how about you just stay out of my shit from now on?"

"You'd never have done this for yourself, so I did it for you. Sorry—kill me for it." She stood up. "You're *welcome*," she threw over her shoulder as she left.

I turned to Seth. "Is there some way we can take the site down?"

"What are you *talking* about, man? After all that work?"

"Well . . . maybe make it so no one can get there?"

"You mean like a 404 message?" He saw my *Huh?* look. "You know—one of those *page not found* error messages you get when you try to go to an old web page that doesn't exist anymore."

"Uh . . ." I didn't want it to look like we just forgot to pay the hosting fee or whatever. "How about if it just comes up as a black page? Until I figure this out?"

"Are you sure you want to do this, because . . ."

Just then Chloe walked by, then stopped, came back, and put her hand on my shoulder. "I'm sorry for your loss," she said quietly. I just nodded and she kept going, then I gave Seth the side-eye.

"Got it," he said. Then he added, "This would be way easier on a computer than on my phone, especially the HTML stuff. So do you mind if I swing by after school and—"

He faded off as he saw me looking across the room, where

Ollie was talking to Assi. Man, what I'd give to be a fly on that wall . . .

I looked back at him. "Huh?"

"Never mind. Looks like your attention is somewhere else."

"I just . . ." I stopped. I was breaking our "don't talk specifics about girls" thing, but I think we were long past that anyway. "I like the way Assi thinks, if that makes any sense."

"So what are you saying?"

"I just really like her mind, that's all."

Seth looked at her across the room. "Yeah, and the rest of her isn't too bad either."

"I'm not fucking blind."

"You might as well be."

I could feel my face scrunching up. "Huh?"

He put his hands to his temples and closed his eyes, like he was getting a psychic message. "Here's what Swami Seth predicts . . . you two are going to dance around each other for another six months, then you're *finally* going to figure it out and get together."

Okay, part of my brain lit up at that, like *You really think so?* But I wasn't ready to go there yet, especially not with the guy who gave my password to my meddling sister.

"I don't know. I just . . . I don't know."

Seth held his finger over his keyboard. "Are you sure?"

"We can always undo it, right?"

He nodded. "Yeah. You just reload the URL into the host server and it'll be back online."

I nodded. "Okay then. Do it."

He hit the Enter key. "Go there on your computer and see."

I did. My site was a black screen with small white letters saying *On Hiatus*. I just looked at it for a minute. "I hope Ollie's happy," I finally said.

"Look, I get why you're pissed at her. But you need to keep something in mind—"

"That my sister just does what she wants and doesn't think about anyone else? Thanks, but I think I already knew that."

"No," he said calmly. "That your sister misses your mom every bit as much as you do. Only she doesn't have an outlet like you do, to honor her and remember her. So maybe getting more attention for your project was her way of helping keep your mom alive, too."

Huh? "She tell you all that?"

He looked shocked. "Me? No way." He paused. "Well, about missing your mom, sure"—even that was news to me, but he was still talking—"but the rest of it isn't too hard to figure out, if you just take a step back and look at the whole thing."

I shrugged. "Maybe." That still didn't make it right . . .

"There's no maybe about it. So don't be too hard on her—she's just trying to help."

She's just trying to help. I'd heard that before somewhere. "Yeah, I know. But something about her sticking her nose in and trying to help me, like I'm too stupid to help myself . . ." I suddenly remembered where I'd heard it. From my dad. About my mom. "God. She's such . . ."

". . . a *mom*," Seth finished for me. "You're right—she is. And half the time, you come off sounding like a dad. I think both you guys are just picking up the slack left when, you know . . ." He shrugged. "Just try not to be too much of a dick about it, that's all."

"Yeah, that's easy for you to say. But right now half the people at school think I'm some sort of Peeping-Tom-with-a-Nikon. I mean, most of them have never even seen my site, but once word gets around."

"Yeah, but—"

"But *nothing*. Some asshole already wrote 'Creeper-Peeper' on my locker with a Sharpie. And the other half thinks my mom just died or something." I took a breath. "That site was my way of remembering my mom. And now it's down. So don't tell me to go easy on her . . . you're wasting your breath."

After Seth left I stayed in my room and avoided Ollie. Which was easy, as she avoided me. Whatever. After a while I got bored and decided to check how things had been going on the site since I'd been outed—even though it was down, I could still go to the hosting page and see everything that had come in up until we pulled the plug.

I looked at the stats—man, there'd been *tons* of page views that day. Normally I'd be super stoked about that but I reminded myself lots of them could be from pissed-off people at school or something. I held my breath as I checked the comments . . .

Hey Jamison, just wanted to say how much I love the idea behind your site. Your photos rock, and so do you!

Mr. Deever looks a lot younger than I would have imagined, but I have to say his images have a certain sophistication beyond his apparent years. And this one . . .

Hi, Jamison!!! Do you have a GF??? ☺ ☺ ☺ (Actually, there were a couple along that line.)

But beyond the fannish stuff, there were another dozen or so requests from people wanting to do their own 9:09 projects in memory of loved ones who'd died. Wow.

And now the site was down.

CHAPTER 24

I believe in living with the camera,
and not using the camera.
—Dorothea Lange

"NICE ESSAY," MS. MONTINELLO SAID TO ASSI THE NEXT morning before class started. "I liked you starting with the mathematical premise of set theory, then segueing into how this relates to a person's life, with brackets standing in for their birth and death . . ." She glanced at me. "Good use of metonymy, wouldn't you say?" I nodded as she continued. "I thought the seed metaphor was apt, and the way you brought it all full circle at the close made for a resonant ending. Well done."

She turned to me. "I'm not as well versed in the visual arts, but I thought that was an evocative image." I just nodded. After all that I didn't have the heart to tell her the site had been taken down.

She turned and walked toward the front of the class while

Assi and I stared at each other for a second, then we both said "Wow . . ."

If I thought this meant Ms. M was going to go easy on us, I was sadly full of crap. She made me defend every thought I had, almost like this was a debate class instead of English. And if anything, she pushed even harder on Assi, calling her reasoning "pedantic" at one point. But we fought back valiantly, and by the end of the hour we felt like we'd won a moral victory, if nothing else.

Even Ms. Montinello seemed to enjoy the verbal sparring. "That was refreshing," she said to us on our way out of the room.

I turned to Assi in the hallway, raised my eyebrows, and whispered "*Refreshing*?"

She laughed. "I know, right?" Swinging on her backpack, she pointed down the corridor behind her. "I have to go by my locker." She paused. "See you at lunch?"

I nodded. "Okay, sure."

As I walked away it hit me that—as minuscule as it was—this was the first time we'd ever really done that. And I didn't mind. Not one bit.

As I walked across the cafeteria I could see people sort of elbow each other and make snide comments, but I did my best to ignore it as I pulled up next to Seth . . . who was sitting at the Unaffiliateds table for some reason. I jerked my thumb toward the fashionista table. "C'mon, man."

He glanced toward where I'd pointed. "Uh, but . . ."

I looked over. No Ollie. But no Sofia or Chloe, either. And no Assi yet, of course. Just Kennedy Brooks and a bunch of girls I didn't really know.

"Dude." I pointed around at our side of the room, including the ULs just a few tables away. "Predominantly stupid, mean, boring, sausage party." I swung my finger to the 7-Up area. "Predominantly smart, funny, interesting, estro-fest."

He rose. "Sorry, I'm new on this tour. Glad I have you for a guide."

We moved to the end of fashion central. As we approached the table Kennedy looked up right when I was looking at her. She didn't pull a face or turn away or anything. And she didn't act all fake nicey-nice, either. She just raised her eyebrows like an eighth of an inch then back down, like *Hi.* Anyway, I forgot about it the moment Assi sat down next to me, because I suddenly realized something.

"I figured it out," I said.

"*Okaaay.* Figured what out?"

"Why your mom called me the happy boy."

"Do tell."

I pulled a pair of imaginary glasses down the bridge of my nose and looked over them in my finest Montinello impression. "I believe that's best left as an exercise for the student." Then I gave her a quick up-and-down glance. "R*efreshing!*"

She laughed and I joked, "Speaking of your mom, maybe we should get her and my dad together sometime."

"You could end up as my stepbrother." She put her hand on my shoulder. "Ooh! That might be . . . *refreshing.*"

We were both cracking up when Kennedy walked by. Instead of the nose-in-the-air routine like the last time she saw us together, she just nodded and said "Hey," like no big deal. And before I even thought about it I said "Hey" back. After she was gone I looked at Assi. "That was weirdly . . . normal?"

"Weird, yes." She shook her head. "But definitely not refreshing."

"So, are we bringing it back or not?" Seth asked.

"I don't know. But if we do, I want it to be different."

He was in my room again that evening, helping me try to figure out what to do with the site. There were some things I wanted to try, so I'd texted him after school and he'd told me to get started writing copy and he'd come over later to help format the new template. Which might seem goofy, but I think we both liked having a project to work on, regardless.

We got to work and after an hour or so things were starting to look a little better. We were working on a new tab on the home page about starting your own project. It led to a page that explained the mechanics of it and the conditions of doing their own (basically just reciprocity—credit and a linkback—plus a notification to us). Then we ginned up a little directory, with links to all the other 9:09s that had already spun off from my site.

I was busy writing some text on my computer while he was updating the site on his, when he asked, "So, which one do you like better?" He toggled back and forth between a couple of different design schemes.

An idea popped into my head—one that was more brother than dad, so I actually considered it. I mean, I was still officially pissed at her. But . . . "Hang on a second."

I went to Ollie's room and said my first real words to her since this whole thing blew apart.

"Hey, Meddlesome Brat, you got a minute?"

She didn't even look up from her phone. "What?"

"Trying to decide between a couple of different design ideas for *what used to be* my site. Thought you might have an opinion." She kept on texting. "Do I really need to remind you why my site is down?"

She got up without really looking at me. "Okay, okay."

We walked into my room and she stopped cold at the door. "Uh, hi, Seth." She tucked her hair behind one ear and tugged at her shirt. I hadn't really noticed but she was wearing super-casual-just-kicking-around stuff—old jeans and a sweatshirt—and no fancy hair or makeup or anything.

Seth didn't seem to notice either. "Hey, Ollie. How's it going?"

She nodded as she walked in. "So where's the stuff you wanted me to look at?"

"Right here," I said, showing her the templates on the screen. "Assuming it even comes back, I don't want it to look home-made. But not too buttoned-down, either. Like indie, but 'smart' indie. If that makes any sense."

She pulled a face. "Are these my only choices? What else do we have . . . ?" Then she dug into it, occasionally stopping to ask Seth something. Pretty soon they were both sitting in front of Seth's computer, working away. She'd look and render an opinion, and Seth's fingers would fly over the keyboard making it happen.

I was finished with whatever new text I was going to add, but they were still in the middle of redesigning the look of the site. I checked the time—almost eight-thirty. "Hey guys, I'm done with my part here—we can paste it in later. I've got somewhere I need to be."

Seth looked over like he'd forgotten I was there. "Huh?"

"I'm taking off," I said.

"You want us to stop?"

I shook my head. "Keep going as long as you want—whatever you think's best." Ollie didn't even look up from the monitor. I almost added *And no zygotes, okay?* but that was way too far toward the dad end of the continuum so I just grabbed my bag and headed out.

As I walked downtown I felt . . . I don't know. Anxious. Almost nervous. Which was weird. I mean, I feel nervous about lots of things, lots of times, but I'd never felt that way about photography before.

When the magic hour struck, the nearest people were a middle-aged couple. I asked, they agreed, and I started shooting. They were nice and interacted with each other—and it should have been fine if not uber-interesting—but every time I'd go for a shot, some part of my brain would be saying *This pic is boring— you should think of something better.* And *No one is going to like this!* And *Oh my God, really? I've seen this image like a thousand times!*

After sixty seconds of this I thanked them and packed up my stuff. I felt like going home and putting my Nikon up for sale on Craigslist, but I decided I needed to drown my sorrows in a big cup of chai first. A couple minutes later I was in the back booth with my drink, reviewing the photos on my camera just to remind myself of how much I sucked.

In the middle of this Assi slid into the booth across from me, espresso in hand. "Like the man said to the horse, why the long face?"

I tried to work up a smile. It didn't stick. "I think my muse left. Or more likely committed suicide after seeing my work."

"You worry too much," she said. "I have a feeling she'll be back."

"Easy for you to say."

She nodded. "It is. Especially when I know I'm right." She tilted her head toward my camera. "So what's going on?"

"Coming down to the corner tonight felt different. For some reason I was like . . . I don't know. Nervous."

"About . . . ?"

"Not sure. When I was taking pictures I kept second-guessing everything. Not fun."

"So what were you doing, before you came down here?"

"Just working on the website. Trying to decide what to do with it." I sort of shook my head and snorted. "If anything."

"But it was going well, right? I mean, before you took it down?"

"It was actually going crazy. That's not the issue . . ." She just looked at me. Maybe raised one eyebrow a millimeter. But it was enough. ". . . or maybe it is?"

She had the same expression she'd had when I'd taken her portrait, like she was looking right through me. Not speaking. Not tipping the scales. Just waiting.

I took in a deep breath. "Okay. Maybe that's it. Maybe the thought of all those people looking at my stuff is messing with my head."

She nodded. "That's understandable."

"All right, but what's the answer?"

She shrugged. "So why were all these people visiting your site?"

"I don't know . . . I got a good write-up from SSA a while back, then that award kind of made things blow up. Plus your essays are great, and the whole 9:09 thing really caught on."

"Maybe all that helped bring them there. But why did people go back?"

I shrugged. "Maybe because they liked the photos, and the other content, too?"

"What were you thinking about when you took all those cool photos, the ones that people seemed to really like?"

"Nothing specific. Just trying to capture whatever it was that made the people special, that made me feel some sort of connection with them."

"But not thinking about who might eventually look at it?"

I shook my head. "Nope. Never really crossed my mind."

She nodded slowly. "So what you're saying is that what got

you here in the first place—what helped you make those award-winning images—was just doing your own thing without thinking about what anyone else thought?"

Remember. This. Moment.

I swear, I almost reached over the table to take her hands in mine, but that would have been way too weird, like something out of an old movie. Instead I heard myself say, "Do you know *how fucking refreshing* it is, talking with you?"

"Is that supposed to be a compliment?"

"Absolutely."

"Then thanks. I guess." She looked serious. "I know it's easy to say, but maybe you should just not overthink it—just do what your gut tells you. You're still doing this for your mom, right?"

"Sure."

"Then all the other stuff—the website and everything—is just a by-product. It's not at the core of your work . . . don't think about it when you're shooting. Think about whatever's in front of you." She paused, and her voice choked a little. "And think about your mom."

CHAPTER 25

A documentary photograph is not a factual photograph per se. It is a photograph which carries the full meaning of the episode.
—Dorothea Lange

WHEN I GOT HOME THE HOUSE WAS DARK AND SETH'S CAR was gone. On a hunch I stopped by the garage and sure enough, my dad was still out there, working away with the radio blaring. He didn't see me come in so I just watched for a minute, and as he was working I caught him looking at the poster of the yellow bike. Twice.

The second time, for like a minute straight.

It struck me that he would probably go through the rest of his life looking at that thing but there was no way he'd ever actually get one—he was too busy worrying about us to do anything for himself, no matter how much we tried to convince him otherwise. Then I thought about everything he'd done for me and Ollie since Mom had died. Like, if he wasn't at work, he was here. Even if he practically lived in the garage once he got home, he was *here* for us. We could find him if we needed him. And he tried to make sure the three of us ate together at least once a day. And on top of all that, he did his best to do the mom thing and check on how we were doing in school . . . and outside of school.

It hit me that even though there was nothing I could do about Mom, maybe there was something I could do for my dad— maybe I could give him one small thing he'd never give himself . . . a little speck of perfect yellow sunlight in his life.

He finally saw me and reached out to turn the radio down. "Hey, son. How's it going?"

I shrugged. "Fine."

He had the cabinet for the old phonograph down to bare wood—stripped and sanded smooth—and he was rubbing some sort of stain on the wood pieces with a rag. Which would have made sense, except the color was red. Not like the reddish-brown tint of mahogany or something. *Red* red.

I don't even know why I cared, but something about it just seemed messed up . . . to go to all that work, and then ruin it with the wrong color. My dad was usually big on "authenticity" when it came to old shit. "Uh, what's with the red color? I mean, it's yours and you can do what you want, but it looks like a fire truck. Is that the way they used to look, back when they were new and dinosaurs walked the earth?"

He shook his head like I was hopeless. "Everyone knows

when dinosaurs were around they used a bird with a pointy beak to play records." He must have seen the blank look on my face. "Never mind." He put down the bloody rag and sat on the stool. "I'm not staining it. I'm giving it an underwash, with a diluted red dye. Then I'll hit it with a mahogany stain. And when I rub the stain out, the parts where I rub it more—like the center of the panels or any of the high points—will have a little less stain so more of the red undertone will show through. It'll give it some contrast between sections."

"So it'll have more variety? More depth?"

"Exactly." He gave me a look like that night at Tacos de, when I'd been promoted. "In the end it's what's underneath—the part you can't see—that really matters."

I could tell—this was supposed to be one of those father-son *Remember this moment* moments.

"Speaking of which," he continued, "earlier this evening I found Ollie and your friend Seth in your room."

I couldn't resist. "Were they playing Gametes and Zygotes?"

He looked confused. "They were doing something on Seth's computer, but I don't think it was a video game. It looked like they were working on that site he helped you with."

"We were working on the website scheme and I thought Ollie might have some ideas . . . she's always going on about the importance of design."

"That's fine, but . . ." Oh God, here it came—a dad moment. "I can remember what it was like, being seventeen . . ." There it was. I tried to head it off with a little creative writing.

"Seth is barely sixteen," I said. "He skipped third grade, but he doesn't like people to know so don't mention it."

"Really?" That took him off course, but only for a second. "Well, I can remember sixteen, too. Same thing. Ollie is a very pretty girl, and—"

I held my hands up. "Whoa. Stop! We are *not* having this conversation. I know all about the birds and the bees and I hate to break it to you, but so does Ollie."

"I hope so. My question's more about Seth. What do you think of him?"

"I'm pretty sure he knows all about them too."

He pulled a face. "Not helping."

"Ollie asked me the same question so I'll tell you what I told her—I think he's a good guy."

"Okay. That's good. I guess. But do me a favor . . ."

"And keep an eye on her," I finished for him. "Mom already asked me to do that, before . . . you know." I tried to change the subject by pulling out my laptop and opening it. I called up the admin version of my site and set the computer on the work-bench. "So, this is the project I've been working on." I didn't want to get into all the grief it'd caused me lately so I just scrolled through the gallery a little so he could see some of my work. "It's . . ." I realized I hadn't really changed the subject at all. "It's in honor of Mom," I said.

He was quiet at first. Then he looked closer at some of the images. "Those are great photos," he finally said. "And I know your mom would be super proud of you." He blinked a couple of times. "Just like I am." He paused as he looked at the heading across the top of the page. "But why is it called the 9:09 Project?"

I just looked at him, channeling Ms. M looking over the top of her glasses. I could tell he got it—after a few seconds he nodded. "Oh . . ."

The next morning Ms. Montinello started class with a question. "So in rhetoric, is there any value in figurative language?"

"Not really," a guy behind me said. "Some people use flowery words to look smart, but they lose clarity."

"Then figurative language is simply 'flowery,' as you so figuratively put it?"

He barely had time to get in a nod before a hand shot up. "Ms. Knudsen?"

"Not always," Assi said. "Figurative language can add depth of meaning through metaphor or analogy. Persuasive writing is not all facts and figures."

The words *euphemism, good,* and *Greek* all appeared together in front of me. All three were some shade of green, of course, which helped group them. But I kept all that to myself . . . right up until Ms. Montinello looked straight at me. "Jamison?"

"Umm . . . there's a reason why *euphemism* means 'good speech' in Greek," I said. "Figurative language helps add emotional connection to your arguments. As opposed to flowery language, which is mostly just shi—uh, *manure.*"

"Good use of 'good speech' in that case," Ms. Montinello

said. "So yes, there is potential value in euphemism." She glanced at the class in general. "What are some of your favorite euphemisms? Avoiding the 'spanking the whatever' variety, if you don't mind . . ."

People started throwing out euphemisms and she started making a list on the whiteboard at the front of the class . . .

Enhanced interrogation techniques
Kick the bucket
Right-sizing
Adult beverage
Collateral damage
Alternative facts
Bun in the oven . . .

While Ms. Montinello's back was turned Assi handed me a small folded piece of paper. Which surprised me because it seemed out of character, but when I opened it and saw *Refreshing!,* I had to smile.

After Ms. Montinello finished her list and turned back to face the class, she said, "As you all know, written communication is one of the cornerstones of this class. But to clarify, written communication should not happen *while* the instructor is actually teaching . . ."

I tried to maintain the same slightly confused expression as the rest of the class. A while later when we were walking out, Assi whispered, "Wow—she really *is* the master."

"You're not kidding. I'm just glad she didn't take it away." But I've got to say, her handing me a goofy little note in class made me happy in a way I couldn't explain.

Lunch was similar to the day before—dirty looks and all—except I didn't have to work as hard to get Seth to move to Fashion Land.

"I checked out the work you guys did last night," I said once we'd grabbed seats, "and it looks awesome."

He nodded. "Cool."

I cleared my throat. "And apropos of nothing at all . . . if my dad ever asks, you skipped third grade and you're a year younger than me."

"Huh?"

"Don't ask. Just trying to pave the way a little."

Just then the object of my deception arrived. I think she was trying to make up for her scruffy appearance last night by going the other way. She had on leggings topped with a long sweater that was like three sizes too big but somehow fit, with a matching knit cap over her re-blonded hair. I don't know much about makeup, but whatever she had on made her look about three years older without looking like "makeup," if that makes any sense.

Ollie sat on the other side of Seth and they immediately started talking about design. A minute later Assi sat down on my other side instead of at her usual table across the aisle. It was like having her pass that note to me—a trivial thing, but it totally got my attention.

I turned to her. "I will gladly pay you Tuesday for a novel chapter today, milady."

"What is the currency of your realm, milord?"

"We use a coin known throughout this land as the taco. Typically paid on the second day of the workweek, hence the phrase *Taco Tuesdays.* I'm prepared to offer you a taco per chapter, for up to five chapters."

Her eyebrows flew up. "That is all my words are worth to one such as yourself?" She waved her arm. "Be off with you!"

I opened my wallet and took a look, then made a sad face. "My patron has been . . . *lackluster* in his support of late, milady. Perhaps a few of your chapters might serve to cheer him?"

She dropped the routine. "There's no way anyone else is seeing it. Not until it's ready."

"Okay. But I was serious. I can't wait to read more."

She shook her head. "Maybe later."

"Kind of chickenshit to get me all hooked and then pull the plug, don't you think?" I couldn't help it. "Almost like a bait and—"

"Don't say it!"

"*—switch.*"

She punched me in the shoulder. "I *said* not to say it."

"Ouch."

We were still goofing when Kennedy walked by. She took in the situation and smiled. That's all. Not smug or mean or sarcastic. Just a normal, friendly *Glad to see you're having a good time* smile, then she was gone. It felt a little strange—on top of yesterday's "Hey"—and I could tell Assi wasn't wild about it, but it was better than Kennedy constantly hating on me for something I hadn't done.

I guess.

* * *

I was studying in my room after school—funny how the desire to keep up with a certain girl can do what no amount of parental pressure can manage—when Ollie came in. I could tell something was on her mind.

"I know things have been rough at school since I, uh . . . *credited you* for your work. I wanted to try and explain, because—"

I just shook my head. "Not now."

She ignored me and sat down. "Look, I just wanted to say—"

"Save it, because—"

"—I'm sorry."

I stopped. "Well, I'll always remember *this* moment."

She ignored that, too. "I'm sorry your site's down. I'm sorry things are weird at school." She took a breath. "I'm sorry for a lot of things. I just wanted to help you, and—"

"Stop right there—that's the problem. I didn't *want* any help, I didn't *need* any help, and I sure didn't *ask* for any help. And yet you decided to 'help' anyway. So what's wrong with that picture?"

She sat there, not saying anything. Then I noticed her eyes were filling. This was worse than the puppy face. She blinked and tears ran down her cheeks. "I didn't mean for all this to happen. The stuff about Mom . . . your site getting shut down . . . people being mad at you . . ."

I held up my hand. "Those people who're mad at me? They're assholes. Forget 'em."

She smiled through her tears at that. "Okay, but the rest of it . . ."

Yeah, she screwed up. Big-time. But it was clear she felt terrible about it, and how long did I want to be mad at her, anyway? "Look," I finally said. "My whole thing with the site was I *didn't* want it to be about me—it was about Mom." She sniffed and nodded. "But now it's all *look at me,* and it makes it seem like I'm milking my mother's death to get some attention for my work. Which is really messed up. Do you see how this might make me, uh"—I paused—"just a tiny bit annoyed?"

She couldn't even work up a smile. "I get it. Completely."

"And *I* get that you were trying to help . . . in your bratty, superior, misguided-but-lovable way." That got half a grin out of her. "But the project itself?" I shook my head. "I don't know *what* to think about it anymore. Like, was it screwed up from the start, that I wanted to somehow use *the specific time that Mom died* as the basis for an art project? Just hearing myself say that sounds all kinds of messed up. Like, what was I *thinking*?"

"You were thinking about Mom. You were missing her. You wanted to honor her. I don't think there's anything messed up about any of that."

"But now that people know who I am, can any of that work?"

She shrugged. "You could get rid of your pic and name on the front page . . ."

"It's too late for that. It's out there, lots of people saw. Like, zillions. Plus it's all over the comments—and there were tons of them after you outed me." I just shook my head. "I don't know."

She thought for a second. "Okay, so now that it's out there, maybe instead of thinking about damage control, we find a way to turn this into a positive." She thought for a lot longer than a second. "Don't say no," she finally said.

"No."

"The comments were going up, right?" I nodded. "So *maybe* people were commenting more because there was an actual person they could talk to, instead of some nameless, faceless 'administrator' guy."

I shrugged. "I don't know . . . maybe. So?"

"So maybe . . . just *maybe* . . . them seeing that you're a regular guy—a teenager instead of some middle-aged professional—might inspire other people like you to try something. Which is sort of the whole point, right?" She wiped her eyes. "I mean, think about it: If *Mom* inspires *you* to do something that inspires a bunch of *other* people, then . . . ?" She looked at me with this hopeful look. And maybe she actually had a point.

"Did you read Assi's piece about the empty set?"

"No. Should I?"

"Yeah, you should." I paused. "I guess what I'm trying to say is, maybe you're onto something."

She actually grinned at that. "And maybe *I'll* always remember *this* moment."

"Yeah, and maybe it's time for my bratty sister to get out of here and let me work."

She turned to go, then stopped. "You know, when you see me, instead of thinking, *There's my bratty sister,* maybe you should think, *My God, it's Ms. Olivia Deever.*"

I just stared at her, like *Huh?* She grabbed a pen off my

desk and started scrawling something on the back of a piece of paper as she talked. "I *said,* you should think, *My God,* it's *Ms. Olivia Deever.*" She spun the paper around so I could read it: *mygodmsod.* That was familiar . . . something about the Pic of the Week . . . on the SSA site . . .

"That was *you,*" I said, "who tipped them off about the pic of Kennedy?"

She nodded. "That was a great pic . . . even if it *did* feature Ms. Perfect. Like I said, I'm just looking out for you." Full crinkle—she didn't even try to hide it.

I'd always thought if I was doing this for the right reasons then I didn't need any credit or fame. But on the other hand, Ollie had a point.

Okay. But if I was doing this credit thing, I was going to do it right.

First off, I edited the Artist's Statement so that instead of saying *My mother passed away at 9:09 p.m. and . . .* , it just said, *Someone very important to me passed away at 9:09 p.m. and . . .* I mean, I could still talk about my motivation for doing this without specifically referencing my mom's death, right? And second, I made a rule—no more pics from school on the site.

That part was easy, but the rest of it took me almost an hour—most of which was finding the right photos. I wanted normal-looking pics, not too slick or posed, but not fuzzy little low-res images. Luckily I found decent photos of each of them.

When I was done, right under my pic—after I'd changed my first name to just J—I put a shot of Assi, with her name and the caption *Writer at Large.* Then Seth. (*Webmaster,* of course.) I was going to leave it at that, but I decided to add one of Ollie, titled *Design Consultant.*

I put the site back online, then I texted Ollie. hey ms od—go look at my website

A few minutes later she came into my room. "So what does this mean?"

"It means what I said—I think maybe you have a point."

"I accept your apology."

"Good. And I accept yours."

She ignored that. "But . . . *Design Consultant?* I haven't done much work on the site."

"You will. Consider it a down payment."

"Okay, well . . . thanks." She looked down. "Look, J. I know I screwed up, putting your name out there. I didn't know exactly what you were trying to do, and I just thought . . ."

"I was trying to bring Mom back, is what I was trying to do."

"Wait. You mean, like, back to *life?*" She actually looked concerned for me, which might be a first.

"No! Well, yes. But not like that. Back to *my* life." I took a breath. "Look, just because she's gone doesn't mean she can't still help me, and maybe inspire me."

She looked back up at me and blinked. "You know, I miss Mom too. Like, every day."

I nodded. "I know you do. Seth and I talked about it, and—"

"Wait . . . what? You guys *talk* about me?"

"Oh, all the time. Daily." She put her hands over her face. "Hourly, even." I looked at the time on my phone. "In fact, it's been fifty-eight minutes, so I need to—"

"Shut up. What does he say?"

"You shut up. He said you miss Mom too, and I should go easy on you."

She waved her hand like she was erasing a whiteboard. "Yeah, I got all that. What does he say about *me*?"

"He says that he thinks that *you* . . ." I paused dramatically.

"Yes . . . ?"

". . . miss Mom too, so I should go easy on you."

"I hate you."

"That's fine." I picked up my phone. "Can you excuse me now? It's time for my hourly 'Ms. Olivia Deever' call with Seth."

"I really hate you."

After Ollie left, my phone buzzed.

hey j, do you have some time later on? i'd really like to talk

It was Kennedy. Wow. Not that getting a text from her didn't get my attention, but in that half second between feeling my phone buzz and reading the screen, the face at the top of my mental *I hope it's her* list was Assi's, not Kennedy's. Which was weird, because the most romantic thing we'd ever said to each other was basically "I really like your writing" and "I really like your photography." And the extent of our physical contact basically consisted of her punching me in the shoulder, more like a friend than a—

That was *it*. Assi was a friend. Maybe a good one. And Kennedy—whatever else she was—hadn't been that to me for years. I put away my phone and got back to work.

Later that evening I was back in my room after dinner looking at my latest disaster of a 9:09 session when my phone buzzed again. u ignoring me?

Uh yeah, actually, I was. The phrase *Get back on the horse* popped into my head, so around eight-thirty I packed up my stuff and hiked downtown.

It's funny. Usually I find myself wishing for a herd of drunken monkey-tamers in pink chiffon or something, but at the moment I didn't really care about the specific subject. I was more interested in just trying to enjoy the process without any expectations. Which was good, because when my alarm went off I was presented with the exact same thing as last night.

They were a different middle-aged couple, but barely—same basic age, same basic look, you name it. They could have been their next-door neighbors.

They were cool with helping me with my "school project" (just like last night) and I started by taking standard "husband and wife standing together" photos (just like last night) and a minute into it I started thinking *Man, I suck* (just like last night). But instead of quitting, I told myself *You're doing this to honor your mom, to document what's happening tonight at 9:09, when she died, not to make some great work of art . . . get your ego out of it and go with your gut.*

My brain called up a picture of two little cartoon smiley faces holding hands, so I asked the man "How did you two meet?" and he told me a boring story about them both working in the same office twenty years ago. I listened and nodded, then the image changed so the smiley faces were a short distance from each other, both looking at a miniature version of them getting together, but from different viewpoints. Like a triangle or something. I turned to her. "So is that the way *you* recall it?"

"Not exactly . . ." Then she told *her* version—much more animated—involving a company party and alcohol and needing a ride home but not really trusting him. They argued back and forth as I fired away, like I wasn't even there. In the end she was laughing at him and he was apologizing to her, then he finally turned to me and said, ". . . And three kids later, here we are. So I guess she decided to trust me after all."

"I guess so," I agreed. After they left I tried to picture myself telling some young guy a story like that, thirty years from now. I couldn't imagine being that age, let alone with a wife and kids and a career and a mortgage . . . I shivered even though it wasn't cold out.

Then I took out my phone.

thanks for the advice, milady. you need to hang out a shingle, because tonight's work went much better. talk to you anon

I heard back almost immediately. i'm so glad! ☺

I walked into Finch Coffee feeling a hundred times better than I had twenty-four hours ago, even though I'd just finished doing almost exactly the same thing. When I stepped up to the counter the barista looked at me and said, "Large chai, right?"

I started to nod, then for some reason I said, "You know, I think I'd like an espresso . . . a double shot." Why not?

She made my drink and I took it to the back booth, where I reviewed the pics I'd just taken. I'd know more when I could look at them on my big monitor, but I could see enough on my camera to tell I'd gotten some good stuff. Scrolling through them in rapid succession was like watching a jerky little film of their conversation, but there were a few magical frames where the single image told a whole story in itself. For some reason I found myself really looking forward to showing them to Assi, because she—

Someone slid into the booth across from me. Without glancing away from my camera I said, "I hope you brought some new chapters."

"What are you talking about?"

I looked up.

It was Kennedy Brooks.

CHAPTER 26

The documentary photograph carries with it another thing, a
quality in the subject that the artist responds to.
—Dorothea Lange

I JUST STARED.

"Happy to see you, too," she said. But she said it with a smile. I found myself starting to grin back—is that why they call it infectious?—and I forced myself to stop.

"Hi, Kennedy. What's up?"

"I texted you. Twice." I swear, she almost pouted. "Are you ignoring me?"

I'm trying to. Why can't you see that? "I've been busy," I said.

She nodded. "I'm sure you've got a lot going on these days." Then she did that goddamn eye thing. "J, we've known each other for a long time . . ."

No. I've known you for a long time. I don't know if you've ever really known me.

"... and I think it's silly that we let something come between us. I ... I want to apologize for overreacting at that party. And afterward, in my room." She looked down at the table. "I think maybe I just had my feelings hurt. I'm sorry."

What can you say to that? "I'm sorry too. Don't worry about it."

"Good." She looked relieved. "I wanted to tell you I saw your website. I think it's awesome." She paused. "I also saw the photo of me you put up." She nodded toward the street. "The one you took right out there. I'm not proud of how I acted that night, but I still think it's an amazing photograph. You captured something about me that"—she blinked a couple of times—"that no one else seems to see. Really."

In that moment, I could totally see how someone could fall head over heels in love with her. I mean, underneath the obvious, there was definitely something special there. Something that—

The thought vanished because she suddenly got up, came around to my side of the booth, and sat next to me. "And here's another pic you might really like ..." I moved to give her some room, but she slid over until she was right up against me. I found myself looking around, making sure that—

"So, remember that glamour session I wanted you to do?" she asked, holding up her phone. "I ended up doing it myself."

Wow. I found myself staring at it as she spoke quietly into my ear. "I'd love to do this again—with you. I've got a few new ideas ... and I'm sure you do too." She kept the phone out as she continued. "I also have some new ideas for a fashion portfolio.

Maybe we could do both of those, sometime soon?" She smiled. "Win-win."

I swallowed. Her phone was still out, and I was still looking. She swiped to another pic. Jesus. It made the first one seem tame. I was acutely aware that the girl in the photo was sitting right next to me. That her leg was pressed up against mine. That her hair was brushing the side of my face. She swiped one last time. Holy fucking shit. It was a good thing the booth was backed up against a wall with no one behind us. The shot left absolutely nothing to the imagination. "This is more what I had in mind," she whispered, "only you could do *such* a better job." She put the phone down and rested her hand on my thigh. "It could be big fun," she said. "For both of us."

Okay. She had my attention, I'll admit it. But apparently my brain was still getting enough oxygen to function. Barely. "Stop," I heard myself say.

She backed away a little and turned to face me directly. "What?"

"Why do you think you have to act this way?"

"What way?"

"Is it because you're insecure? Because you don't really know what you want? Or because you *do* know, and you think the only way to get it is to manipulate guys into helping you?"

She gave me the look. You know the one. "J. What are you *talking* about? We're just sitting here having a conversation, and all of a sudden you—"

At first I was nervous, talking to her like that, but now I was pissed. "*Stop.* Just fucking quit with the innocent routine, okay? Instead, maybe try this—maybe quit leading guys around by the dick and just be straight about what you want to accomplish. Who knows . . . maybe they'll actually help you. Not to get into your pants, but just because they might actually *like* you as a person and want to help." Wow. Did I just say that? I softened my tone. "Seriously, Kennedy. What do you want?"

For a second I thought it might go like the last time I'd asked her that, when she'd told me she wanted me to leave. But she seemed to take the question seriously.

She was quiet for a long minute. "I want . . . ," she finally said. "I want to feel like I have an anchor." She sighed, and for the first time in years she seemed like the Kennedy Brooks I used to know. "I feel adrift."

I nodded. "I get that. I've done my share of drifting." I paused. "We weren't hanging out then, but you should have seen me after my mother died. I didn't know which way was up."

"I'm so sorry you had to go through that. But you seem pretty anchored now, like you know who you are."

"I think what people seem like on the outside and what they are on the inside can be really different. Like . . ." I paused. "Like, to me you seem to have *everything.*"

She laughed, but there wasn't much humor in it. "Honestly? Here's what I have . . . I have a bottle of cheap vodka hidden in my room—so my parents don't smell it on me, if they'd even care—and I drink it alone most nights. Not for fun. So I can get to sleep."

Wow.

"Oh yeah, I also have a set of parents that never seem to praise me—or punish me—no matter what I do. Like, I could be getting all Fs on my report card or land a full ride to Stanford, and I don't think they'd notice either way. I mean, why'd they even have me? Seriously, I would kill to get grounded, just once. Just so I knew they gave a shit."

Double wow.

"And . . . I never really talk to guys. Or, they never really talk to me. They come up to me and ask me out while staring at my boobs, or they try to talk me into getting high—because they think it'll 'loosen me up' or whatever. Or they'll complain about their boss or their guy friends. But they never really talk to *me*. About *me*. Or about *anything* important to me. I used to try, but . . ." She shrugged. "I pretty much gave up. And it's sort of the same thing between me and most girls. Well, kind of the opposite, but the same. So, yeah . . . I have everything." She looked down and did that humorless little laugh again. "Mostly, what I have is loneliness." She looked up at me. No eye thing. "But I meant it, J—you seem to know who you are."

I thought about it. Pretty much everything she'd said about being lonely applied to me—for totally different reasons, of course—from before my mom died until recently. So what had changed . . . ?

"I don't know about that. I'm lonely as hell at times—a *lot* of times—but I think I found something I'm good at. No, I found something I *care* about . . . and maybe that's why I'm halfway good at it. If I even am." And it hit me that this—more than anything—had changed the way I felt about myself.

"You are," she said matter-of-factly.

I waved it away. "Fine, whatever. I'm not here to mansplain stuff to you. You know yourself way better than I do. Most guys probably pay you compliments to try and, you know . . ."

She nodded. "Yup."

"But I'm going to tell you something because it's true, and because I think you need to hear it. From someone who isn't trying to blow smoke up your ass. It's this: You have a serious talent for modeling. Which has very little to do with how you look. Like, there are attractive people everywhere. But ninety-nine percent of them can't do what you can do. Which is to have this presence in front of the camera that says, 'I don't give a *fuck* about the camera, I'm just being me. Take it or leave it.' That's the thing you can't fake. I think you'd probably be a great actor, too, for the same reason." I looked at her and nodded. "Really."

She gave me a half smile. "No smoke?"

"None."

"Then thanks. Seriously." She paused. "Are you seeing anyone?"

Huh? I started to shake my head, then stopped. "Honestly, I don't know . . . maybe."

"You *don't know*?"

Which was actually a really good question, but I ignored it. "Look, either way, I don't think I should be the one to do your portfolio. With or without clothes." I took out my phone and started searching . . . there it was. The local photo studio. And they still had the $999 portfolio special. I copied and sent it. "I just sent you a link to someone," I said.

"Okaaay . . ."

"They seem good . . . their prices are reasonable"—I nudged her out of the booth and stood next to her—"and I think they might be a better match for you. I meant what I said—you're really good at it. It's up to you to decide what you want."

I kissed her on the cheek. "Good luck."

I'd be lying if I said I didn't think about her on the way home. At first part of my brain was all *What did you just do?*, imagining what might have gone down if I'd played it differently. (And I had some compelling visuals to go along with that, believe me.) But beyond that, when she'd been talking about the street shot I'd done of her—and when she was telling me what her life was really like—I got the distinct vibe that we had some sort of connection. Maybe not exactly a BF/GF thing, but maybe . . . something?

I don't know. I was such an idiot about this stuff.

One thing I *did* feel semi-certain about was that evening's 9:09 shoot, but you never really know until you know. The first thing I did when I got home was make a sandwich, open up my computer, and import the pics. Then I sat down and started going through them.

At first they looked a lot like the night before, but as I kept reviewing I found myself starting to nod my head occasionally, and near the end of the shoot I found one I especially liked. The man held his hands in front of him—palms up, like *Huh?*—while the woman had her arms wide and her mouth open, clearly scoring some major points in the debate.

It reminded me of a scene from an opera or an old movie, where she was telling the tale and he was literally the sidekick, making the occasional snide comment to the audience. I converted it to black-and-white, lightening her and her expressive hands. This made it feel like there was a spotlight on her, with him catching some of the reflected glory on an otherwise darkened stage.

I decided to title it *How It All Began.* On one level it seemed like a comic image, but on another I hoped it told a deeper story, about love and commitment and the passage of time.

I was really happy with it. Or maybe I was just happy with the fact that I'd *done* it, after last night's miserable experience. Either way, I did something I don't usually do—I sent it to someone else before I'd even posted it.

Hey, I'm pretty stoked about this so I wanted to send it to you right away. As proof of your talent, not mine. This is from tonight's 9:09 shoot, which was starting to feel like last night until I recalled your advice, then things really improved. I meant what I said earlier—you should go into practice, Dr. K. ☺

I didn't get a response but by then it was pretty late. I put the image up on the 9:09 page and went to bed. And after my experience at Finch you're probably thinking you know what *I* was thinking about as I lay there in the dark. But you'd be wrong.

When I woke I found myself checking for messages. Nothing. I got some breakfast and found myself checking again. Which was stupid. I mean, do *I* hop out of bed every morning and immediately write a breathless reply to whatever came in during the night? Not even. Maybe she slept in. Or maybe she missed the message. Or maybe there was a glitch and it didn't even get delivered, or—

Stop! We've already been down this road, with you-know-who. Just get on with your life.

I got caught up on my homework. I cleaned the kitchen. I even did the laundry. And you'd better believe I was on the corner of Fig and Gardena well before 9:09 that evening, camera in hand. And you'd better believe that afterward I went to Finch and milked a large chai for at least an hour before I walked home. Alone.

And you'd also better believe I thought about the same thing as the night before.

So I was actually happy when Monday rolled around. I hustled over to AP language five minutes early. I might as well have walked. And stopped for a beer. And a cigarette. Because one of Ms. Montinello's most vocal students was nowhere to be seen.

Same deal with lunch. I hung by myself at the end of the table while Ollie dominated the conversation with Seth.

When I got home from school I broke down and sent her a quick text. hey, u weren't in class. hope ur not sick?

No reply. After dinner I thought about texting her again—or even calling—but that smelled like the hey, u ignoring me? thing, and I was determined not to be that guy.

So I was a little surprised when eleven o'clock Tuesday rolled around and she walked into language class like everything was fine. I said "Hi," she said "Hi," and she took her seat. And it wasn't like back when she was pissed and sniping at me in class or anything. But something was different. Like, Ms. Montinello was debating the value of parallelism in a speech and I said it could help draw the reader in on an emotional level.

"It's like a musical connection," I said. "You know how in some songs there's a hook or a riff that plays before each verse, to get you ready . . . ?" I was losing it, suddenly feeling all alone.

I looked her way but she was looking at the teacher, like everyone else.

"Thanks for that, Mr. Deever. Anyone else care to add to the discussion?" I swear, she even looked at Assi as she said it.

Nothing. Zip-zero-nada.

"Well, okay then! Moving on . . ."

Lunch was the same nonstory. Seth and I sat at the end of fashion central. Ollie on the other side of Seth. And even though I left some room before the end of the table, Assi was at the next table, talking to the girl next to her. I was in the middle of choking down a deep-fried "burrito" that'd never been within a thousand miles of Mexico when my phone buzzed. I was all excited for exactly one second until I saw it was Ollie.

taco tuesday tonite?

I glanced over at her and shrugged, but inside I was grateful for an excuse to ask.

I moved over next to Assi, but she kept talking with the other girl. I waited, feeling like a total dork loser just sitting there looking at her shoulder. Finally I said, "Hey . . ."

She turned and looked at me. "Hey, J—what's up?"

I was going to make a stupid joke about gladly paying her Tuesday for the chapters I didn't get last week or something, but I suddenly had that feeling where you realize you're talking but nobody's interested in listening. Just like in language class today. "Um, it's Tuesday, and, uh . . . we're thinking about going for tacos tonight."

She nodded politely and said, "Thanks. I have some things I need to do, but have fun." Then she turned back to her friend. Like I wasn't even there. Somehow it was even worse than if she'd said *Screw you!* I felt this weird pressure behind my eyes like . . . like I don't know fucking *what,* because I'd never felt it before. But other than when my mom died, it might be the worst feeling I'd ever had in my life.

I moved back to my old seat and took out my phone. she's busy. go without me

no can do—u know that!

I had zero interest in chaperoning her and Seth. really not feeling it tonite

She didn't even bother texting—she just leaned out where I could see her behind Seth and gave me the saddest puppy-dog look.

Screw it. ok—we'll just be the three amigos i guess
that's no fun
sorry. but unless u want me to bring dad, I got nothing
okay, no worries

No worries. I think you can find that phrase in Wikipedia under *Famous Last Words.* Right next to *Hold my beer.*

A little before seven o'clock I drove Ollie to Tacos de. Seth was already inside, parked in one of their worn vinyl booths. He got out and let Ollie in, and I sat across from them. We'd just started discussing the critical issue of what to order when Ollie looked up toward the door and waved. I turned.

Sofia.

I kicked Ollie under the table but she totally ignored it. "Hey, Sophie!" she said. "Glad you could make it."

Sofia grinned. "And miss Tacos de Tuesday? Are you kidding?"

It felt so old-school, but I hopped out and let her take the inside seat of the booth—either that, or I'd end up looking across at Ollie's smug face all evening. And really, it was no big deal—we got food and hung out, and half the time Ollie talked to Sofia across the table while Seth and I talked school stuff or computer stuff or whatever. Might as well have been in the cafeteria at school. Without the pain of LaRue's history class afterward.

We were about done when Sofia said, "We're having a Christmas party next Friday night. I hope you guys can make it?"

Ollie and Seth were nodding and saying *Sure!,* but I just kind of sat there. She turned to me and laughed. "Hey, you made quite a splash last time. Don't tell me a troublemaker like *you* isn't going?"

Going to a party was the last thing I felt like doing but I didn't want to get into all that, so I just shrugged. "Is that skeleton-bartender dude going to be there again?"

She leaned back against the corner of the booth and looked at me. "Would that be a good thing or a bad thing?"

"Oh, es muy bueno."

"Good, because he wouldn't miss it. That's my cousin Roberto—he's a crack-up."

"Cool. I really like him." I stood up and looked at Ollie. "You about ready? I have a few things I need to do."

I drove in silence for a while, but I had to say something. "Look, I did you a favor by tagging along so you could hang with Seth. I don't need you trying to get me a date."

"Seems to me that's exactly what you need."

"If that was the case, I could have asked Kennedy. I'm pretty sure she would've gone."

She looked at me like, *You're kidding, right?*

"Can you keep a secret?" She nodded. "I mean it—no blabbing to your little fashion-forward friends." She nodded again. "I had coffee with Kennedy on Friday night. And she hit on me, pretty hard." Her eyes opened wide.

"Wow."

"She wanted me to shoot her new portfolio. Among, uh . . . other things." I paused. "But we started talking. And guess what? Yeah, she seems like she has it all together, but her life isn't perfect either, any more than ours is. Not even close."

She cocked her head at that. "Okay . . ." Ollie wasn't exactly a member of the Kennedy Brooks Fan Club, but I could tell on some level she was sympathetic. She looked over her shoulder at the empty backseat. "But still, by virtue of the fact that she's not here with us, I'm assuming you turned her down?"

I nodded.

"Don't take this the wrong way, but why?"

"Uh, Tacos de, with horchata and pan de muertos? After the Día de los Muertos party? When you sat there and lectured me about the Wily Ways of Wicked Women?"

"I remember. You bailed on the hottest girl in school to save your loving sister from a fiery death behind the wheel of Seth's car." She looked apologetic. "Which I'm still really grateful for, by the way."

"If that's true then quit trying to set me up."

She ignored that. "But I was safely at home last Friday night. So why did you bail on her then?"

I shrugged. "Maybe I learned a lesson? Maybe all your wisdom sank in?"

"Maybe." She glanced at me. "But probably not."

CHAPTER 27

*While there is perhaps a province in which the photograph
can tell us nothing more than what we see with our own
eyes, there is another in which it proves to us how little
our eyes permit us to see.*
—Dorothea Lange

AFTER I TOOK OLLIE HOME I GRABBED MY GEAR AND WENT to the corner. Nothing amazing happened, but I've learned that the biggest secret to getting good stuff is just putting yourself out there—night after night—so that when something amazing *does* walk by, you won't be at home wasting time vegging on the internet and miss it.

And after I was done shooting I went to Finch and hung out for a while. For the same reason.

Later that night after doing some homework I went to check on my site. You'd think I'd get used to it, but I was always a little amazed when I saw that it was still doing so well. In fact, it was taking on a life of its own. There were *dozens* of other people doing their own 9:09 things and posting their results, including one eighty-six-year-old man who had arthritis so bad he was bedridden most of the time. His photographic territory was limited to the view from his third-story apartment window in downtown Brooklyn, where he documented street life on that hundred-foot section of sidewalk in honor of his wife, Jessica— they'd been married for sixty years before she'd died of cancer. And his work was *amazing*. Without trying to sound corny, that was the kind of stuff that made me glad I'd decided to start a website in the first place.

On a related note, I heard from the arts editor at Vista Grande's alternative weekly paper, the *VG Vanguard*. She'd found out about my website and my photos somehow, and I got a message from her saying the *VeeGee* wanted to do a little piece on me, sort of a "Local Artist Does Good" thing. Cool. I figured we'd chat by email or whatever, but she wanted to see the project in action.

She met me at my corner the next evening a little before 9:00 and mostly hung in the background observing as I photographed three women walking back to their car after catching a movie at the indie art house down Fig Street. I asked them what they thought of the film and managed to capture a few good frames as they discussed it.

Afterward we went to Finch, where we grabbed coffees and she interviewed me about the site and my work—why I was doing it, how I got started, what I wanted to accomplish. When we were done I asked her about *her* writing process—I'd noticed she didn't use a recorder but took lots of written notes. In the middle of her telling me how she typically structured an article for the *VeeGee* I found myself really wishing Assi were there—she would have loved the whole discussion.

Before she left, the editor asked me to send her a few images that "best represented my work," and I promised to send her something right away.

Several options came to mind, but by the time I got home I'd made up my mind. I sent it, with a message: Thanks again for taking the time to interview me. I'm sending you a high-resolution file of an image I think best represents what I'm trying to do. I thought for a minute, added a title for the photo, and pressed Send.

As nice as all that was, none of it changed anything at school. Assi was like she was back when I'd first met her . . . quiet, polite when spoken to, but with zero reciprocation. Nada.

I tried talking to her. Like, at lunch I asked when I could maybe see some more chapters in her book. Her reply? A shrug, followed by, "I don't know. I'll let you know if I ever finish it."

As she turned to go I tried to make a joke of it and I called her milady. She spun on me and said, "What do you want?"

"Hey, I was just kidding around, and—"

She held up her hand. "No. I mean, what do you fucking *want*?"

Huh? What do I want? Uh . . . *I don't want to feel like shit? I want things to be like they used to? Or maybe I don't want to walk around feeling absolutely fucking awful anymore?*

But before I could put any coherent sentences together and actually get them out of my mouth, she stalked off.

"I want my money back," I said to Seth. "You're not as good a wizard as I thought."

"What do you mean? Your website crash or something?"

"No, *that's* doing great . . . for what it's worth." Honestly, I didn't really give a shit about it anymore. I tilted my head toward Assi, at the far end of the next table. "I meant, you predicted six months of dancing around before we got together."

"Oh. That was Swami Seth, not Wizard Seth. I'm a way better wizard than a swami."

"No kidding. Because the whole thing is apparently over before it even began."

"Ouch. So, how are you with that?"

"Seriously? Awful. And confused. I mean, it's not like we were ever a thing, so how can I be so bent because we're a nothing?"

"I don't know. The rules of logic don't exactly apply to relationships."

"No kidding. And speaking of weird, check *this* out . . ." I told him about Kennedy and our conversation at Finch—along with the offer to do her "glamour shoot"—and how I'd basically told her *Yeah, no.*

"So now she hates you?" he guessed.

"You'd think, but that's what's so weird. Now she's nice to me. Not throw-herself-at-me nice, just low-key normal nice. Like we're semi-friends or something."

"Dude, I'm not a genius about this shit like your sister is, but it sounds to me like this is something more than 'mean girl messing with your head' stuff. I mean, maybe she actually *likes* you."

I snorted. "Or maybe she likes what she thinks I can do for her."

"Maybe." He shrugged. "Or *maybe* she finds herself attracted to the one guy at school she can't lead around by the, uh . . . nose."

I shook my head slowly. *"Great."*

He studied me for a minute. "You know, I'm required by the Guy Rules to point out that you're acting like having the hottest fucking girl in school be interested in you is somehow a *problem.*"

"No, the problem is . . ." What *was* the problem? "The problem is, she's not the hottest fucking girl in school."

He considered this for a second.

"Look," he finally said. "Ollie and I aren't a thing. At all. But yeah, I'd be upset if she suddenly lost all interest."

"Because . . . ?"

"Because maybe we're a potential thing. And that's worth something too." He watched me as he said it. "So, what do you think about that?"

"I think you skipped third grade."

And I felt like I'd *flunked* third grade. Over and over. I mean, I had no idea what to do with myself.

In language I tried to keep a low profile while staying engaged but it felt like riding a bicycle built for two all by myself—I was either in back pedaling away with no one steering or I was up front steering but no one was back there helping me get over the hills. Either way it sucked, so I basically stopped interacting in class unless I was called on.

I also gave up trying to interact with Assi on any level, because besides breaking my heart, the whole freeze-out routine was messing up my brain, too. I don't mean I turned and ran every time I saw her coming. I just started treating her the way she treated me—like two people who're in the same class but don't have anything in common.

And she stopped going to Finch.

Completely, as far as I could tell. That part made me sad. For her, I mean. Because she used to go there all the time and write or do homework or whatever—back before she even knew me—and now she didn't. I almost wrote her about it, but that'd be stupid. She didn't need my permission to go hang at any particular place. She could do what she wanted, and what she wanted apparently didn't have shit to do with me.

I didn't go there as often either. I'd been making it a regular thing lately, but if I went there every time I did a 9:09 shoot that'd be like an extra hundred bucks a month out of my savings.

And speaking of money, I'd contacted the manager at Vista Grande Screens and told him I'd be available to work lots of hours over winter break.

It wasn't like I had anything else going on.

I wasn't kidding about the whole thing screwing with my attitude. Take US history. We were finally sneaking up on the 1930s, and Mr. LaRue was big on the "practical impact" of programs like the FSA, WPA, TVA, and the rest of that whole between-the-wars alphabet soup.

Anyway, he was rambling on about them—for like the third goddamn time—and I was gazing out the window. There wasn't much to see, but way in the distance was this cool little cinder cone mountain rising above the mesa. I think my brain likes it because it's almost perfectly symmetrical—the kind of shape you'd get if you asked a little kid to draw a mountain—and way more interesting than LaRue. So I'm looking at the mountain, imagining it as part of a cartoon scene, when out of nowhere I hear, ". . . so perhaps *Mister Deever* can inform us as to the tremendous practical impact of whatever's so interesting outside the window."

The class went dead silent.

I saw an *F* and an *S*. Dark brown and black. Like the dirt on a farm after you've tilled the soil. Like the fields on a mesa. Fields where pea pickers camped, almost a hundred years ago. I opened my book to the photo . . . I knew where it was by heart, of course.

Talk about telling a whole story in 1/100th of a second. Badass, with a perfect yellow *B*.

"You see that cinder cone, way out there?" I said, pointing to my little cartoon mountain. "Near the base of it is where Dorothea Lange took *this photograph*"—I had a hard time leaving out the f-bombs as I held up the book and showed *Migrant Mother* to the whole class, like I was the teacher—"while she was on assignment for the Farm Service Agency, under FDR. And it was *this photograph*"—I showed the book around again, in case anyone missed it—"that resulted in the federal government rushing thousands of pounds of food to starving migrants from the Central Valley." I slammed the book closed and turned to LaRue. "Is that enough practical impact for you?"

By the time Friday—and winter break—finally rolled around I was so messed up I actually considered going to Ollie and saying *I'll talk to Seth for you if you'll talk to Assi for me.* But I could see several ways that could turn into a complete fuckstorm so I left it alone. And besides, I was having a hard time caring. About anything. I hadn't been down to the corner for three or four nights and I hadn't updated my site in even longer. I totally wasn't feeling it.

Honestly, I wasn't feeling *anything*. I mean, my site blows up but before I can even enjoy it, Ollie outs me and screws it all up and half the people at school think I'm some weird photo-stalker dude. And then this thing with Assi . . . man, that hit me harder than I could've imagined. I was walking around all day feeling like I was ten seconds from bursting into tears at any given moment. Jesus, what was up with *that*?

Right on cue, Ollie came into my room. "Don't say no, but I want you to consider going to Sophie's party tonight."

"No."

I got ready to say *no* again the instant she opened her mouth to give me the inevitable argument. But she just sat there, waiting.

Finally I said, "Why—do you need a ride?"

"No, I can get one, but if you go I wouldn't mind getting a ride from you."

"Do you need me to go so you're 'with a group,' to keep Dad happy?"

"No, I asked a friend from school to go."

Aha. "Is this another attempt to hook me up with Sofia?" She started to look defensive so I added, "Look, I know she's your friend. And I actually think she's really nice. But now's not a good time."

"I figured that much out. I told her you're out of rotation."

"*Out of* . . . Never mind. Then why?"

She shrugged. "Why does anyone go to a Christmas party?" Then she did it again—she just sat there while I thought about it. She's really mastered the art of tactical waiting.

It was the beginning of winter break. After a *really* shitty week at school. It might be good to get out of the house for a while. "I'll think about it," I finally said.

We left the house around seven o'clock.

"Thanks for giving me a ride," Ollie said on the way over.

"No problem. Just don't try to drive someone else's car home. So who's the 'friend from school'? Chloe?"

She gave me a funny look and I did a face palm. "It's Seth, right? I knew it! Look, I don't know what I don't know, but don't make me lie to Dad's face. He'll know, and—"

"It's Assi."

CHAPTER 28

I realize more and more what it takes to be a really good photographer. You go in over your head, not just up to your neck.
—Dorothea Lange

"*ASSI?* WHAT THE FUCK WERE YOU—"

"Turn here," she said, ignoring my outburst.

Instead I stomped on the brakes, bringing us to a dead stop in the middle of the street. "What the hell's going on?"

"I asked Chloe but she's out of town tonight," she said calmly. "I needed someone, so I asked Assi."

"So who was your ride?"

She looked behind us. "You need to either drive or pull over." I started driving. Slowly. "Seth," she said.

"So he'd have to pick up Assi or whoever first before he came by to get you, right?" Dad's overall dating rules for Ollie could be condensed to "No getting in a car alone with a boy."

"Yeah. But you're driving, so we're her ride. Which is why you need to turn here."

"Does she know this? That I'm going with you?"

"No. She didn't really want to go at all, but I talked her into it. And I had to promise her a ride."

"Shit."

She looked confused. "I don't really understand what the big deal is . . ."

"I figured Seth already told you."

"Told me what? He doesn't tell me everything you guys talk about . . . we're not an item or anything."

I had to laugh. "An *item*? That's like something Grandma would say." She didn't see the humor in it. "Anyway, if you haven't noticed, Assi and I are pretty much the *opposite* of an item. Just don't go making a big deal of it, okay?"

She nodded. "Okay. Sorry."

When we got there, Ollie went up to get her. When they came out toward the street Assi looked at the car and must have seen me, because she stopped and said something to Ollie, then started back to her house. Ollie caught up to her and they talked for a minute, then they both came out to the car. *Great.*

Ollie hopped in front and Assi got in back. "Hi," I said.

"Hi," she replied, looking at the floorboard.

She didn't say another word all the way to Sofia's. When we got there I parked and shut off the car. *Screw it.* I looked at Ollie and jerked my thumb toward Sofia's house. "I'll see you in there later." She nodded and got out. After the door closed I turned to Assi. "I'd like to talk to you for a minute."

"There's nothing to talk about."

I took a deep breath and let it out. Then I heard Ms. Montinello's voice . . . *At times like these, a change of venue may be in order.* "Okay. I have to go run a quick errand. Do you mind going with me?"

"How long will it take?"

"Fifteen minutes." She raised an eyebrow. Something about that gesture just fucking wrecked me. "Okay, twenty, tops." She still looked doubtful. "I promise, the party will still be going strong when we get back."

She didn't say anything so I started the car. "You want to sit up front? I feel kind of stupid chauffeuring you around."

"I'm good where I am."

I swear, I came *this close* to bailing out and just going to the stupid party, but I shook my head and put it in gear. Whatever . . .

As we drove back toward town I asked, "So, what happened with us?"

"Nothing."

"Seriously? I felt like we were becoming pretty good friends—maybe more—then all of a sudden it's like you don't even know who the fuck I am." I paused. "This is worse than when you were sniping at me in class. So what happened?"

"Nothing."

I didn't try any more conversation until we were almost there. As I slowed down to turn in I said, "So, you know the rules of the no-lie drive-by?"

"I really don't want to go there."

"I don't either, but I think we need to." I thought she might get out when I pulled up to Happy Jack's drive-thru speaker, but she just slumped down in her seat. I ordered two Happy Burgers, well done. With extra grilled onions, also well done. That ought to take some time.

After I placed the order I turned around to look at her. "Okay, so what's going on?"

"Face forward," she said quietly. I turned back around, glancing at her in the mirror. She leaned back in the seat and closed her eyes, then took a slow, deep breath. "Last week you texted me, to thank me after getting some good pictures. You sounded so happy . . ." She stopped for a second. "I decided to come down to Finch to see if you were there. As I was walking by the front of the place I looked in the window. You were sitting in a booth with Kennedy Brooks. Right up next to her, like 'get a room' close. You guys were looking at something on a phone, talking away and . . ." She stopped. "Do I really need to go on?"

"That's it?" I was suddenly, bizarrely happy. And it must have showed in my voice.

"Is there something funny about what I just said?"

"Not at all." The line inched forward—there were still a few cars in front of us. "So, how would you feel if I were going out with Sofia?"

"Look, I don't really care who you—"

"You're under the no-lie oath. Nothing but truth."

"Okay, I'd be upset." She sounded angry. "Is that what you want to hear?"

"How would you feel if I were going out with Kennedy?"

"I'd be *really* upset."

"Why the difference?"

"If you were with Sofia . . . Well, she seems really nice and I think she's probably a good person, so I'd mostly be upset because if you were with her then you couldn't be with me. But if you were with *Kennedy* . . ." I glanced in the mirror in time to see her slowly shaking her head with a scowl on her face. ". . . I'd be *so mad* . . . at *you* . . . for being manipulated by her. I'd also be mad at myself for even liking someone so gullible." She paused. "It'd be a whole different level of mad."

No kidding. "So earlier that day—the day you saw us in Finch—she sent me a text saying she wanted to get together. I ignored it."

"I remember that day—she smiled at you in the cafeteria."

She didn't miss much. "What *I* remember most about that day was you passed me *this* in language class . . ." I took out my wallet and found it, then handed it back to her. A folded scrap of paper I'd been carrying around with the single word *Refreshing!* written on it in her neat handwriting. "And what *I* remember about lunch is joking with you about your novel. And how happy I felt." That reminded me of something. "Which is the same reason your mom called me 'the happy boy.' You know why I was so damn happy at your house?" I could feel myself getting worked up. "Because I was with *you.* It's that fucking simple."

She was silent. We were moving up in line, so I kept talking.

"Kennedy sent me another text that evening and guess what?

I ignored that one too. Then I went down to the corner and took some halfway-decent photos—which is when I sent you that excited text. Then I went to Finch. After a while Kennedy showed up, which was a complete surprise to me. It took me about two minutes to figure out what she really wanted."

"Yeah . . . *you*."

I shrugged. "That's what Seth thinks, but I think she's more interested in using me as her photographer—she thinks I can help her become a model or something, plus the fact that I work cheap. I don't know about her liking me."

"I do. I saw her, mashing up against you."

"She was trying to bribe me, showing me her naked selfies and hinting I could take more, if I did her new portfolio for her."

I looked in the mirror. Assi was righteously pissed. *"And . . . ?"*

"And I sent her a link to a local photo studio, saying she should use them instead."

That got her attention. "What did she say to *that*?"

"I don't know, because I said 'bye' and walked. End of story." I called up the texts with Kennedy from that day. The let's meet up text was at 4:17, the u ignoring me? one was at 8:02, and the link to the studio with my message try these guys was at 9:43. I handed her my phone. "Look."

She read them and handed it back. "Why does she think she can act like that around you?"

We moved up again, to the window.

"We've known each other since elementary school. I had a big crush on her when we were kids and she knew it. I think she tries to use that to get me to do what she wants. And it might even have worked at one time. But compared to you, she's—"

Right then Mr. Stoner Dude handed our order out the window. "Here you go, man. Sorry for the wait, but like, I stuck some extra fries in there for you guys." He snorted, like that was hilarious.

I paid for the food and was about to pull out of the parking lot when Assi suddenly said, "Pull over!" I found an empty slot and pulled in. Assi got out of the car.

"What are you doing?"

"Get out," she said.

I got out. "Are you all right?" I was starting to get worried.

"I'm not sure yet." She got into the driver's seat and pointed to her right. "Get in."

What the . . . ? I went around and got in the passenger seat.

She drove around the parking lot and back into the drive-thru. When the guy asked for our order over the speaker she said, "Two large Cokes. I want forty-seven ice cubes in each one." Her voice took on a threatening tone. "I'm going to count them. God help you if you get it wrong."

The stoner's voice came back. "Uh . . . like, okay, man . . . Large Coke . . . forty-seven ice cubes. Uh, got it."

"*Two* large Cokes. Forty-seven cubes *in each one.* Don't make me come in there . . ."

"Uh, no way, man . . . No worries, I got this . . . uh, thanks."

"You're scaring him," I said. She gave me the side-eye. "And me," I added.

She pulled forward a little—there was no one in front of us—
and turned to face me. "Your turn. So, what do *you* think?"

"About . . . ?"

"Us."

There. She'd said it. "What do I think?" *Tell her. All of it.*
Some of which I didn't even know until I heard myself say it. "I
think . . . I think you sit there in class every day and you say exactly what I'm thinking and if it's not exactly what I'm thinking
then it becomes exactly what I'm thinking once I think about it
and that makes me mad and weirdly attracted to you at the same
time and you're really smart and you're really funny although the
funny isn't as obvious as the smart because your sense of humor
is really dry and understated but it's still there, and"—I turned
in my seat and looked directly at her as my mouth kept going on
automatic pilot—"and you're different and unique and whatever
the polar opposite of phony is—where's my mental thesaurus
when I need it?—but whatever you are you're completely you
and no one else and even if you sometimes act like you're mad
at the world I can tell you're really just guarded about it because you don't have that victim thing going on it's more like
a quiet confidence and on top of all that—I shouldn't be telling
you this—but on top of all that, something about you is *just so
unbelievably hot.* Don't take this the wrong way but the first time
I saw you I said you had a little Che Guevara in you but really
it's more like Frida Kahlo because you're really creative but kind
of intense and . . . I don't know—it's like Frida and Che had a
love child and somehow she ended up in twenty-first-century

California as a teenage girl who is just"—I was trying hard not to abuse the word *hot*—"who is just . . . absolutely . . . captivating." I took a breath. "So that's what I really think."

I was sort of expecting her to say something in return. Hopefully something along the same lines, or maybe not, but *something*. She didn't say a word. She leaned over and kissed me. And not a quick little *Thanks, I think you're sweet* kiss, but a crazy-ass dangerous kiss, exactly the kind of kiss you'd expect if you were to be kissed by the gorgeous bastard love child of a sensual groundbreaking artist and a violent communist revolutionary.

A kiss with closed eyes and open mouths.

A kiss like we were absolutely starving to death.

A kiss that seemed to go on forever but wasn't nearly long enough.

Somewhere in the middle of all this a car pulled into the drive-thru behind us and honked their horn. Assi pulled away and looked at me.

"We need to go somewhere and continue this discussion."

CHAPTER 29

You know, so often it's just sticking around and being
there, remaining there, not swooping out in a
cloud of dust . . .
—Dorothea Lange

WE PULLED OVER TWICE ON THE WAY BACK TO SOFIA'S.

When we finally arrived it was hard to believe we'd left only an hour before. We were right back where we'd started—in the same parking spot, in fact—but *everything* was different. I don't mean just our relationship. I mean my *hair* felt different, my *shoes* looked different, the goddamn steering wheel in my mom's forest-green Subaru *Outback* was somehow different.

And all of it was *totally* different from anything I'd ever felt with Kennedy.

As we got close to the front door Assi reached out and took my hand. I glanced at her and she whispered, "Is that okay?"

I shook my head. "No." I waited two seconds. "It's awesome." I gave her hand a squeeze.

"You're such a little shit." But her eyes were gleaming.

The front door was already cracked and we could hear music, so we walked in. It was almost a repeat of the Día de los Muertos party, but with a holiday twist—the music was Christmas music and the lights and decorations were Christmassy instead of spooky and no one was in costume or death makeup, but it was still a big-ass party with a BBQ and music blazing away and everything.

"These guys have the *best* parties," I said to Assi as we walked through the front room toward the backyard. "Is it too late to revise my position on going out with Sofia?"

She raised an eyebrow. "I don't know . . . is it too late to revise my position on letting you live?" But she kept a grip on my hand so I figured I was okay for—

"There you guys are!" It was Sofia, standing near the sliding glass doors that led outside. Then she noticed our hands and her eyes widened. "Oh. Um . . ." You could see her switch gears. ". . . Maybe I'll start a fire in the kiva for you two."

"You don't have to do that," Assi said.

Sofia reached out and threw a switch high on the wall next to the door. "Done. My dad's a builder, remember?"

They exchanged looks. "Thanks," Assi said quietly. "That's really nice of you."

Sofia smiled, then nodded toward the backyard. "Enjoy."

We made our way through the crowd to the far back part of the yard and sat on the built-in bench next to the kiva, where a fire was already going. Assi maneuvered us to a dark corner where there were a couple of cushions and we resumed where we'd left off in my car. It was like we were under a spell—we couldn't get enough of each other.

Eventually we came up for air. "This is *so* nice," she murmured as she lay back against me. I nodded in agreement and leaned back against the bench, staring into the fire. We snuggled like that for a while, and at some point she took my hand and said, "Remember the last time we were here?"

"Of course. That was really nice."

"What were you thinking, back then?"

"Honestly? That you were pretty awesome. How about you?"

"Well," she said quietly, "*I* was actually thinking that *you* were pretty, um . . ."

"Pretty what?"

"Stupid."

"Jeez!" I closed my eyes and leaned back. After a minute I felt her shaking. I opened an eye—she was cracking up and trying not to make any sound. "You think you're so damn clever . . ."

"One of us has to be." After another minute she said, "So what's on your mind right now?"

"*Really* refreshing thoughts about you," I said. "*And . . .*"

"And . . . ?"

I grinned. "And I can't wait to read Astrid's take on all this."

She looked confused. Or tried to. "How could she even *have* a take on this? Her story's set on the other side of the world. With different people. It's fiction—there's no connection."

"Yeah, but a lot of authors say their real life 'informs' their writing."

She scooted even closer. "Then I think we need to do some more research . . ."

I tried to look offended. "Wait. That's all I am? Research for your book?"

She nodded, straight-faced. "Pretty much."

I let go of her like she was radioactive and moved away. "Be that way."

She slid over next to me and did this totally cute thing where she bumped her butt against mine. I don't know why, but it made me feel unreasonably good. "Sometimes I think I use writing to help me deal with what's going on in reality. Like maybe the story is research for real life, rather than the other way around?"

I thought about that. "Hmm. Sometimes photography helps me make sense out of stuff that makes no sense."

She was quiet for a minute. "Like your mom?"

I swallowed and nodded, suddenly not trusting myself to speak.

"If you ever want to talk about it," she said quietly, "I'm right here."

It was strange to even contemplate—talking to someone about my mom. But if anyone . . . "Thanks," I finally said. "And I'd do the same for you. About your dad."

She nodded, her eyes shiny. "I know . . ." She faded off.

This was getting way too serious. I backed up and gave her a look. "So, Ms. Knudsen, is there any truth to the rumor that your novel is almost finished, and—"

"What novel?" a nearby voice in the dark said. "*What* rumor?"

"The rumor that little sisters are the nosiest people on the planet," I replied.

Ollie stepped into the little circle of light around the fireplace, Seth behind her. "Hey, we finally found you," she said. "Where were you guys?"

Talk about a loaded question. "We got some food," I said, "and now we're just hanging out, discussing writing." All true, right?

"We were discussing the *difference*," Assi said, giving me the side-eye, "between fiction and nonfiction. And how one thematically informing the other does *not* mean they're synonymous."

Ollie slowly shook her head, like we were hopeless. "School's out, you guys. Let it go. You can nerd up again soon enough." She tilted her head toward the food and the music. "Time to have some fun for once."

The four of us walked back toward the lights and noise of the party, where we ended up on the patio with everyone else, hopping around to the music. By the time the music finally quit, we were ready for some food.

We went over to the BBQ, where they were serving tri-tip and beans, along with a big platter of dessert tamales. We each got a plate of food and found seats on a bench a little way from the patio so we could talk.

I remembered the time the four of us went out for tacos, and how it wasn't weirdly awkward because we didn't have one couple in need of a room while the other was shoe gazing. So I acted like everything was normal. I speared a chunk of tri-tip and held

up my fork. "Man, this is awesome. Like, *so much* better than—"
I was about to say *than Happy Jack's crappy burgers,* but I stopped.

"Better than what?" Ollie asked.

"Better than the cafeteria food?" Assi said, in an attempt to help bail me out.

I laughed. "Yeah. Better than that, even."

Ollie raised an eyebrow. "I'll tell the chef you said so."

Assi and I kept things on the downlow for the rest of the party, by unspoken agreement. The four of us hung out and ate and talked and listened to music until it was time to go.

I had Assi and Ollie with me on the drive back into town—except Assi was up front this time—and I spent most of it wondering about the drop-off routine. Like, should I make some excuse to walk her up to her house? But would her mom be watching? So maybe I should kiss her good night in the car? (With Ollie there? Too weird!)

Assi solved it for me. When we pulled up in front of her place she turned toward Ollie in the backseat—while resting her hand on my thigh—and said, "Thanks for inviting me. This was way more fun than I'd expected." She gave my leg a squeeze and let go as she turned back toward me. "You too, J. Thanks. This was awesome." Then she got out and went inside her house.

Ollie moved to the front seat and we headed home. After we'd driven a couple of blocks she said, "See? That wasn't so bad. I don't know what the big deal was about taking Assi. So . . . what did you guys do after you dropped me at Sophie's?"

"Went to grab a bite." I realized how stupid that sounded in light of all the amazing food at the party. "I, uh, wanted to talk to her about a couple of things."

I was expecting her to ask what we talked about and I was deciding between *school stuff* and *website stuff*, when she simply said, "Where?"

"Where what?"

"*Where* did you get food?"

"Oh. Happy Jack's." Then I added, "Just a couple of burgers and cokes," as if that somehow made it seem normal.

She studied me for a minute. "You guys are totally an item." It wasn't really a question.

"I don't know." I thought about it. "No, yeah. We are."

"I *thought* you two looked pretty cozy back by that fireplace." She broke out in a big grin. "J—that's awesome! And she's awesome, too . . . the more I get to know her, the more I like her."

"Yeah, she does that."

"So why were you hiding it . . . doing the 'just friends' thing?"

I shrugged. "I don't know. I didn't want it to be weird. With you and Seth, I mean. Like, if she and I were all over each other . . ."

". . . then we might freak out," she finished. "Which is probably why Mom and Dad never showed affection in front of us."

"What are you talking about?" We used to catch them kissing in the kitchen all the time, usually over a sinkful of dishes. When you're ten you think it's gross. When you're twelve you roll your eyes and tell them to knock it off. By fourteen you ignore it. And now, in hindsight—

"Exactly," she said, interrupting my thoughts. "No permanent damage done, right?" She paused. "And besides, I don't think Seth likes me 'in that way.' "

"You're kidding me, right?"

"No. So save me the trip to Happy Jack's and the ten dollars and just pretend we're there, okay? Enlighten me." She gave me a look that was more serious than puppy. "Please."

"Um, if by 'in that way' you mean when a guy thinks you're cute *and* smart *and* funny *and* nice *and* he has definite romantic inclinations toward you . . . then yeah, he likes you 'in that way.' " I shrugged. "Not that he's even close in his opinion of you, but that's his problem."

"So, uh . . . why—"

"—doesn't he show it? Let's see." I started counting on my fingers. "You're a freshman. He's a junior. He's your older brother's friend so maybe he feels weird about that whole thing. You're a fashionista and he lives in jeans and T-shirts, so maybe he feels he doesn't fit in or maybe he's intimidated. And I'm guessing you haven't given him any definite signs so maybe he has a fear of rejection. Remember, he's almost as much of a nerd as I am." I cleared my throat. "And—as long as we're supposedly in the no-lie zone—maybe because I asked him not to."

"You *what*?"

"Hey, I was just looking out for you." I explained the whole deal about making Seth promise not to hit on her, and why. "But I'm pretty sure we're beyond that now anyway."

"Why?"

"Because just the other day—during our regularly scheduled 'Olivia Deever' talk—he mentioned that yeah, he could see the possibility of someday thinking about you 'in that way.'"

"So do me a favor . . ."

If I hadn't been driving I would have folded my arms and squinted. "Yeah . . . ?"

"Clarify. To him. About that promise no longer applying."

"You're kidding, right?"

She shook her head. "I'm serious as a fucking heart attack." Wow. I pulled over, right then and there. "What are you *doing*?" she asked.

Instead of answering I sent a text, then handed her my phone to read. dude—i think u know this but just to clarify, ur promise to never hit on my bratty sister no longer applies (although god knows why anyone would want to). so fly free, young bird—and don't say I didn't warn u

She handed it back. "Thanks, J—you're a good brother."

"Remember this moment." I paused. "And something tells me I owe you, anyway. For, uh"—I jerked my thumb over my shoulder, back toward where we'd dropped off Assi—"you know."

"What?" She looked at me with a *Who . . . me?* face, but there was a nano-crinkle.

"Shut up," I said.

"You shut up." She nodded at my phone. "Anyway, thanks. And I think Mom would approve. . . ."

* * *

I actually *like* thinking about my mom, as long as I'm remembering all the good stuff. Which is part of why I miss her so much. She *got* me. Me and my nerdiness and the goofy way my brain works. Whenever I was in a new situation and feeling stressed—like the first day of middle school or joining a new soccer team or whatever—she always found a way to make me feel okay about it. And that was awesome.

But when someone asks me to "talk about it," they usually mean "talk about when your mom died." And that was the complete opposite of awesome.

Because I was there. I was the *only* one there. Dad had been camping out at the hospital all day, and he'd brought me down for a visit. (Usually the visits were more like he'd take us to the hospital cafeteria and we'd all get dinner—because no one felt much like cooking—and then we'd stop by and see Mom for a while before he took us home. Half the time she was asleep, and we all knew better than to wake her once she was sleeping. That was the only time she didn't hurt.)

That evening was a Friday and it was just me and Dad. Ollie was staying overnight with a friend—she did that a lot when Mom was sick. Dad had to go do something, I don't even remember what, and he offered to take me home while he ran his errand. But Mom was awake so I said I'd stay with her until he got back and then we could go home together.

It was around nine o'clock and Mom and I were in her hospital room talking—about stupid stuff like how I was adjusting to high school—and she was getting tired. I knew the signs . . .

she'd talk less and listen more, then she'd just nod between my sentences without talking at all, and then she'd drift off.

But this was different.

Labored breathing. The phrase is so overused it's a cliché, but a lot of people don't know what it actually looks like. If you really want to experience it, lie flat on your back and have someone put a sack of cement on your chest. Then breathe. Or try to.

That's what my mom was doing. It seemed like it took all her strength to draw in her breath, then it was forced out of her body in a quick gasp.

I stood up, freaked out by it. "Are you okay?" Which may have been the single stupidest thing I've ever said. She reached out and took my hand.

"I'm fine." She took a couple more of those strange breaths. "I love you, J." *breath* "And Ollie." *breath* "And your dad." *breath* "Very much."

"I know, Mom. We love you too." She didn't answer. She concentrated on her breathing, like someone attempting to do fifty push-ups but they're stuck at forty-nine, trying with everything they have to lift themselves just one more time.

I panicked. *"Mom."*

"Please . . ." *breath* ". . . don't . . ." *breath* ". . . forget me."

I just stared at her as she took another breath.

"Promise me . . ."

I nodded furiously. "I promise, Mom. I promise! But you can't—"

She looked at me and took one last, labored breath.

Fifty.

Somewhere in the back of my mind I heard a buzzer go off and a machine start beeping—then a nurse rushed into the room, followed quickly by another one—but I barely noticed any of it. *She's gone,* this little voice in my head kept repeating. *She's gone forever.* I stumbled out into the hallway and called my dad. It all seemed so unreal . . . it was hard to punch in his number because my hands were shaking so bad. I remember standing there, crying my eyes out—with some guy sitting in a chair nearby—and finally blurting out, "Dad, Mom died." Just three little words.

Then I went back into her room where the doctor showed up and officially set the time of death. At you-know-when.

That's what I was thinking about when my phone buzzed. (Actually, I'd been lying in bed trying *not* to think about it, as I realized that the second anniversary of her death was coming up. Which only made it that much worse.) I looked at my phone. Assi. I pulled the covers over my head and put her on speaker—turned way down low—with the phone lying right in front of my face.

"Hi," I said, barely above a whisper.

"Hi," she said quietly. "So . . ."

"So . . . ?"

"Um, how are you?"

"I'm fine."

"No you're not."

"Okay, you're right. When you called, I wasn't doing so well."

"Why? Did it have anything to do with us? Tonight?"

"What? No! In fact, you're the most amazing thing in my life."

She got really quiet. "So . . . ?"

"So . . ." I took in a breath and let it out slowly. "Something came up and I was thinking about my mom. About her dying, I mean. I was trying to get it out of my mind when you called."

"I'm so sorry. Really . . ."

"Thanks, but don't be. When I looked at my phone and saw it was you, I suddenly felt better." I cleared my throat. "So, how are *you* doing? We didn't really get a chance to talk, after . . ."

"After our research?"

"Yeah. That. But before you say anything I need to tell you I'm in bed—in the dark—talking to you on speaker. Under the covers so no one else can hear. Just in case you were wondering."

She laughed. "Oh my God, I'm doing the exact same thing!" She paused, and I could hear the smile in her voice as she spoke slowly. "So, *yeah* . . . "

"I agree. So, um, *yeah* . . . "

"So . . . ?"

The heck with it. "Okay, I'll go first." I felt like I was back in the no-lie drive-by, which I discovered was way easier to do in the dark, under the covers, than sitting in your car. "I had an awesome time tonight. Once we got everything straightened out at Happy Jack's, I mean. And at the party, too." I paused. "And this might sound stupid, but I started missing you the minute you got out of the car."

"That doesn't sound stupid at all," she said, really softly. "In fact, I'm super happy to hear that because I almost crawled all over you right there in your car. For the same reason. But I didn't really want to do that in front of your sister."

"She knows."

"She does?"

I laughed. "I think she sort of knew before we did. But anyway, I told her on the way home."

"Told her what?"

"That we're kind of an item."

She laughed. "That's so old-fashioned."

"I know, right? But that's what Ollie called it, so . . ." I was getting off track. "Who cares what you call it, are you okay with it? The concept, I mean. If we're, like, a thing?"

"Yeah. I mean yes, absolutely. Completely. And I like the term *item*." She got really quiet again, but in a totally different way. "I mean, if you think about the topology of it, it's actually sort of . . . refreshing."

Man, there is *nothing* as sexy as an intelligent woman.

CHAPTER 30

*And in this language will be proposed to the lens that with
which, in the end, photography must be concerned—time,
and place, and the works of man.*
—Dorothea Lange

"I'M HUNGRY," OLLIE ANNOUNCED FROM THE BACKSEAT. For a second I was reminded of our family trips where the four of us would be going down the highway—sometimes in this very car—and every hour someone would announce a burning need for either food or a restroom.

"Anyone else?" I asked.

"Some coffee might be nice," Assi said, sitting next to me.

I looked at Seth in the rearview mirror. He shrugged. "I could eat."

"There's a coffee place up in Soledad next to a bunch of fast-food joints, right off the freeway," I said.

"You're right," Ollie added a few seconds later, looking at her phone. "How'd you know?"

"Dad and I made this trip a bunch of times and we always stopped there. It's at the halfway point, and it's right at an off-ramp."

"Sounds like a plan."

Speaking of plans, the first piece of the puzzle was the money. Once I'd finally decided to do it, I'd started looking online and prices were all over the place. There was no standard Blue Book listing for stuff like this, it was whatever someone thought it might be worth—asking prices started at "high" and went up to "forget about it." Luckily I'd been working crazy hours all break, which helped a little bit. Between that, what I had at home, and my savings in the bank, I could scrape together a few thousand dollars. Ollie probably would have pitched in if I'd asked, but she was so broke she made me look rich. Being a fashionista comes with a price.

The second piece was learning to ride a motorcycle. I watched everything I could online, then started looking for someone who could teach me. I didn't have to look far—it turned out Seth's older sister Nicole rode one. I didn't have a lot of spare cash lying around so I sent her copies of the head shots I'd done for Ollie, Sofia, and Chloe, and told her I'd swap a photo session for some lessons. And she actually went for it.

When she'd said I was good to go after a few lessons I was

jazzed until she continued, "By that I mean you're good enough to get out on the road and learn. Barely. So take it easy and avoid stuff like nighttime riding and hiking someone else for a while. And for God's sake, stay off the freeway—that's not the place to learn." I just nodded, like *No worries.*

The third piece was the big annual Brit Bike show, on the weekend before school started back up after winter break. My dad might have asked me to go with him, like we used to, but he had to go to LA for a work conference. He used to go on business trips three or four times a year, but he stopped after Mom died— this was his first trip away in a couple of years.

Once I thought this crazy idea was even a possibility, I got with Seth and we hatched a plan: I'd drive the two of us up and he'd drive the car back. That—plus my riding lessons with Nicole—was the entire plan. Pretty simple. But then Ollie found out and immediately invited herself along. Duh. And of course Assi got wind of it and ended up demanding to go—double duh—and it morphed into a road trip.

It turned out having the girls with us was really helpful once we got there. The times I'd gone with my dad, we'd spend the whole day looking at every bike in the show. This was different. *I* sure didn't want to waste an entire day looking at old British motorcycles, and the others had even less interest. Plus it was at least a three-hour drive back to Vista Grande, so I was on a mission—find what I was after and get going.

But the place the show was held—the expo halls at the fair-grounds in San Jose—was huge, filled wall-to-wall with bikes and thousands of people walking around looking at them. You could spend hours scouring the place and not see everything.

Before we'd left I'd taken a pic of the poster in the garage. When we got inside the show I held up my phone and said, "This is what we're looking for." It was a midcentury classic British single-cylinder motorcycle—a 441 Victor Special, made by BSA during the mid-to-late sixties—with the gas tank painted yellow. The perfect yellow. I texted the pic to each of them and told them what it was. "The good news," I added, "is they were all made in yellow. So if it's not yellow, it's not it. But anything with a yellow tank deserves a closer look."

"What if we split up and each take a different section of this place?" Assi said. "We'll text you if we find anything."

"That's a great idea. Everyone good with that?"

The others nodded and we headed out. I went to my wing and started going up and down the rows of motorcycles. After a while I began to get at least a glimmer of what my dad saw in them. It wasn't the performance or the reliability or anything practical like that. I mean, Nicole's bike—a midsize Suzuki—beat the pants off everything in the room when it came to that stuff, but it just looked like a machine. These things were more like works of art.

Unfortunately, none of them was the particular work of art I was looking for. After an hour of striking out we met up for lunch at the big concession area, grabbing burgers and burritos and sitting at the long tables. As I sat down next to Assi I asked, "Anything to report?"

"Nope. Not about the bike, at least. But Ollie and I squeezed in time for a nice talk."

I glanced over to where Ollie sat with Seth, a couple tables away. "About . . . ?"

She grinned. "Not you, if that's what you're worried about."

"I'm not worried." I was worried. "So . . . ?"

"About your mom, among other things."

A hundred thoughts went through my mind, but they all sort of led to the same place. "I'm glad. But surprised. She doesn't ever seem to want to discuss it."

Assi gave me a funny look. "She says she got the idea to talk to me from you."

"Yeah, well . . . I just thought maybe you guys might have . . ." I sort of trailed off as I shrugged.

"I know what you meant. You're a good brother. And a good boyfriend." She reached over and held my hand. "Losing your mom really affected her . . . I think she's just good at covering it up. Maybe that's why she threw herself into the whole fashion thing, and maybe her schoolwork, too. To keep busy . . . to give her something to do."

I thought of my dad, out in the garage, bringing old things back to life. Then I thought of myself, standing on the corner night after night with my camera, looking for . . . something.

"I have this theory that everyone has some minor-league superpower," I said. "And I think one of yours is providing clarity. Among other things." I glanced around the room, then leaned closer to her and said, "This is like a bizarre science fiction movie where we're back at the high school cafeteria . . . except everyone's gotten *really old*."

She gazed at the crowd. We were definitely the youngest people in sight. "I wonder which one's the middle-aged version of Kennedy Brooks?"

I looked around. "There she is!" I gestured toward a woman in her forties or fifties who'd gone full cougar, dressed in her twenties and wearing makeup in her teens, with hair blonder than Ollie's. She was with a guy who was doing the same basic thing, squeezed into a leather jacket he'd probably had since high school.

Assi laughed. "Yeah, and she's with Beal Wilson." Then something caught her eye and she grew quiet. "Oh my God," she whispered as she tugged at my sleeve. "There's *us*."

It was an older couple, in their seventies at least. They were sitting at a crowded table, but they only noticed each other. He helped her unwrap her sandwich and they started eating, then she made a joke and wiped his mouth with her napkin and they both laughed.

I felt myself suddenly starting to tear up. The combination of seeing them and thinking about my parents and how they'd never have that—never be able to grow old together—and then thinking about Assi and me . . .

I reached over and took her hand. I started to say something but I was having a hard time with it, so I just looked at her and squeezed her hand. She squeezed back and nodded. It felt like a whole conversation without words. Then she fanned at her eyes and looked away.

* * *

After another hour or so of nothing, I finally got a text. hey j, i think i found one!!! west hall 2nd row from back. nice one—hope you saved your pennies It was from Ollie. I finished walking the row I was on, then headed over.

She was right. It was really nice. I'd heard my dad use the phrase *nut-and-bolt restoration* before, but this was the first time I really got it. This thing looked like it was right off the showroom floor even though it was over a half century old. And it was priced like it, too. There was no way.

I was pretty bummed, thinking we should just pack up and go home, when my phone buzzed. It was Assi. is this it? i'm way back in the far right-hand corner. i think he'll deal . . . She'd sent a pic. Yup, it was the right model. bingo! on my way, I sent back.

As I walked up I wished I hadn't just seen the perfect one, because this one suffered in comparison. I don't mean it was wrecked or dented up or anything, and judging it against the pic of the bike in the poster it seemed like it was all there, with all the original parts. It's just that this one looked like a motorcycle that had actually been ridden quite a bit—and then maybe hosed off before it was taken to the show—as opposed to looking like it came out of a museum.

After looking it over, I turned to the guy sitting nearby and got why Assi said he might haggle. He didn't have the millionaire-cowboy look of the guy selling the uber-polished bike. He looked more like my dad when my dad was puttering in the garage on

a Saturday, and he had a small stable of other bikes with him—
most of them with the same well-worn look.

"Does it run?" I asked.

He just tilted his head toward the sign in front of it . . .

BSA 441 VICTOR SPECIAL

ALL ORIGINAL

RUNS STRONG

I nodded and bent over to inspect it closer. Like I even had a
clue as to what I was looking for. Mostly I was stalling, thinking
Am I really going to do this? But the more I thought about it, the
more it felt right. I mean, regardless of the price, in some ways
this one was better for my dad. Because he didn't want something that was already museum-quality. He wanted to roll up his
sleeves and restore it himself, "becoming one with the machine,"
like he always said. Plus, they *weren't* the same price. Not even.
The sticker on this one said $3K, which was less than half the
other one. I could afford this one—barely. (I never thought I'd be
grateful I'd spent most of the last few weeks selling popcorn at
the movies, but at this point every dollar counted.)

Finally I stood up from the bike. Assi walked over. "What do
you think?" she asked quietly.

"I hate to say it, but this is probably as good as I'm going to
get. I saw another one that was fully restored but it was seventy-
five hundred bucks."

She looked at me. "If you want, I could lend you a little and
maybe—"

I held up my hand. "You're awesome, but no. Plus, for my
dad the restoring is half the fun."

"So do you want to get this one?"

I nodded. "I think I do." And as I said it, I realized it was true.

"Then offer him twenty-seven hundred."

So I did—under the condition that it started and ran fine—and he took it. We wheeled it outside to fire it up, and the first big difference I noticed was that, unlike Nicole's bike, this thing didn't have an electric start. He stuck in the key and went through an elaborate routine where he pushed this and pulled that and jiggled something else, then finally stomped on the kick starter a few times and it roared to life.

As soon as it started Assi held out her hand. "Give me your car keys," she said, yelling to be heard over the engine. I handed them over. "I'll be back in a while," she added, and took off.

The guy shut it off. "We still need to sign the forms," he said, nodding back toward the building. We went in and did the paperwork and I handed over the cash.

"You need to teach me how to start it," I said after we were done with everything.

He gave me some confusing instructions about a "tickler" and a "valve-lifter" and "top dead center," then must have seen my face because he said, "When you get home, look on YouTube—they've got tons of videos showing how to start one of these old thumpers."

"If I can't start it now, I'm not *getting* home."

"Didn't you bring a truck?"

I shook my head. "I'm riding it home."

"Where's that?"

"Vista Grande."

He did a slow shake of his head. "You got balls, son. Gotta give you that." He sighed and jerked his thumb back toward the door. "Let's go."

It was way more complicated than starting a lawn mower, which up until then was the only engine I'd ever started manually. It took me a while to get it right, then I made him hang around until I did it twice more. After it fired up the third time he gave me a little two-fingered salute and said, "I need to get back to my bikes," then went inside.

I decided to take it for a quick spin around the back parking lot before I went to find the others. That's when I realized that not only did the British drive on the wrong side of the road, they also shifted on the wrong side of the bike! Seriously, the gearshift lever and the rear brake pedal were swapped, left and right. And forget about blinkers—there weren't any. And—once I talked my right foot into shifting instead of braking—I discovered this thing had four gears instead of six like Nicole's Suzuki, and they were spaced a *lot* farther apart. Man, there was going to be a big learning curve, all the way home . . .

Just then Assi stepped out the back door with my helmet in her hand, which she must have retrieved from my car. And another one in her other hand. She caught me staring at the second helmet and said, "Just bought this inside. I'm going with you."

"Not a good idea. I barely know how this thing works, the shifter and the brake are on the wrong sides of the bike, and I'm not great at starting it yet."

"In that case, you definitely need me along."

"Thanks, but you're probably better off going back with Seth and Ollie, because—"

"They already left," she said. "I told them to take off when I gave them the keys to your car, and said we'd see them at Seth's tonight." She hefted her helmet and grinned. "Let's go."

CHAPTER 31

*One should really use the camera as though tomorrow
you'd be stricken blind.*
—Dorothea Lange

HAVING ASSI ON THE BACK WAS TERRIFYING AT FIRST. I'D
never hiked anyone before and it took me a while to adjust to
the extra weight, and cornering was pretty scary until I finally
figured out I could just roll on the throttle and lean into it like
normal. But all that was balanced out by having her right up
against me with her arms wrapped around me. Believe me, I got
used to *that* in no time. What wasn't so cozy was flying down
the 101 in a T-shirt. Assi hadn't brought anything really warm so
I'd given her my jacket. So having her cuddle up close behind me
had a practical side too.

Adding to the fun factor was the ride being a lot rougher
than I'd expected. The suspension was really stiff and you could
feel every bump in the road, plus that thing *shook*. There was one

little mirror on the left side, but the bike vibrated so bad once you got over twenty miles an hour that the image was just a blur.

We'd gotten a late start after all the paperwork and starting lessons, and by the time we'd been on the road for an hour or so the sun went down and it started to get cold. I switched on the lights and learned another lesson—the electrical system wasn't exactly state-of-the-art. The faster I went the brighter the headlight was, but when I backed off the gas it was just a dim yellow glow. Luckily I had to ride this thing about as fast as it would go just to keep up with freeway traffic, so as long as I kept it at full throttle I could almost see the road.

Until it started raining.

It began with a sprinkle, but I figured it'd let up soon so I kept going. Well, you can scratch "weatherman" off my list of possible career choices because the more we rode the harder it rained, until we were slogging through a downpour. And if anything, the traffic was getting worse. There weren't necessarily more cars, but now it seemed like half the vehicles on the road were big trucks.

"This sucks!" Assi yelled behind me.

I nodded, but we were in the middle of nowhere—in the rain and the dark—with no shelter in sight. I didn't really see any choice except to keep going, keeping an eye out for a gas station or fast food or anywhere we could get out of the weather. We were near the end of a long downhill and I was in the right lane, staying a couple hundred feet back from the big rig in front of us because it was throwing up all kinds of crap from the wet road.

Passing on our left was another big truck that was hauling

something under a tarp. I don't know what was going on with it—maybe his mirrors were bad or he couldn't see our shitty little light in the rain or he was drunk or *something*—but all of a sudden he started moving into our lane. I don't mean drifting over the line a little, I mean he fucking pulled into our lane like we weren't even there. It all happened so fast. I didn't have time to get on the brakes—which probably saved our lives because there was someone behind us—so I just ran off the road, to avoid getting *shoved* off the road by this asshole. At sixty miles an hour.

The dirt shoulder was really rough and bumpy. It was all I could do to hang on to the bike, and Assi had me in a death grip—I couldn't really see what was coming up. We went over some deep ruts and through a couple of bushes before I finally got it under control and we came to a stop.

"Are you okay?" I had to yell over the pounding rain.

She nodded.

I pointed up the road. "Is that an overpass?"

"I don't know. Maybe."

"Okay. Hang on." I waited until I couldn't see any headlights behind us, then pulled back onto the road until we got to the overpass. I pulled over underneath it and took my helmet off.

"Holy shit," I said, still stunned by the whole thing. "Are you sure you're okay?"

"I'm fine." She got off the bike and looked at me. The front of my shirt and pants were totally soaked. "You're shivering."

I was trying to think of a clever reply when she took out her phone and started scrolling. "There's a motel three miles ahead. We need to get somewhere warm and dry."

I didn't argue—I was so cold I felt numb.

"Try to get a room next to the laundry," she said when we got there. She pointed toward the strip mall next to the motel. "I thought I saw a CVS over there . . . I'm going to get some supplies. Need anything?"

"Uh . . . a new pair of underwear after that truck pulled into our lane?"

"Yeah, no kidding. Text me our room number when you get one." She gave me a quick kiss. "Then climb in the shower and warm up. And leave your wet clothes outside the bathroom."

Our room . . .

The old guy at the front desk looked at me funny when I walked into the lobby, but when I explained we were on a bike and got caught in the rainstorm he suddenly became a lot more sympathetic. "Got a Harley myself," he said. "A Fat Boy. But there's no way I'd be out in this weather. Whatcha riding?"

Who the fuck cares? I'm dying here . . . "Uh, BSA Victor Special."

"A 441? You're kidding me, right?" I just shook my head. "No shit? I gotta see this!" He came around the counter and headed toward the front door. I couldn't believe it—here I was, soaked to the bone, and he wanted to go look at a stupid bike. As soon as he saw it he started talking. "Man . . . when I was a kid, *this* was the bike we all wanted. I can't believe you have one, let alone the guts to ride it on the freeway." He laughed, like it was the funniest joke ever. "At night! In the goddamn rain!"

Ha fucking ha. "Yeah, that's me—pure genius. Uh . . . do you suppose I could get a room? We're pretty cold, and—"

He finally got it and headed back inside. "Oh, sorry. Sure, we'll fix you right up."

"Near the laundry, if you can?"

"Sure, no problem . . ."

He was actually pretty cool after that. Like he didn't ask about my age or ID or who the other half of "we" was. Just had me fill out the form and said "Don't worry about it" when I told him I didn't know the license number of my bike. "It's not like there's another one of those here tonight," he added, laughing.

As I walked into the room I texted Assi. room 112—next to laundry. i'll leave it unlocked

great! is there a microwave?

yeah. hitting the shower—see u soon

ok! ☺

Ten minutes later I was feeling like I might survive. At first even lukewarm water made my skin tingle and burn, but eventually I could stand warmer water and began to thaw out. Once I felt halfway human again my thoughts turned to . . . you know. Okay, I was excited, but also totally nervous.

I mean, we were going to be in a motel room.

Together.

Overnight.

Man, this was brand-new territory for me. Like, what was she expecting? What was *I* expecting?

I got out and dried off, then wrapped the towel around my waist and left the bathroom . . . to get hit in the face with a package.

"Here," Assi said. "Not that you're not cute in that towel, but I think this'll work better." I tore open the plastic wrapper—it was a thin white terry-cloth robe. "Sorry, but that was the cheapest one they had."

"No, this is great." I looked at her. She had that drowned-rat thing going on too. I pointed behind me. "You need to get in there and get warmed up."

I didn't have to ask her twice. She went into the bathroom, then cracked the door and handed out her wet clothes. "Your clothes are next door in the dryer. Maybe put these in along with them? There's a pile of quarters on the dresser . . ."

"Sure."

I put on the robe and took her clothes to the laundry to throw them in the machine. Then I went back to the room and took a look at the small stash of supplies she'd bought. By the time she came out of the bathroom—wearing a robe like mine, with her hair up in a towel—I'd heated up some chicken soup and had it on the little table, along with a sandwich I'd split in half.

I pulled back her chair and waved at the table with a flourish, like a waiter at a fancy restaurant. "Soup and sandwich, milady? Nothing better when you're cold and hungry." I dropped the act. "At least, that's what my mom always said."

"I think she was right," Assi said as we sat down to eat. We must have been hungry because neither of us said anything for a couple of minutes.

Finally Assi asked, "So, what was she like?"

"Who?" I asked absentmindedly, still concentrating on my food.

"Your mom."

I stopped eating. "Oh." I put down my plastic spoon. "Um . . . she was great."

Assi lifted an eyebrow. "I pretty much knew that, seeing as how she helped raise you."

I didn't say anything, until she fired up the look she'd given me when I took her portrait. Hard to hide from that. "So . . . imagine you're in a foreign country. Not on vacation, but living there. Permanently. Only you don't speak the language, and no one there speaks yours—no matter how long you study it, you never quite get the hang of it. Imagine how that might feel."

She nodded again. *Still* serious. "My guess is you'd feel incredibly lonely."

"But now imagine there's one person who speaks both languages. They're like a bridge between you and everyone around you. They can tell you what everyone else is saying . . . what they're thinking. And they can understand what *you're* thinking, and help you to get that across to everyone else."

"That'd be awesome."

"It is. Or at least it was." I was quiet for a minute. "My mom was really cool. I mean, she had synesthesia and could geek out on the relationship between abstract things like colors and letters and numbers, so she totally got the nonlinear way my brain sometimes works. But she also had Ollie's social sense—she always had good advice for when I was in some awkward situation and didn't know how to deal. And even if there was no good answer, she could make me feel like at least *someone* out there understood me. Like I wasn't all alone."

Assi didn't say anything, she just watched me. "So when she died," I went on, "not only was my mom gone, but there was no one left who could even help me talk about it. Like, how do you tell people that your mother was the most important person in your world? That she was your translator, your bridge, your interpreter? I mean, I was fucking *lost* for a while. And guys aren't allowed to talk about shit like that. So . . . they don't."

"And I'm guessing that after enough of that," Assi said quietly, "you don't have any friends left. Not real ones, anyway."

Bingo.

"Not that I had a lot to begin with, but no, you don't." Then I took a breath and told her something I'd never told anyone else, ever. I told her about the night my mom died. All of it. I tried to explain how it felt, being the only one with her when she took her last breath. When I finished we were both quiet, then she seemed to gather her thoughts.

"You've done so much this past year . . . Your photography. The website. The 9:09 Project, which seems to have a life of its own now. And"—she caught my eye and held it—"there's us."

I just nodded.

"And on top of all that, you have friends now. Real friends. People who care about you. So I think your mom would be really happy for you." She fanned at her eyes for a second and her voice got a little wavery. "And . . . and super proud of you."

Hearing that last part put a massive lump in my throat. I suddenly realized that *that*—more than anything—was what I needed to hear. To feel. To *believe*, in my gut.

And now I did.

"You're the absolute best," I said when I could finally talk again. "And you know what she'd be most proud of?"

"What?"

I pulled her around the table and onto my lap and kissed her. Which, when you're both wearing nothing but robes, is even more awesome than it sounds. "The fact that I'm with you. Oh my God, she would have *loved* you."

She looked down and said, "Insert self-deprecating reply here," then stood up. "I need to make a phone call."

She went into the bathroom while I cleaned up our little dining area, then I sent Ollie and Seth a quick text so they wouldn't worry when we didn't show up tonight. Five minutes later she walked out.

"I'm guessing you called home?" I asked.

"Yeah."

"Everything okay?"

She nodded. "I didn't even lie—I just gave her a carefully edited version of the truth."

"I don't want you to get in any trouble. I feel bad enough about getting you soaked and half frozen and stuck here in the middle of nowhere. I didn't really know what I was getting into and—"

She held up a hand. "Stop. I pretty much forced you into taking me, remember?" She laughed. "Here's a little secret—when I got on the back of your bike I was sort of praying for rain. Although getting run off the road by a truck sure wasn't part of the plan." She kind of shivered. "And I had no idea it would be so *cold*."

"You're still cold?" I looked around for the thermostat. "Do you want me to turn up the heat?"

She shook her head. "Can you hold me?"

I could, and I did. And a whole flock of thoughts flew through my brain.

"I . . . I know we're going out, and we're like a thing, but . . ." She froze. *"But?"*

"But I want you to know that you're more than that. *Way* more. You're . . ." I felt totally awkward, not sure how to say what I was feeling. "It's not like *Well, no one really comes close* or something. Because you're *it*. You're in a set all by yourself."

She smiled. "Well, now that you put it in sexy mathematical terms like *that* . . ."

"You know what I mean." I pulled back a bit to look at her. "Don't you?"

She raised an eyebrow. "So are you saying, Mr. Deever, that you envision yourself in a long-term, exclusive relationship with one such as I?"

"Yes, I'm saying that. Exactly. Well, there's no *such as* you." I pulled her closer. "There is only you."

CHAPTER 32

The visual life is an enormous undertaking,
practically unattainable.
—Dorothea Lange

WHEN WE GOT TO SETH'S THE NEXT DAY TO STASH THE bike in his garage, Ollie and I had an interesting discussion. Not about where Assi and I had spent the night. Not about getting our story straight in case Dad asked about our weekend when he got back on Monday. Not about how she was doing about Mom, after opening up a little with Assi. And not about the fact that she seemed more proprietary about Seth in some indefinable way.

It was about the bike.

I'd parked it in the back corner of Seth's garage and Ollie was checking it out. *"You know . . . ,"* she said slowly, like whatever it was, she didn't really want to bring it up.

"Yeah?"

"Well, I know it's perfect in the picture and everything, *but . . .*"

"But what?" I was pretty sure I knew, but I wanted to hear it from her.

"But it's not the perfect yellow, is it?" she finally said. "It's a little muddy. Like maybe it has some brown or dark green in it?"

I nodded. "Yeah, I think you're right."

"So . . ." She looked concerned. "Do you think Dad'll mind?"

It's kinda late for that now. But I didn't say that. "I guess we'll find out."

Later that evening at my house, Seth and I had an even more interesting discussion. Ollie had disappeared to do whatever fashionistas do when school's starting back up the next day, and I told Seth my plans for the 9:09 website.

"You *what?*"

"I want to retire the site," I said.

"Why? It's doing better than ever . . ."

"Exactly. It's accomplished what I set out to do. It's reached its natural end point." I could tell he didn't get where I was coming from. And to be fair, a month ago I wouldn't have either. "Look at it this way—if my mom were here *right now,* what would she want me to do? Stay and take a picture on that same stupid corner for the rest of my life—like I'm paying some sort of penance—or progress to other things?"

"Yeah, but . . ."

"I've gotten more out of that project than I ever expected, and it's made me feel more connected to my mom than ever. Feels like it's time to move on."

"But . . ." He got quiet. "Look, I don't want to say *But what about the children?* but, well . . . you've helped a lot of people deal with whatever shit they're going through. Just like the project helped you."

I nodded. "Yup . . . and you had that part figured out way before me. So I'm thinking we could convert the site to a *Start Your 9:09 Project thing.*"

"We've already got a little do-it-yourself page on the site."

"Sure, but imagine if the whole website was about *that,* not about me and my photography. So people can sign up, dedicating some kind of creative project to the memory of a loved one. And maybe build some sort of community around it, where they can give positive feedback and encourage each other somehow . . ."

He started nodding and I could see the wheels turning. "Yeah . . . we could have a forum, where people can post their stuff and ask questions and get help or inspiration or whatever. And maybe a gallery of what different people are doing . . ."

"Yes! That all sounds awesome." I thought back to when I freaked out over forgetting my mom's birthday and first realized I had to put my feelings *into* something. "So . . . I think I have a tag line I want to use at the top of the revamped site."

"What?"

"I want it to say *Put Your Grief to Work.*"

I'd come up with that after talking with Assi about what the project had done for me. Like, using grief as an engine to drive creative work is way better than just boxing yourself off . . . especially if the work helps connect people. And once you realize you're not alone in your grief—that others go through it too—it seems to lighten the burden a little.

Once again I thought of my dad—putting his grief into re-animating old mechanical art that would otherwise be doomed.

And Ollie, with her deep dive into fashion.

And Seth, with his computer wizardry.

And Assi, with her writing.

And . . .

And maybe me, with my photography.

"You see things differently than other people," my mom said as she handed me the book. "And so did she. Some people think that's a curse, but it's not." She gave me her special crinkly half smile. "It's a gift. It makes you unique, and it can make your work unique. *If* you let it."

It was my fourteenth birthday and I didn't completely understand everything she was saying, but as I flipped through the book, something about the images made by Dorothea Lange spoke to me.

"I'm not saying copy her," my mom went on. "But maybe she can be an inspiration . . . anything that makes you want to go out and take photographs is a good thing." That grin again.

"And if you really pay attention, maybe she can teach you how to see without a camera."

But I was a kid, and I *wasn't* really paying attention. Because there's always tomorrow, and the next day, and the next.

Until there's not.

If I'd known I'd only have another year with her, would I have paid more attention? I honestly don't know. But I do know that *now*, I'd give absolutely anything to be able to go back and have that conversation with her again.

It was more than a little weird going to AP lang the next day. I mean, the last time we'd been there Assi and I were totally ignoring each other and not even talking, let alone getting along. And here we were a few weeks later, in that same room . . . same seats, same teacher, same students. But now we *were* talking. And, uh, getting along.

Considering it was the first time we'd seen each other since I'd dropped her off after our road trip the day before, I thought we did a pretty good job of paying attention in class and not making goofy faces at each other or texting or passing notes or whatever. But after class ended Ms. Montinello had us wait behind.

"You know," she said after everyone else had filed out, "I think it's great you two have finally figured out your differences . . ." I was waiting for the *but*, but there wasn't one. Instead she added, ". . . and I have the feeling you're really going to be good for each other."

We looked surprised, because we hadn't really told anyone anything. "Thanks," Assi said, "but, um . . . I'm not exactly sure what you're talking about?"

Ms. Montinello just gave us a look over her glasses like *Who do you think you're talking to?* and waved us out the door.

Once we were outside Assi and I stared at each other. "Didn't you find that almost a little, uh, scary?" I asked.

She smiled. "She *is* the master, after all . . . and underneath it all, I think she's just an incurable romantic."

So yeah, some things changed, but some things didn't. As I was walking across the cafeteria at lunch to meet up with the others, I heard the self-satisfied prevaricating voice that could only belong to one Beal Wilson. "See?" he called out behind me. "I didn't need your help to get a taste of that little hot pocket after all."

I spun on him. He was sitting with Riley at the UL table. "What the *fuck* did you just say . . . ?"

"I said, I didn't need your help to get a taste of that little—"

I cut him off. "I *heard* you. What I meant was, what's the implication of the sewage spewing from your lips?" I was glad Seth and Ollie were already sitting across the room or things could get ugly. Shit, from the way I suddenly felt warm all over, things might get ugly anyway. People were starting to look.

"I'm just saying she and I had a good time at the movies last week, during break. But I guess it was more of a *feel* than a *taste*." He was about to say something else and I took a step forward when his gaze shifted over my shoulder and he stopped cold.

"What's up?" Assi said, coming up behind me.

"This asshole's talking shit about Ollie. Says something happened between them at the movies." Ollie and Assi had gone to the movies a couple of times over break—for free, since I was working there—but this was the first I'd heard anything about Beal being there.

She laughed out loud and looked down at him. "Tell me all about it, lover boy. I was there too, remember?"

He kind of choked. "Well, uh, of course you're going to cover for your friend. But we know what happened, right, Riley?"

Riley shrugged and nodded, then Assi looked up. Tristan was approaching. She took a few steps and cut him off before he could sit with Beal and Riley. "Hey," she said, smiling. "You were at the movies with these guys the other night, right?"

"Uh . . . sure?"

"Cool. So, did anything happen between Beal and the girl I was with? You know, the blond?" She held her hand shoulder-high to indicate Ollie's stature.

"Uh, no," he said, looking confused. "Well, I think he said hi to you guys or something."

"Or something," Assi agreed. "But there was no grab-ass kissy-face stuff or anything?"

He shook his head, surprised. "No."

"You sure?"

He hesitated, then nodded, like he'd decided the truth was the path of least trouble. "Yeah, I'm positive. Nobody touched her."

"Good." She turned back to Beal and Riley, who hadn't said

a word. "You losers choose to act in a way that no girl on the face of the earth would find attractive. Like, *ever*. Then you get all butt-hurt because guess what? *No girls find you attractive.*" She shook her head in disgust. "It's like you're trying to win the Darwin Award for *Least Likely to Pass On Your Genes*." Her glance took in all three of them. "Look, I get that you're nervous around girls. Guess what? We're nervous too. But don't go around treating girls like shit just because you want to look tough in front of your boys, or you'll be celibate for the rest of your short, stupid lives."

She leaned toward Beal, her dark eyes flashing. "Do you know *why* they call me AK-47?"

He tried to look all defiant but his face was bright red, like he'd been slapped.

She nodded over toward where Ollie sat. "Try that shit again and you'll find out in a hurry."

As we were walking away I held my hand out and she slapped it. "That was awesome," I said. "I'd been trying to talk sense into them for weeks, and you got your point across in like thirty seconds. How do you do that?"

She shrugged. "I just try to talk to them in a language they understand."

Later that afternoon I was working in my room—trying to keep up with Assi on our AP language reading—when I got a message from the arts editor at the *VeeGee*.

The issue with the article on you comes out tomorrow. We're printing it tonight, so if you'd like some advance copies you can pick them up at the Vanguard offices any time after 6:00 p.m.

I was going out that evening anyway so I decided to swing by beforehand. They were a little out of the way so I took the car, which turned out to be a good thing.

When I got there they sent me around back to see the production manager. I told him what I wanted and he pointed to dozens of bundles of papers stacked up against the concrete block wall. "Sure, take what you need," he said.

I was going to grab four or five copies, but when I actually saw the issue I went back to the production guy. "This is going to sound crazy, but I'd like a couple of bundles."

He shook his head. "That's two hundred copies. It's a free paper, but even so—don't you think that's getting a little greedy?"

"Yeah, but I'm not going to keep them—I'm going to distribute them." I told him what I had in mind.

"Hmm . . ." He thought for a moment, then shrugged. "Sure, why not—knock yourself out."

I loaded the bundles in the back of the Subaru, then checked the time. Yeah, I could make it to the corner by nine o'clock if I hustled.

Between my job over winter break and everything else, I hadn't done a 9:09 shoot in quite a while. I knew with the project ending there wouldn't be any more and I was okay with that—mostly—but for some reason I wanted to do one final one.

Maybe I just missed standing on the corner, waiting to see what the universe was going to toss my way. Sometimes joyful, sometimes sad, sometimes both. You never knew.

When my alarm buzzed two women were walking toward me, bundled up against the cold. I spoke to the one closer to me. "Hi. Would you mind if I took your photograph? It's for a school project, and—"

"Are you absolutely sure about that?" the other woman asked.

Huh? I looked over at her. *Oops.* "Sorry," I said, feeling kind of stupid. "Sometimes people freak out when I tell them the truth. So I just default to the 'school project' approach and they're usually cool with that."

Ms. Montinello smiled. "That's okay. I understand." She turned to the other woman. "This is Jamison, he's a friend from school." Something about that made me feel sort of like when my dad had promoted me.

The woman put her hand on her heart and nodded, almost a bow. "Hi, I'm Stephanie. And any friend of Grace's is a friend of mine."

I nodded back. *Grace?* Who knew? "Well, uh . . ." I held up my Nikon.

"J's doing a photo project," Ms. Montinello explained to Stephanie. "It's remarkable—I can show you some of his work online later. And apparently we've stumbled upon it at the appointed hour, such that we can serve as his subjects should we so desire."

Stephanie looked at me and read my mind. "Yeah, she's like

this all the time, not just when she's teaching." She looked at Ms. Montinello and they had some sort of silent conversation, then she turned back to me. "And yes, we so desire."

"Great! If you could stand over there . . ."

Okay, it wasn't the most amazing, bizarre, animated photo session ever. But it was authentic, and it was warm, and it was real. And that showed. As I worked I actually forgot she was my teacher and just focused on capturing these two women as they were enjoying their evening together. Near the end Ms. Montinello said to Stephanie, "You know, these might end up on his website, which I understand is quite popular."

I shook my head, still shooting away. "I'm ending that project. You two are my very last 9:09 subjects." Then I mentally reviewed what I'd taken so far. Yeah, there was definitely something there. "But I'm fairly certain this'll end up as a feature on my next project, whatever that is."

Ms. Montinello's eyebrow went up. "Oh?" She and Stephanie had been standing side by side, but she reached out and took Stephanie's hand, moving much closer. She looked at me and nodded. "Well, in that case . . ."

The next day I got to school early to take care of something, then went to class. The morning went pretty smoothly and I even got through most of language more engaged than the day before— and Ms. Montinello was her same old uber-linguistic-teacher-nerd self—but near the end I had a hard time concentrating because I was excited about lunch.

Assi and I walked into the cafeteria together and I studiously ignored the stacks of *VeeGees* placed on plastic chairs just inside each door, leaving it to her to make the discovery. Which she did, almost immediately. She stopped cold inside the door and stared at the top copy like she couldn't believe what she was seeing.

It was the portrait I'd made of her that night at Finch—the one in warm tones of black-and-white that highlighted her eyes—and looking at it I was really glad I'd used a tripod, because they'd printed it big. I mean, it wasn't just *on* the cover—it *was* the cover. The whole thing. With the title across the bottom:

"This Girl Is Not a Kalashnikov," by Jamison Deever

She picked it up, still staring at it. Then she flipped to the article and skimmed it, then back to the cover. "Wow," she finally said. "I'm torn between being super embarrassed and a tiny bit upset and almost giddy . . . all at the same time. And I guess I have you to thank for that." She held up the paper. "When did you decide to submit this photo?"

"Back when you were either hating on me or fucking hating on me. I'm not sure which."

"You mean before the Christmas party at Sofia's?"

I nodded. "Yeah, like a few days before."

She looked down at the paper in her hand. "Then why? I mean, we weren't exactly friendly at that point."

I shrugged. "That didn't change *this*," I said, tapping the image of her face.

Speaking of girls who formerly hated me, just then Kennedy

Brooks came through the door and smiled at Assi. "Must feel pretty good, having your face all over the place."

Assi seemed surprised that Kennedy would talk to her but she managed a shy smile. "Actually, I didn't know anything about it until just now." She glanced at the photo. "But yeah, I guess it feels okay."

"Well, congrats. To both of you." Kennedy nodded at the paper. "It's a wonderful photo."

After she left, Assi and I turned to each other. "Wow."

That evening I went out to the garage and found my dad doing his postjob cleanup. It was like a ritual—whenever he was done with a project he'd clean up the entire workbench and put everything away before he started something else. I was dying to tell him what that something else was going to be, but Ollie and I had decided it had to wait just a little longer.

"Hey, Dad. Guess this means you're finished with the record player, huh?"

"It plays cylinders, not records. But yeah, I just fired it up and it works great."

I nodded. "Cool."

I guess my lack of wild enthusiasm about his antique-phono-whatever was showing. "Have a seat," he said, "and I'll show you." It wasn't exactly a question so I sat on the stool and waited, kicking myself for stopping by the garage in the first place. He set the finished machine on the bench and I had to admit, that thing was pristine. Gorgeous even, like a work of art you'd see in a museum. The wood seemed to glow from the inside out and all the machinery was shiny and bright—like it was new—but it also had this timeless quality about it, like it was saying *I was here long before you, and I'll be here long after.*

But—thinking back to the original pile of rusted, grimy parts scattered across the workbench—the most surprising thing of all was that I'd had no idea in the world it could ever look like this. I found myself respecting my dad even more, that he could see the potential in something that seemed so crappy a few months back. How did he do that . . . ?

He started talking as he turned a crank on the side of the machine. "Before they had disc records, they made recordings on wax cylinders. This is an Edison cylinder player, made around 1900." He paused. "And you're right—they don't sound perfect, that's for sure. But there's something about it. Check this out."

He reached for a small cardboard box shaped like a tube. "With the *really* early cylinders—before they had a way to mass-produce them—they'd make multiple copies of a song by having a bunch of machines like this in the room with the musicians, only the machines were set to record instead of playback. They'd start them all recording, then they'd perform the song and when it was over they'd reload the machines with blank cylinders and do it all again." He removed the cylinder from the padded box, holding it with a couple of fingers inside it. It was light brown, about the size of a toilet paper tube. He pointed to the really fine lines on the surface of it. "These grooves in the wax—where the music lives—were literally formed by the sound energy coming from the singer's mouth." He held it up. "This was in the room with the singer when the song was performed. It's like holding an autographed novel from a hundred years ago—you know the book was held by the author."

He carefully put the cylinder on the player and pushed a lever, which started it spinning. "This is 'Ave Maria,'" he said over his shoulder as he lowered the needle. Some scratchy surface noise came from the phonograph's brass horn, then I heard a thin-sounding violin, accompanied by a quiet, tinkling piano. I thought *Okay, is this it?* Then a woman's voice started singing.

Oh. My. God.

The sound may have been tinny and old-fashioned, but there was something about it that was just so *real.* Everything was so exposed . . . almost like I could see her in the room singing. Like I could hear the rustle of her dress as she moved. Like I could feel exactly what she was feeling. And when she hit those high notes near the end . . .

I don't know why but the song reminded me of my mom. As far as I knew she didn't sing or listen to opera or religious music or whatever. But something about hearing that haunting voice from over a century ago—like a ghost, standing in the garage next to me and my dad—made me feel like my mom was right there with us.

When the music stopped my dad blinked and a drop ran down his cheek. "So no," he said. "It's not perfect. But sometimes perfection is overrated."

CHAPTER 33

The viewer must be willing to pause,
to look again, to meditate.
—Dorothea Lange

THE NEXT DAY AT LUNCH, ASSI AND OLLIE AND SETH AND I were hanging out with a tray full of burgers and fries and everything was fine . . . right up until Assi proclaimed the ketchup-to-fry ratio too low for optimum consumption.

"Be right back," I said as I stood up.

I didn't intentionally walk by Kennedy on my way to the counter, but as I passed near her she got up and came over to me.

"Sophie tells me you and AK-47 are—"

"Her name's Assi."

"Okay, Assi. Well, apparently you guys are officially going out and—"

"Which by the way means *beautiful goddess*," I added.

She just stared at me. I could tell something was on her mind, but at least there was no eye thing or fake smile or "shy" look. "I meant what I said yesterday about the portrait on the cover of the *VeeGee*," she said. "I thought it was really good."

She was clearly upset about something. "But . . . ?"

"But . . ." She let out a breath. "But I thought maybe I would be the one who . . ." She suddenly stopped, then said quietly, "Who do you think told the *VeeGee* about your photo project in the first place?"

That threw me. "*You* did? But why—" It was my turn to stop, while my brain connected the dots. "Oh. You thought if they covered me and my work they'd probably publish some photos of you, since I did that whole portfolio of you."

"Maybe," she admitted. "But . . ." She paused. "But it was more than that." Then she just looked at me and blinked two or three times. "Jesus, J—what happened?" she finally whispered. "I thought maybe . . ." She wagged her finger back and forth between us.

Wow. I could tell she wasn't jerking me around. Which actually got to me, in a bittersweet way.

"You zigged when I zagged, I guess." I looked her in the eye. "But I'm happy where I am. Really happy."

Was she tearing up? Shit. She *was*.

"Look," I said. "I actually think you're really special, and I think there's a lot more going on inside you than you let on." That night on the corner of Fig and Gardena came back to me, and I realized what I saw in that image. Underneath her act—if you bothered looking close enough to see it—she seemed so much older than everyone around her. Like a woman surrounded by twelve-year-old boys. "I'm the last person to give love-life advice, but I think you need to find someone who appreciates you for *you*. For everything about you, not just your looks. Take that college dude . . ."

She rolled her eyes. "Please. Like I haven't heard this shit before? You think he's too old for me, and—"

"No. He's way too young for you."

"What?"

"Emotionally, that guy's an adolescent." I paused. "Remember that girl who always raised her hand in class?"

She nodded slowly, eyes wide.

I pointed at her heart. "She's still there, inside you. And she's fucking amazing. If you want to find someone who's worthy of you, maybe start by looking for someone who's interested in *her*."

She just stood there, staring at me. For a second I thought she was pissed off, and I braced for the blowup. Then I thought she might full-on cry, which would have been even worse. Instead she surprised me. She sort of halfway smiled. Not the fake "look how cute I am" thing, and not her patented hundred-watt grin or some other carefully curated version of herself that she presented to the world. Just a sad little smile. And yeah, it kinda melted my heart.

"Thanks," she finally said. "I mean, you could've totally ripped me a new one after the way I treated you earlier. Or you could have just blown me off. Or kissed my ass, because I might let you take naked pics of me or whatever. But you didn't do any of that. You told me the truth—with no smoke—and you tried to help. Like a friend." She glanced across the room. "Do you think your girlfriend would mind if I gave you a kiss on the cheek?"

"Honestly? She'd fucking kill you. And then probably me."

She actually laughed at that. "Don't tell her, but I think I'm starting to like her. So, consider yourself virtually kissed. You're a good guy, J Deever."

She turned and left, and I walked back to my table. Without any ketchup.

Assi eyed me. "What was *that* all about?"

"I'm not sure. I think maybe she's a little jealous."

"*She's* jealous? Of *me*?" She had that *Yeah, right* look on her face.

"Absolutely. And of me. But mostly, of *us*."

"Uh, not to put too fine a point on it, but she could have any guy she wants." She made a dramatic pause that was half joke, half threat. "Well, except for one."

I ignored it. "Yeah, but what she really wants is what we have. Which is something she's never had." I paused. "I actually kind of feel sorry for her."

Assi full-on snorted at that.

"I'm not kidding," I said. "Remember that 9:09 pic I took of her . . . ?" She nodded. "That sort of sums it up." I told her about Kennedy's boyfriend grabbing her just before I'd taken the photo. "So yeah, I feel sorry for her. I told her I hoped someday she'd find someone who thinks about her the way I think about you." I grinned. "And as much as I hate to admit it, my attraction to you isn't just about how nice or funny or smart you are."

She raised an eyebrow. "It's not, huh?"

I shook my head. "Nope. For what it's worth, Kennedy Brooks—on her best day ever—isn't one percent as hot as you. Not even close." I leaned in and whispered something into her ear. Something completely true . . . if not the sort of thing you went around telling people every day. Then I looked her in the eye and nodded. "Seriously."

She did a great job of not responding but I could see her blush. Finally she picked up one of her fries and examined it.

"Sorry," I said. "I guess I forgot to get more ketchup."

She popped it into her mouth. "These are perfect just the way they are."

My dad opened the envelope and read, *"Go to the most endo-thermic place within our living space . . ."* He face-palmed. "Oh no—not one of these!"

When we were kids Ollie and I used to make up scavenger hunts for our parents' birthdays—with really corny rhyming clues—but it'd been a while since we'd done one. Two years ago my dad didn't have any sort of birthday because it was a week before my mom died and he was pretty much living at the hospital. Then last year—when he'd turned forty—he didn't want much of a celebration, plus we were all thinking it was the one-year mark since Mom had died. But Ollie convinced me that this one definitely called for a scavenger hunt.

He went to the kitchen and opened the freezer, where he found another envelope. *Be wise, beware, use me with care . . .*

And off he went to find another clue in the knife drawer. We ran him all around the house—with a dozen alternating clues from me and Ollie, until he found one that said *Stop this woeful procrastination—seek out twelve-centimeter radiation!*

He opened the microwave to find a key taped to a note that read *Don't do this alone—go check your phone!*

He checked and saw a text . . . 4 b-day 41: 441!

He just looked at it. "Huh?"

Ollie sent him another quick text. look in the **garage, dummy!**

We followed him to the garage, where there was an old sheet covering something big, with an envelope attached. He opened the envelope. It was a card featuring a goofy dog with a helmet and a wagging tongue riding a motorcycle, and we'd signed it *Happy Birthday to the Best Dad in the Whole Wide World! Love, J and Ollie*

He read it and was quiet for a moment. "Thanks," he said. Then he held the card up. "You know, this is all any parent really wants. Well, that and a crazy scavenger hunt with *really* ridiculous clues. I'm almost afraid to see what's under here, because—"

"Just open it!" Ollie and I both said. He pulled the sheet off.

"Oh my God . . ." He stood there staring at it. Until that moment I was worried maybe he'd figured it out, but—unless he was a way better actor than I thought—he was totally taken by surprise. "I don't know what to say."

I pointed to the one on the poster. "It's not quite like that one yet, but I think it has potential."

My dad nodded, almost to himself. "*Oh* yeah. Imagine this after a total nut-and-bolt restoration . . ." He was practically drooling.

I indicated the bike. "I don't know if the paint fades over fifty years or if the color in the poster is off, but in real life it's not exactly the perfect yellow, is it?"

"Well . . ." He studied the bike—*his* bike—for quite a while. Then turned back to me. "It's *my* perfect yellow."

I was thinking about that when he decided to get all parental on me. "And I'm sure you're dying to try and ride it, but I think you ought to wait a couple of years. Besides, this is hardly the bike to learn on." He thought for a second, then got one of his oh-so-clever dad ideas. "I'll tell you what . . . These big singles are a bear—there's quite a technique to getting them going. Especially when they're cold. So, when you can start it, you can ride it." He obviously assumed we'd had it trucked here. "Deal?"

Ollie was shaking her head at him. "Uh, Dad . . ."

I jumped in quick before she could say anything. "Deal!"

I grabbed the key out of his hand, punched the button that opened the garage, sat on the bike, and put the key in the ignition on the left side, under the front of the seat. *Gas on,* I said to myself, seeing a little cartoon picture while I repeated what I'd learned from the guy who'd sold it to me. I reached down on the right side, under the gas tank, and turned the petcock. *Kickstand up.* I kicked the stand up and out of the way. *Find neutral.* I pulled in the clutch, stepped down on the shifter a few times, then put my right toe under it and gently clicked up once. *Flood the carb, so the mixture's rich.* I pushed the tickler button on the right side of the carburetor several times, until I could smell gas. *Get some gas to the engine.* I kicked the starter through a few times, easy. *Ignition on.* I turned the key. *Find top dead center.* I slowly kicked the starter until it met resistance. *Open the valve lifter.* I pulled in on the compression release lever. *Get it just past top dead center . . .* I rotated the starter a little more until I was past the point of compression. *. . . and kick!* I jumped up and stood on the starter for all I was worth, making sure not to open the throttle yet.

Pop. Pop. Pop-pop-pop-pop-popopopopop . . .

I gave it some gas. *Braaaaarrr . . .*

I don't know. Maybe it was the earsplitting sound of that thing as it came to life inside the garage, but I couldn't resist. I pulled in the clutch, stomped it into gear, and—with my dad yelling *Hey, wait a minute!*—I gunned it and roared out of the garage, down the driveway, and into the street.

I went down the block and back, then rode into the garage and shut it off. The silence, as they say, was deafening.

"Well," I said quietly, "I guess I'm almost ready."

My dad stood there for a minute, staring at me. "Where'd you learn to do that?" he finally asked.

For a second I considered saying *Well, I rode it a couple hundred miles with this totally amazing girl on the back, nonstop except for when we got caught in a storm and almost got killed by a crazy trucker and had to stop at a funky little motel where we stayed up*

most of the night talking and making love before we got up the next
morning and finished the wild ride. That's where I learned to handle
this thing . . .

But instead I said, "Do you really want to know?"

Maybe it was the magic of having the bike from his poster
come to life right in front of him, but he just grinned and said,
"Maybe later."

"Good call."

"Hate to interrupt the bro-fest," Ollie said, "but I have to
meet someone." She gave my dad a hug. "Happy birthday, Dad!
You really are pretty awesome . . . for an overage grease monkey."

"I love you too," he said as she walked out of the garage.

After she left I turned to my dad. "Uh, just between you and
me, Ollie's sort of going out with Seth."

He nodded. "I thought that might be the case."

Wow. This was like being in the no-lie drive-by with my dad.
Or maybe I'd been promoted another step. "And, well . . . he
didn't really skip a grade."

"Yeah, I'd sort of figured that one out too."

"So you're not mad I lied to you?"

"No. I was actually happy when you told me that, because
I knew you were trying to help your sister." He got really quiet
for a second, like after we'd listened to that old recording. "That
was always a big deal to your mom—that you and Ollie became
friends. She'd be so happy to see you two becoming partners
in crime rather than you ratting on her or trying to play the
overprotective parent." He cleared his throat. "And speaking of

parental pride, I thought that article about you was great." He pointed to a copy of the *VeeGee* on his workbench.

Seeing that brought something else to mind. "Okay, one more thing. I have a girlfriend."

He nodded at the paper, with the photo of Assi on top. "Her?"

"Yeah." I might've been grinning. "I think you'll really like her. I know Ollie does."

He glanced at the paper again, then nodded thoughtfully. "I'm really happy for you." He let out a sigh, then sat down. "You know, sometimes it feels like Mom died, then I blinked, then you were both grown up."

On the one hand he might have a point, but on the other—if I'm still going by the no-lie rules—there's no way in hell. "Don't worry," I said. "I've got lots more stupid ideas for you to talk me out of."

"Good. Being a dad's the only job I really care about, and I'm not ready to be out of work just yet." Then he pointed to the paper and smiled. "So, when can I meet her? And it'd be good to see Seth again too, now that he's had a status upgrade."

Hmm . . . the anniversary was coming right up. It might be stupid, but this was one idea I wasn't going to give him a chance to talk me out of. "Soon, I think. Real soon."

CHAPTER 34

The contemplation of things as they are, without error of confusion, without substitution or imposture, is in itself a nobler thing than a whole harvest of invention.

—Dorothea Lange

HEY, IT'S BEEN A WHILE. SINCE I'VE BEEN HERE IN PERSON, I mean. I just wanted to say we're not over you—I think about you every day, and always will—and for what it's worth, we're still trying to look out for each other . . . with wildly mixed results! But mostly I want to thank you for getting me started down this path, because it's been an anchor for me and kept me from blowing out to sea. And . . . I think maybe I'm finally learning how to see without a camera.

I placed the small bundle of flowers on her grave and went to get some things from my car.

Assi was the first to arrive, driving her mother's car because she had some supplies to bring. (Earlier we'd debated for all of thirty seconds the idea of having her mom come along, but we'd ended up quickly looking at each other and shaking our heads violently. I mean, just imagine her mom and my dad—would that be like the most cringe-worthy sitcom setup *ever*? Yeah, no.)

She pulled up onto the grass near me and waved. "Can I park here?" she asked as she got out of the car.

"No, but we can unload first."

As I walked over to help I held my finger up to my lips, like *Shh*. She looked around. "Uh, everybody's dead, so . . . ?"

I shook my head. "It's not that. I just don't want to get interrupted." *Again.* "I have something I've been wanting to tell you, but I can't seem to find the right moment."

She grinned. "You snooze, you lose."

"Not always. Remember that night when you—"

She wagged her finger at me. "What's the first rule of Fight Club? If you ever want—"

"Stop." By now I was standing right in front of her. "I only have a few things to say."

I held up a finger. "I'm in love with you. Completely. That should be obvious to anyone within a hundred miles. You're the most alluring, confounding, fascinating person I've ever met, and I find myself thinking about you constantly."

Another finger. "I love *you*. As a person. Everything you are, everything you stand for. You have so much integrity . . . just trying to live up to you makes me a better person."

One more. "And beyond that, I really, really, really *like* you. You're just so much fun to be with, and . . ." I paused for a second as it hit me that this was the key to the whole thing. ". . . and you're absolutely my best friend in the whole world." Pause. "So there."

She just stood there for a moment, then wrapped her arms around me without saying anything. And *I* stood there—for longer than a moment—just basking in the feeling of being with her. When she finally pulled her head back her eyes were wet but she was smiling. "Wow. If I'd known it was going to be like *that*, I would have let you say it sooner." She reached into her backpack. "Now it's my turn."

She took out a stack of stapled pages maybe two inches thick. "I'm finished," she said, handing it over.

"I'm honored."

"It's an early draft—it's not perfect by any means."

"As a wise man once told me, perfection is overrated."

"I agree. But I'm finally ready to have someone look at it and . . . I think you should be the first." She smiled. "You were always good at constructive commentary."

"Oh man, I can't wait—I know what *I'm* doing tonight." I couldn't resist. "So, how does it end?"

She wiped her eyes with the back of her hand and gave me a look that was surprisingly fierce, almost a challenge. "It doesn't."

We unloaded her supplies and she moved her car to the little gravel lot at the end of the row. When she got back I had her stuff arranged on a blanket on the grass. Like a picnic. But not.

She walked up behind me and put a hand on my shoulder. "How are you doing? Are you going to be okay with this?"

"I'm good." I glanced across the grass at the gravesite beyond the blanket. "All things considered." I checked the time on my phone—the others would be here soon, and there was something else I wanted to do before they got here. I took her hand and started forward. "Come on," I said. "There's someone I want to introduce you to . . ."

It was wonderful and it was sad and it was sweet. And I cried like a baby. Mostly because they could never meet in real life, which just broke my fucking heart. But like Assi had said in *The Empty Set,* sometimes the best we can do is to carry someone with us as we go through life. And maybe when you expose them to someone new—if only through stories and feelings and dreams—you're not just keeping them alive, you're expanding their influence on the world instead of seeing it diminish.

And that would have to be enough, because that was all I had.

My dad watched as Assi gathered everything she needed on the blanket in front of her—the burner, the long-handled copper pot, the sugar and finely ground coffee, the tiny cups and saucers. "What did you say this was called?" he asked.

"Ahweh," Assi said. "It's the Lebanese version of Turkish coffee." She looked shy. "I learned to make it from my mother."

My dad nodded.

"Who you are never to meet," I added quickly. Assi and Ollie and Seth cracked up, while my dad just looked confused. Confused but—for the first time in quite a while—maybe actually happy.

We were full. I'd brought a big container of massaman curry with steamed rice and vegetables from Thai Sister—my mom's favorite dish from her favorite restaurant. My dad had brewed a jug of Thai iced tea to go with it, which I'd packed in my car since he came on his bike. And Ollie and Seth had sweated away in our kitchen the night before, making a pecan pie. It was actually kind of funny watching them work together, the fashionista and the nerd. But between the two of them they'd made a pie my mom would've been proud of.

Assi handled the ahweh preparation almost as well as her mother, although I could tell she was nervous—she stuck her tongue firmly into the corner of her mouth as she poured each steaming shot. When everyone had a cup in front of them, she held hers and nodded to me.

"To Mom," I toasted. "We love you, we miss you, and"—I blinked a couple of times as I remembered her final words to me—"and we'll never forget you."

Everyone raised their cup and there was a ragged chorus of *To Mom!*, then we all took a sip.

While the others were busy drinking coffee and eating pie, Ollie came over and plopped down next to me. "You know, I never got the chance to say thanks," she said quietly.

"Hey, I just invited everyone. I didn't even cook—you're the one who made the pie." I punctuated that with a big bite. "Which is awesome," I added, talking around a mouthful of food.

"Gross." She pulled a face, then said, "I meant about letting me horn in on your present to Dad." She looked over at him. "He seems almost happy."

"He deserves it. God, it's been a shitty couple of years."

"You're not kidding."

It was the second anniversary of Mom's death, which is why I'd chosen the day for our own private little Día de los Muertos at the cemetery. I didn't know what else to say so I changed the subject. "Anyway, I'm not actually giving you half of Dad's present. You owe me thirteen hundred and fifty dollars of design work on my next website."

"That'll buy you a day's worth."

I shrugged. "So? I'm charging you a thousand dollars per head shot now."

"Shut up."

"You shut up."

I leaned back on my elbows and looked at everything around us. At our dad. At Seth. At Assi. And at our mom, just beyond the grass. Yeah, there were holes in our life. Well, one huge one, which had rippled out and made several smaller ones. Holes that might never be completely filled. But there were also things that had come into our life. New things. Unexpected things. Wonderful things, even.

So it wasn't perfect. Not even close. But it was something.

And maybe my dad was right—maybe perfection was overrated.

Beyond that, I still carried my mom with me—more now

than ever. Doing the project to honor her taught me to really observe . . . to see things differently, and more deeply. And learning to see like that has made me feel more resilient . . . made me believe that even though there've been some tough times, we can face whatever lies ahead.

I lay back on the blanket and closed my eyes, enjoying the warmth of the sun.

"Hey, Ollie . . ."

"Yeah?"

"Remember this moment."

A NOTE FROM THE AUTHOR

I wrote this book in part because there were things I was interested in exploring, including using art to help recover from loss, the concept of perfection, and having synesthesia, a condition that causes a person to experience one sense through another. (I have it and have seen it portrayed somewhat differently than my experience of it.) I hoped this would be a story made even more authentic through being informed by reality.

Be careful what you wish for.

I was a few months into the initial draft—well past the place where Jamison's mother has died from metastatic breast cancer—when my mother was diagnosed with metastatic breast cancer. She'd had cancer fifteen years previously, but the treatment was successful and she was considered disease-free. Fortunately I lived near her and worked at home, so I could take her to most of her various medical appointments—a few times a week, for a few years.

I say "fortunately" not for her, but for *me*. I wouldn't trade those last few years with her for anything.

It wasn't nearly as depressing as it sounds. Those "doc dates" usually included lunch afterward, often with my wife, and thanks to some very skilled medical professionals, my mom remained largely symptom-free throughout almost all of it. Laughter being emotional therapy, my goal was to make her laugh as often as possible.

She was claustrophobic, so during nuclear bone scans she'd have me sit right next to her and read to her throughout, to distract her. I would often end up joking with her too or reading from a work in progress. (Never from this book, however.)

And then, after all the joking and lunches and doctor visits, everything fell apart. The ambulance arrived at her house, the EMTs examined her, and the head EMT talked to me. (This was in the spring of 2020—the early days of the pandemic.) I was informed that if they took my mom to the hospital, she would be there for the duration, and there would be no visitors. I said, "So you're essentially saying if I put my mom in your ambulance, I'll never see her again and she'll die in the hospital, all alone?"

The EMT gave me a complicated look, then finally said, "Yes." I thanked her for her honesty and told them they could leave.

We moved my mom into our house. After her oncologist made a house call and told us what we were facing, we called hospice, brought in a hospital bed, and tried to make her feel as comfortable and loved as possible.

All this was concurrent with this book being readied for publication. Mom being here in hospice overlapped my first big round of revisions. Writing was a solace, but there was a period when I couldn't really focus on the words on the screen. My wife and sister and brother were godsends. At one point when my sister offered to help, she said, "It's not lost on me that you're trying to work on a book about a boy who's lost his mother . . . while your mother is dying in the next room."

Stories come in all sizes. There are stories about people doing huge, heroic things and saving lives or even saving the world. This story is not that. This is the story of one boy who's lost his mother, and his stumbling, fumbling steps—with the help of a few good friends—toward reentering life, using art as a tool to aid in his recovery. In other words, it's a love story.

The vast majority of us don't get to save the world, but many of us have suffered a loss—even more of us than usual, since the COVID pandemic—so exploring recovery seemed worthwhile. The specifics don't matter—Jamison uses photography, I use words, you use whatever works for you. What matters is, with creativity and with the help of good people, we can perhaps steer ourselves away from the empty set and back into life.

Thanks for taking the time to read this quite personal novel. I hope you enjoyed it.

ACKNOWLEDGMENTS

Everlasting gratitude to the three women without whom this would just be a collection of random words and not the book you have in front of you: my beautiful and brilliant wife, Wendelin (also my best friend, my first reader, and the love of my life); my rock-star agent, Ginger Knowlton, who believed unwaveringly in this story—and in me—from the beginning; and my editor, the phenomenal Beverly Horowitz, who knew exactly where the soul of this book lay, and who helped me chip away the stone to reveal it.

Thanks to the small group of early readers who gave their time and attention to providing feedback: Amy Goldsmith, life-long librarian and probably the deepest reader (and rereader) I've had the pleasure of knowing . . . thanks for the love and attention you gave this story. My sister, Leslie Parsons—artist, writer, and editor—who had my back throughout the writing of this. And Bob and Ruth Montaño . . . you two are truly the best—muchas gracias, muchos besos y abrazos.

Thanks also to those who supported me along the journey: My brother, Eric Parsons (also a writer) for always being supportive . . . and for listening to me ramble incessantly about reading and writing. Caradith Craven . . . an amazing librarian, serial overdoer, and book talker nonpareil. Bill Simpson, whose voluminous, vociferous, and vibrant emails kept me sane during the process (or drove me insane . . . either way, it helped!). And Steven Frenzel (also a writer), whose FB posts and email sign-offs alone could comprise a hilarious volume or two. Thanks for the much-needed sanity, peeps!

I'm so grateful for the wonderful team at Delacorte Press . . . Rebecca Gudelis, who kept the train on the tracks throughout. Hannah Hill and Lydia Gregovic, who provided insightful editorial feedback. Barbara Perris and Colleen Fellingham, copyeditors extraordinaire. Tamar Schwartz, Managing Editor, who oversaw all aspects of this project. Ray Shappell for the bold cover and Cathy Bobak for the artfully rendered interior design . . . and the rest of the team at RHCB.

ABOUT THE AUTHOR

MARK H. PARSONS is a writer and musician living on the Central Coast of California with his wife (also a writer and musician). They have two sons, with whom they occasionally make loud music under the name Risky Whippet. He enjoys the three R's—reading, running, and rock 'n' roll.

MarkHParsons.com

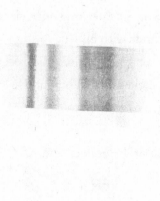